A BRIG AND HOPEFUL PLACE

A Romance
By
Jean-Paul Pare'

© 5/2024, by Jean-Paul Pare'

Table of Contents

Copyright Page 1

A Bright and Hopeful Place 7

Playlist 11

CHAPTER 1 | Joseph Guillaume (Joe) 13

CHAPTER 2 | Maxine 21

CHAPTER 3 | Joe 33

CHAPTER 4 | Maxine 37

CHAPTER 5 | Joe 41

CHAPTER 6 | Maxine 53

CHAPTER 7 | Joe 63

CHAPTER 8 | Maxine 75

CHAPTER 9 | Joe 77

CHAPTER 10 | Maxine 87

CHAPTER 11 | Joe 89

CHAPTER 12 | Maxine 97

CHAPTER 13 | Joe 103

CHAPTER 14 | Maxine 111

CHAPTER 15 | Joe 127

CHAPTER 16 | Harold 129

CHAPTER 17 | Joe 133

CHAPTER 18 | Maxine 141

CHAPTER 19 | Joe 145

CHAPTER 20 | Joe 151

CHAPTER 21 | Maxine 157

CHAPTER 22 | Joe 163

CHAPTER 23 | Harold 167

CHAPTER 24 | Maxine 171

CHAPTER 25 | Joe 177

CHAPTER 26 | Maxine 185

CHAPTER 27 | Maxine 191

CHAPTER 28 | Maxine 197

CHAPTER 29 | Joe 211

CHAPTER 30 | Joe 219

CHAPTER 31 | Maxine 225

CHAPTER 32 | Maxine 231

CHAPTER 33 | Joe 239

CHAPTER 34 | Maxine 243

CHAPTER 35 | Maxine 251

CHAPTER 36 | Joe 257

CHAPTER 37 | Maxine 261

CHAPTER 38 | Joe 263

CHAPTER 39 | Arlene 271

CHAPTER 40 | Joe 277

CHAPTER 41 | Joe 283

CHAPTER 42 | Maxine 291

CHAPTER 43 | Joe 293

CHAPTER 44 | Maxine 297

CHAPTER 45 | Arlene 301

CHAPTER 46 | Joe 307

Little boxes on the hillside
Little boxes made of ticky tacky
Little boxes on the hillside
Little boxes all the same
There's a green one and a pink one
And a blue one and a yellow one
And they're all made out of ticky tacky
And they all look just the same"
–Little Boxes, Malvina Reynolds
Well, she's all you'd ever want
She's the kind I like to flaunt and take to dinner
But she always knows her place
She's got style, she's got grace, she's a winner
She's a lady
Oh, whoa, whoa, she's a lady
Talkin' about that little lady
And the lady is mine
– She's A Lady, Tom Jones
I want you
I want you so bad
I want you
I want you so bad
It's driving me mad, it's driving me mad
–I Want You (She's So Heavy), The Beatles

Dedication

This one's for the family. You stood by me at my worst, and you support me for my best. I love you all.

For mom.

For dad. Wish you could have seen this one, Pops.

For Mr. Auten, for starting it all. All I ever learned about writing I learned from Scraps.

This is a work of fiction. Any similarities to real people, events, and places is purely coincidental and are products of the author's imagination.

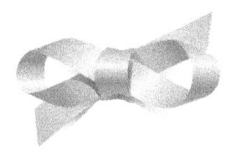

Playlist

Follow along with the Spotify Playlist. Scan the QR Code below or follow the Spotify link. https://open.spotify.com/playlist/62fnZm5cJPXt7psrfxupuy?si=233af9ade8b44f1

Acknowledgments

MANY PEOPLE HELPED me on this journey, but I really have to shout out to Alexis for doing the heavy lifting on this one. Without her, this book wouldn't have gone past the first two chapters. She gave me a deadline, which is what I needed. And she encouraged me to write the story of Max and Joe. She helped in more ways than I can imagine. She helped bring this book to life.

Also, to all the people I've met in the rooms. You know who you are. I love all of you. Without you, this wouldn't have even started.

And like I said earlier, my family. All you siblings know what you've done, and I thank all of you for being there when I needed you most. You're awesome.

And I want to shout out to Judi. A dear friend.

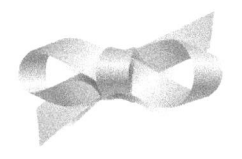

CHAPTER 1
Joseph Guillaume (Joe)

HE DIDN'T KNOW WHY she couldn't just get off his back about it, already.

"I just can't understand why you don't put the seat back down when you get done, Joe." Arlene said over the phone. "It's not that hard. It takes two seconds."

"I don't know, I'm sorry. I was in a hurry, Arlene," Joe responded. He didn't need this. Not at work. Not today. He looked up from his desk in the middle of the flooring section, and saw a slim redheaded woman looking at some laminate samples. He started to say "Arlene, I–"

"You're always in a hurry, Joe. You never slow down. I've been trying to get you to take things slow but you charge full speed ahead with every damn thing," she cut him off and started rambling. Joe ignored her. When Arlene got like this, the best thing to do was just agree with her and maybe she would calm down.

"Okay," he said. "Can we talk about this later? I have a customer. I promise I won't do it again."

"Fine," she said with an acerbic finality. "But you know we'll have this discussion later. Call me back." She hung up the phone.

"Great," he said. He looked down at his red Bennet's apron, soiled with a coffee stain. Not a great first impression. He wore a blue polo shirt and tan slacks and looked at the stain on his thigh. What was that from, he wondered? Oh yeah, the black grout bag that burst on him when he was putting it up. Why the night stock guys weren't more careful with the packing knives he didn't know. So one of the bags of black grout opened up as he was trying to put it up on the shelf and bam, it spilled all over him.

So here I am, disheveled, dirty pants, just getting off the phone after arguing with a woman for fifteen minutes about a two-second marital error. Looking like a low-budget Jake from State Farm. Fuck.

He wiped his pants off as best he could, stood up, and approached the customer. She had her back to him, and Joe could hear Joan Jett coming from her earbuds.

I hate myself For Loving You—Joan Jett

He noticed her fine clothing—a white designer blouse and an equally designer red skirt that clung to her curves. Nice looking broad, he thought. Married broad, he observed, noting the expensive rings. Not that it mattered to Joe. The thought of any kind of encounter beyond flooring sales with this woman was out the window. So he asked, "Can I help you?" in his best salesman voice, and she turned around.

She was even prettier from in front, he thought. "Hi!" she said in a cheery voice, a bit louder than she should have. And then she giggled and took the ear buds out. "Sorry, I was blaring the music and wasn't paying attention to what was around me."

"It's totally fine. I like Joan Jett," Joe said. Those brown eyes are going to send me, he thought. "What can I help you find today?"

"Maxine," she said. "Maxine Colston." She shook his hand. The warmth of it made his heart jump. He looked at her hand, and noticed her fingernails were the same red as her lipstick.

He drew his hand away and flexed it. "I see you're looking at hardwood."

Maxine noticed the hand flex and smiled, turning back to the shelves. "Yes, I have an empty house, a husband that doesn't care how much I spend, and a twenty-four-year-old floor that needs replacing. Can you help me with that?"

"Sure," he said. "Let's go over what you're looking for."

He described what she was looking at before, laminate hardwood faux flooring. "This is trash. You don't want it in a kitchen or a bathroom. It's just MDF fiber smashed between cardboard. If it gets wet, you'll have to replace it."

"I don't think I'll have to worry about that," she said. "Nothing in that house has been wet for a few years."

"You don't cook?" he asked. "Or use the bathroom?"

"I do," she answered. "But when your husband just sits in his room and plays online poker most of the day, it's kind of hard to feel like doing anything but ordering out."

"I see," he said. He had her pegged right away as another bored housewife, spending hubby's money.

"So, I'm not looking to break the bank," she said. "I see your hardwood is pretty pricey, how good is it?"

"Yes, how about vinyl planks? It's the best of both worlds. Hard, durable, strong, and waterproof."

He led her to the rack where two dozen planks were arrayed along the wall at the back of the flooring section of Bennet's Hardware. He could see his boss coming toward him. Jamie Bennet was a tall, lanky man, with his black and silver hair gelled into perfection as always. "Here we go," Joe thought. Here comes the fake smiles and glad-handing.

"Alright," Joe continued. "Here's all the samples we have, but there are more in a catalog we'd have to order. These are the most popular, though. How big is your area?"

"I don't know," she said. "It's a kitchen, a living room, three bathrooms, including the master of course, and a den slash dining room. I haven't decided what to call it yet, since we don't use it for a dining room anymore, and I have a bunch of shelves I bought from Ikea that I use for my books."

"You read a lot?" he asked.

"All the time. It's my second favorite pastime. Besides running of course."

That's what it was, Joe thought. He admired her taut lithe legs, flat belly, the curve in her waist. She was totally out of his league for sure. Even if in some alternate universe he could bag a woman this pretty, he was still a married man and wouldn't dream of it.

"Do you have any ideas?" she asked.

"Yes, I do. But I would have to see the space first. When are you available for a fitting?"

"A what?" she asked.

"A measurement," he explained. "A consultation where I come out to the house, measure the rooms, make some designs, and then come back here to write up the estimate?"

"Oh, yes, I'm sorry. You need to come to the house, I should have thought of that," she said.

"Can we not come to your house?"

"Yes," she said. "I just have to make sure my husband is gone. He doesn't know I'm doing this yet." She paused in thought. "Not like he would give a shit anyway, but that's beside the point."

"Would Tuesday be a good time?" he asked. He led her over to his work desk to start the file on Maxine Colston. "Around noon?"

"Yes," she said. "And in the meantime, I can get an idea of what I should pick out of the three samples I have here." She showed him the small hardwood squares.

Just then, Jamie came by, and said, "Hello, Jamie Bennet, they call me JB." he said, shaking her hand. She introduced herself to him.

"Nice to meet you, thanks for coming in," he said affably. Jamie liked to think of himself as the perfect boss, and was always glad-handing the customers. "I see you're buying some flooring. Listen to Joey here, he's the best."

"Jamie, we talked about that," Joe said, referencing the Joey remark.

"Hey," said Jamie, "Who's the boss?" He raised his hands and said, "I know, I just like to get a reaction."

"Whatever," Joe said. "Just let me sell the pretty lady some flooring,"

Maxine noticed the "pretty lady" remark and flushed. Joe instantly felt embarrassed. He started to backtrack.

"I'm sorry, no offense."

"Oh," she smiled, blushing at the compliment, "It's okay. So Tuesday, noon?"

"Yes, what's your address?"

She gave him an address on Shady Lane Court.

He thought for a moment. "Shady Lane, that's the cul-de-sac about three blocks down from me. I walk past your place all the time on my morning walks. Pretty nice place. That was part of Phase One, if I remember right?"

"Yes, back in Two Thousand when they bought the old Sycamore Farm," She raised an eyebrow in intrigue. "You live in White Pines too?"

"Yes, Oakmont court," he answered.

"Oakmont, what house is yours?"

"Fourth on the left from the entrance sign. The gray house with the azaleas every spring."

"Oh my God, your wife did so good with all of those," she said. "All the different colors, it's so pretty."

"Thanks," he said. "But she didn't have anything to do with it. That was all me. I've had a green thumb since I was a kid. You should see the backyard."

"Maybe one day I should," she said. "You did a great job. I need some TLC in my yard. I should hire you to come by and make it pretty outside as well as inside."

"I don't know about that," he said. "Let's focus on flooring first and see how that works out. If you want, I can hook you up with Jodi, she's our garden guru."

"Sure,but first things first," her face was a glow of delight. "I should go," she said, taking a business card from him. She looked at the date and time of the consultation and nodded. Then she added "I have more shopping to do. The hubby's bank account won't empty itself."

She shook his hand again, then shook Jamie's hand. "Good to meet you both." She turned and walked toward the doors of the large hardware store, past the checkout where two young girls were being lectured to by Barb, the older white-haired head cashier.

After she left, his coworker in the next cubicle, Derrick said, "Well, that's a hell of a lead, big guy. Good going."

"Yeah," Joe agreed. "And boy, do I need it. I'm right on the verge of that top bonus. And that three grand is going to push me over the top for the down payment on the ranch I have in mind."

"Still on that, huh?" Derrick laughed. Joe had been talking about his ranch in the desert idea for the last ten years. "Why are you still holding on to that pipe dream, man?"

"I've got something in the works right now that'll make that dream come true. With that two grand I'll finally be able to get it."

"What about Arlene?"

"What about her?" Joe said sarcastically. "What she doesn't know won't hurt me."

"But she'll find out eventually. You don't just spend all your savings on a ranch in the desert and not have her notice. Besides, she's going to have to live there too, remember?"

"If the deal goes through, I'll tell her, obviously. I want it to be a surprise."

"Oh it'll be a surprise for sure," Derrick said. "What makes you think she wants a ranch in the desert, anyway."

"We talked about it when we were first dating, she said it would be fun."

"Dating is different, Joe. Y'all are married now. She's taking care of two kids and a house. You really think she wants to move across the country to take care of a horse ranch? And didn't she grow up on a farm?"

"Listen," Joe said. "I put some feelers out a few nights ago. When I get word they were successful, I'll let her know and we'll talk about it then. If it doesn't, she's none the wiser."

Derrick laughed, "What if she says no."

"Then we do something practical like pay an extra house payment on the place we have and I shelve my dream of being a cowboy for a few more years." He put Maxine's file in the new client's drawer of his desk. He hoped this one would pan out. He really needed that bonus. Maybe he should lay on the charm a bit more, but then thought better of it. Don't open that door, Joe. Because once it opens, that road leads exactly where you think it does.

"I wonder if she has a cute single friend," Derrick said, breaking Joe's thoughts.

"You're incorrigible, you know that?" Joe chuckled. "How about I find out the next time I see her, then you and the friend can have a whirlwind romance while the two married people watch with envy."

"Sounds like a plan, Stan," Derrick shot finger guns at Joe. Then he stopped and listened into his earphone as Jamie called him up to the office. "Gotta go. Big man wants to talk about lumber prices. Talk to you later, Joey."

"Hey!" Joe said, bristling at the 'Joey' remark.

"I know, I just like to get on your nerves with it. What are coworkers for?" He stood up from his desk, a gray cubicle next to Joe's cubicle, and walked out of the room to have a meeting with the boss.

Joe looked at the Colston file and thought Man, I hope this works out—a whole house. Bonus for sure. But then the worry crept in. What if Arlene found out about the New Mexico offer he'd made a few nights ago? It would end in an argument either way. Just once in his life, he wished something good would come up for him without complications. Until then, he would have to keep dreaming.

CHAPTER 2
Maxine

SHE STEPPED OUT OF the hardware store and moved to her silver Lexus, her mind floating with possibilities. That man was handsome, she thought. She got in her Lexus and just sat there, thinking about the strength of his handshake. At how it had seemed to envelope hers, and how it had flexed.

"Be cool, Maxine," she said. Just be cool. She looked down at the ring on her finger, the impenetrable bond of matrimony she had held for twenty-four years to a man who barely held her or touched her or even talked to her anymore.

And this Joe is coming over to her house on Tuesday. Shit. I have to get Harold out of the house someway. Maybe he'll do it for me. I'm sure I could be upfront and tell him I'm changing the flooring, what would he care?

The answer was, he wouldn't. He couldn't give two shits about what's going on in that house any more than the man on the moon. But Joe, those blue eyes of his, and his calm yet sultry voice. She could listen to him all day. Did that man not know how sexy he was?

"Obviously he's happily married," she said. His wife probably goes after him every day. That square jaw, the set of the muscles on his arms, and the way his butt looked in those khakis. Goodness, she could eat him up. Why wouldn't his wife be doing the same thing? "I have to get my mind out of the gutter," she said to no one in particular. "Mind out of the gutter, Maxine."

She picked up the phone and called her friend Carrie, who she'd known since childhood.

Three rings later, Carrie answered, "Hey, girl!"

Maxine asked, "Hey, got time for lunch?"

"A few minutes," Carrie answered. "What's the occasion?"

"I just wanted to have lunch with a friend. Do I need a reason? My treat."

"Well, when you put it that way I'm in."

Maxine smiled. "Good." She couldn't wait to talk to her friend. It had been too long since they'd been able to catch up. "Angelo's in fifteen minutes?"

Carrie said, "I'm Just stepping out of the shower. Make it half an hour. See you then?"

"Perfect. See you then."

She put the phone back down on the seat next to her. She hadn't left the parking lot. If she hadn't broken that stupid kitchen floor tile with the coffee cup this morning, she wouldn't have even been in this place. She started the car and left the parking lot.

Why did he have to bring up her husband? The man who hadn't done much besides barely speak to her and ordered her to run his errands for the past two years. She thought when her daughter went off to Cornell two years ago, that he would be all over her. She thought wrong. He had barely touched her.

She knew she shouldn't cry, shouldn't bemoan her lot in life. She had created it after all. She signed the papers, she had said the 'I do's', had had the baby, raised her daughter to be a caring, loving human being, and then that baby had grown up and left the house. Maxine knew when the car drove down the road she would be alone. Her job of motherhood was done, and she wouldn't know how to be a wife to a man who no longer knew how to be a husband.

That had been two years ago, and as Maxine drove into the pizzeria's parking lot, she noticed that slow salty tears dripped from her eyes. She pulled a tissue out of her purse and dabbed her eyes.

She looked at herself in the rearview mirror, saw blotchy red eyes, and redid her makeup to make herself presentable. She would die before she showed she was crying to her best friend.

"She's going to know anyway," she said to herself. She got out of the car and went to the doors of the Pizza shop. She waited in the lobby for a few minutes until her best friend Carrie came in the door. She was a tall, thin brunette, wearing black jeans, a purple low neck tee shirt, and black sandals.

After a brief hug between the two, a young italian woman with dark hair and pretty eyes led them to a booth. They sat across from each other, and Carrie said, "What's up?"

The waitress asked, "What can I get you started with?"

Carrie ordered an Italian lager, a light brew that would be perfect for the pizza she planned on ordering. Maxine ordered a Pinot Grigio. The girl wrote this down on an order pad and walked away with a smile.

Maxine said, "I just wanted to see a good friend, that's all."

Carrie said, "You've been crying again," in a voice that made her seem like she was about to do violence.

Maxine wiped her eyes, "You could tell. I knew it."

"What did he do? Did he hit you?" Carrie asked, referencing Harold.

"No," Maxine said. "He would never hit me. It's just..." She trailed off.

"Just what?"

"I don't know what I'm doing anymore, Care," Maxine said, using the nickname she had given her friend so long ago.

"I don't get it," Carrie said. "What's wrong with your life? I'd like to know."

The waitress came back, drinks in hand. She took their order. Carrie ordered a small pepperoni and onion pizza and Maxine ordered the Chicken Parm.

The young lady left. Maxine looked around at the other customers. It wasn't too busy, but she kept her voice low anyway, but loud enough to let Carrie hear over the Italian music playing low over the loudspeakers.

"So, like I asked," said Carrie. "What's wrong?"

"Nothing," Maxine lied. "Well, everything. What am I doing with my life anymore?"

"Okay, what brought this on?"

"I'm just depressed, maybe. All I do is drive around and spend Harold's money. I order stuff online and when it comes i just put it on the shelf and never use it. And then I'll go to stores and order things and then second guess myself. What is that?"

"What store did you go to this time?"

"The hardware store," Maxine explained. "This morning I was doing dishes and a coffee cup fell on the floor and broke some tile. Cracked it to shit. Then I got to looking around the house. The carpet was worn down, the hardwood in the dining room needed replacing and then I thought why not go shop for flooring. Maybe Harold could do it in between sitting on his ass playing poker all day."

"So you went to look at flooring. What did you find?" Carrie held out her hands, waiting for samples to give her thoughts on.

"This," Maxine pulled out Joe's business card and put it in front of Carrie. Carrie sipped her drink, looked down at it.

"What's this?" she said dubiously.

"The guy selling the flooring," Maxine said.

"Max," Carrie said. "We're not in the fifties anymore, hon." She held up the card, with the embossed name 'Joe Guillaume' in block letters. "Joe?"

"Yes," she blushed. "It got me thinking, that's all."

"Thinking about what?" Carrie gave her the side eye that she was famous for. She always looked at Maxine that way when her friend was about to make a bad decision.

"Isn't it obvious?" Maxine whispered.

"No." Carrie said flatly. "No, girl. You can't. I forbid it."

"What?" Maxine asked innocently. "It's just a flirtation, that's all. Can't I just have a little fun with the guy?"

"Flirtation is one thing, hon. But a minute ago you had a look that said you're about to make a bad decision, and soon."

"I am not," Maxine said defensively.

"You are," said her friend. "And I won't allow it."

"Allow it?" Maxine chuckled. "It's my life, you know."

"We are just speaking hypothetically, here, right?" Carrie asked.

"Yes," Maxine said with a sigh of resignation. "Of course. I'm just playing around. Trying to get some excitement in my life. God knows Harold doesn't do that anymore."

"And you think flirting with this guy is going to do that?"

"Maybe?"

"Didn't you try something a few years ago with that Foodway produce guy?"

"Yes, and you know how that worked out." Maxine remembered the bald strong armed clerk that manhandled the apple boxes in the grocery store that one time right before the onset of Covid.

She had asked him if the cucumbers were firm and he just looked at her and said, 'Yeah, I guess' before walking away. She had told Carrie about it that day, embarrassed and heartbroken.

"Hon," Carrie said, "you want to get some excitement, try it out with Harold. Maryanne is gone, it's just you two in the house. You're hot, he should be all over you. What gives?"

Maxine sighed sadly. "I tried a couple of times, but he's just not into it. He'd rather be making money online than do anything with me. It's sad when a bunch of cards are more exciting than your wife."

"Maybe he's talking to someone else, you ever thought of that?"

"He's not talking to anyone. I've checked," she said. "I even went in one night and looked at his browser. It's all just stock pages and his poker app."

"No porn?" Carrie asked incredulously.

"Not even one picture," Maxine said. "It's like he has no libido. And I would have been okay with that. At least it would have shown me he wanted to do something like that."

"So he's maybe got a problem," Carrie said. "Have you thought of that?" She pointed down to her pelvis.

"It's a possibility," Maxine answered. "I've tried to get him to talk, but he clams up, says 'guys don't talk about their emotions', and then he walks away. It's like I'm a stranger in my own house. We're roommates at this point."

"Well then you have a rich roommate footing the bills, Maxie." She used her own nickname for Maxine this time.

"Rich or not," Maxine said, "I just want him to touch me."

"And you've said this?"

"Yes," Maxine answered. "But his idea of touching me is a hug every now and then and a peck on the cheek. Which really does it for me, I can tell you." There was sarcasm in that last sentence.

The waitress brought their food, set down the pizza in front of Carrie, a couple of napkins, forks, and then set the chicken dish in front of Maxine. She didn't have an appetite, but she figured she would soldier on and eat as much as she could before getting a to-go plate that would add to the others in her refrigerator.

"Here you go, ladies," the petite young girl said. "You need anything else, let me know."

They smiled at her, said, "Okay," and let her go. They both dug in, eating in silence for a minute.

Carrie finally said, "Okay, so you think an affair with jazz up your life, is that what you're telling me?"

"Yes," said Max. "I just want some excitement. And if I can't get it from Harold, why not from some other guy?"

"Why not?" Carrie said sarcastically. "Maybe because it would ruin your marriage? You think Harold wouldn't put you on the street if he found out?"

"How would he know?" Maxine explained. "He doesn't come out of his room. He rarely leaves the house. I have to go out and get everything for the guy anyway. Why can't I have a discreet liaison with someone during the day? Hell, he never touches me now to begin with, you think he would know?"

"You're not actually thinking about this, Maxie," Carrie looked at her seriously now. "I mean, you sound like you've given it some thought."

"Not really," Maxine explained. "It's fun to consider it, though."

"So tell me about flooring guy," Carrie said.

"Well," she answered, "He's cute in a disheveled dad bod sort of way. Salt and pepper hair, a bit of stubble. Ruggedly handsome." Maxine chuckled.

"Oh boy," Carrie said, rolling her eyes. "And?"

"And these strong hands that made my own look like a child's. And you should see how he flexed his hand. Oh my God." Maxine said, dreamily, as if describing her perfect man.

"What are we in a Jane Austen novel all the sudden?"

"Actually," Maxine defended herself. "He's just a good guy, and handsome in a middle aged dad sort of way."

"I get it," Carrie said. "He's good looking and can shake a hand. Welcome to salesmen everywhere. Don't get involved, Maxie. He was being nice. It's his job."

"I know. But, he's off the table for sure," she said.

"Let me guess."

"He's married."

"He's married?"

"Yes," Maxine said. "So he's off limits, I know."

"Hella off limits. Why didn't you lead with that?"

"Because I know how you get."

"Because I know what I'm talking about," Carrie said harshly. "Remember the last husband I had? Ran off with some yoga trainer? Yeah, bad idea, Maxine. You step out and Harold finds out, you lose everything. He steps out on his wife? He loses everything. What were you thinking? You want to spend the rest of your life living under a bridge?"

"I was playing around with the idea in my head, that's all," said Maxine. "Relax. It's not going to happen."

"It better fucking not," Carrie said. "You do that, you're both screwed. And most guys who have an affair don't leave their wives. I'm guessing this one won't. He's got too much to lose." She took another bite of pizza and continued. "If you want to have an affair, I can't stop you. But why not go down to the beach and have a fling with a summer tourist. Or the college in town. Pick up a football player half your age."

"Didn't you do that a few months ago?" Maxine joked.

"We're talking about you, here, not me."

"I don't want to do that, Care, and you know it. I'm playing around, anyway. This is never going to happen. So please, let's stop talking about it."

"Okay," Carrie said. "See that it doesn't."

"Good. What's up with you these days?" Maxine asked. "Still dating the doctor? Or was it an ER nurse?"

"He's a resident," Carrie smiled. "But his job comes first and I haven't seen him in a few weeks so I think he ghosted me."

"Unlucky in love again, huh?"

Carrie shrugged her shoulders dismissively. "It's not like he was going to be the love of my life, anyway. He was just a guy, you know?"

"Yeah," Maxine agreed. "But he made you happy at least?"

"For about a minute," her friend said.

They continued to talk about love lives of the bored and infamous for the next half hour. Their subjects ranged from current events, men, other people they knew in town, boys, and made an appointment to go shopping together next week. In the back of her head throughout the discussion though, she thought of a handshake, flexing fingers pulling her hair, and a hardware smell that wouldn't go away.

Maxine stepped out of the restaurant and started walking to her car. She looked into her purse and held the business card in her hand. It had his name, "Joseph Guillaume, Flooring Sales," in large block letters next to the red Bennet logo. His store phone number and extension were there, and his cell number.

I should text him, she thought. Just a note on how excited I am to get the measurement done. Test the waters, see if he was interested in her. Probably not. He did call her pretty, though. But that was just as Carrie said. Salesman speak. He wouldn't be interested in her any more than Harold was.

There was a honk behind her as she realized she was standing in the middle of the parking lot, lost in reverie. She waved at the driver of a white Nissan and moved out of the way, "Sorry!" she yelled, hoping he could hear her through the tinted window. He drove past and parked. She got into her Lexus and sat for a minute, looking at his card again. "No," she said to no one. "Probably not a good idea.

Even if it was going to happen, it's just a bad idea all around. Too much trouble there, Maxine. Too much trouble indeed." She put the card back in her purse, gave up on the idea, and drove toward home, toward Harold.

A BRIGHT AND HOPEFUL PLACE

Little Boxes—Malvina Reynolds

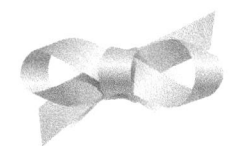

CHAPTER 3
Joe

AT THE END OF THE DAY, Joe put his paperwork and files together, stacked where he could find them for the next day. He was meticulous, making sure he knew right away when he walked in the door the next morning what he had to do, who he had to call, and what he had to process in order to get the work done most efficiently. Maxine's file was on top, a single sheet that had name, address, phone number and a few ideas of the flooring she wanted. He looked at it.

He thought of her momentarily. Pretty gal, he thought. Married gal, he thought. Then he looked at his hand, saw the yellow gold band on his third ring finger. He sighed

Married guy.

She was just being nice, a little too nice maybe, but nice all the same. She's a customer, Joe. And that's all she would ever be, you know this. And even if it did happen, in whatever alternate universe, he would be fired for even going down that road. He could see the future of that decision. Jamie would have his ass if he was caught having a liaison with a customer, a client, especially one that was going to spend over ten thousand dollars in the store, and maybe more if she was a good customer.

So he pulled out his phone, looked at the texts, and saw one from Arlene.

Hey. stop by the store and get
nuggets for Joey. microwave fries too.

He texted back:

ok. Anything else?

A few minutes passed as he picked up his briefcase and his phone dinged again.
Arlene:
Yes. Go to the LS, get vodka
You know what kind
He almost said, "No, get it yourself. You're the one who drinks it." but then he thought she had already had a few shots already and wouldn't be able to drive. He had laid down the law with that to her several times. "No drunk driving. Ever.

You start, you stay home or wherever you are. I'll pick you up or you don't come home at all," he had said to her. He had made it quite clear that there was no negotiation on that topic. He didn't mind her drinking, but getting behind the wheel of a car was a big no no. A divorce no no. He had experienced too much pain with drunk drivers in his life, he wasn't about to have any grief with her about it.

And she had agreed.
So he texted her back:

sure np.

So this was how it was going to be tonight. Again. Tipsy Arlene sitting in front of the TV, watching whatever mindless show she had on, while he cooked microwave nuggets for the kids. Then the cleanup, then getting her off the couch and leading her to bed, where she would pass out at nine o'clock, like clockwork.

Could he blame her? Yes, and no. He remembered three years ago, when she started drinking more heavily. It began after her father had died of COVID. When she got the news, she was inconsolable for days. All she did was drink and sleep. And Joe let her. He let her grieve in her own way.

Her mother Catherine had to come to the house to help her. Arlene barely ate, barely spoke. Her father was everything to her. She was his baby, and he was her biggest hero. If there was any man she truly loved on this earth, it was him.

Thomas Richards was everything you could want in a man: strong, ambitious, gentle, and a devoted father to Arlene and her older brother, Tommy. He was the quintessential man's man, owning a sprawling seventy-acre farm three hours away, renowned for producing some of the best corn you could ever eat. Salt of the earth, old-fashioned, and intimidating as hell—especially when Joe had to ask for Arlene's hand in marriage.

In Thomas Richards' world, no blessing meant no marriage. There were days Joe secretly wished Thomas had said "No." But here he was, married to Mr. Richards' daughter, with two kids, a house in a soul-sucking housing development, a good job, a mortgage, two cars, and all the trappings of the American dream.

Trappings—exactly the right word. Every day felt stifling, a constant reminder of how trapped he was by obligation, responsibility, and a cage he had unknowingly built for himself over the years. A sense of duty to those he cared about weighed him down, leaving him yearning for something more.

He left the store, got in his car and sat for a few minutes. He looked at his phone. *I'll call her and tell her they were out of vodka*, he thought. *I'd just go to the grocery store. Get the nuggets, get one of those deli sandwiches for himself, or maybe on the way home stop for tacos and just treat the kids to that. Say he couldn't get there. Say they were busy. They didn't have her kind. Tell her to get her own Goddamn vodka when she was sober. She had a car. Why didn't she get it during the day?*

Because she had been drinking during the day. That's why. Arlene prescribed to the adage that it was five o'clock somewhere. Even though five o'clock started at ten for her sometimes. He would have to talk to her about it. Tell her he was worried, that deep down he wanted to pour all of it down the drain. Tell her to get help. Go to therapy. Go to meetings. Go to rehab. Go to anywhere where there wasn't this clear liquid that was driving a wedge between them.

But he didn't do that. Amidst protests, she would cry and cajole and tell him she needed it to get over her father's death, she needed it to calm her down to get the kids taken care of. She needed it to make her happy. And any number of reasons someone who tries to justify drinking to oblivion.

So he bided his time. He enabled it. He went to the liquor store, bought a large bottle of Absolut, her favorite, paid the clerk, and ignored the look he gave Joe because Joe had been in every other day the past few years.

"For the wife," Joe explained, like always.

"Uh huh," said the clerk, handing him back Joe's debit card.

Joe walked out, feeling judged, wanting to punch the fat shop clerk in the mouth, maybe smash the bottle over the clerk's bald head.

But instead he went to his car, slammed the driver's side door, started up his white Hyundai and pulled out of the parking lot of the store to go grocery shopping.

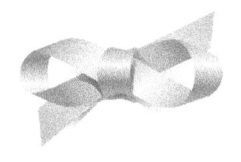

CHAPTER 4
Maxine

• • ⚜ • •

"HEY, HON?" HAROLD HAD called from his office. She had just walked in the door, put her purse down on the tan sofa, and heard him call for her. "Now what," she thought.

"Yeah, baby?" She walked down the hall to his office. He sat behind the large curved screen on his brown mahogany desk and looked up.

"Good, you're back," he said with a smile. "Where you been?"

"I had to run some errands and then I went to lunch with Carrie. What's up?"

"Hey, we need some toilet paper, and there's no milk in the fridge. I ordered a pizza too, so you gotta go pick it up."

"Okay," she sighed. "But couldn't you have done all that?"

"I was playing today," he said, dismissive.

"Right," she smiled as sweetly as she could. He had been in here over eight hours and probably had only gotten up to go to the bathroom. That's how he knew about needing toilet paper. "Okay, sure. I'll go. Let me change clothes and I'll leave in a few minutes."

"Good," he said, going back to his monitor. "That's my girl."

She closed the door, stood there a moment, and turned to go down the hall.

"Don't forget the TP!" she heard Harold yell from the door.

I really should, she thought. Let him wipe with his hands, or whatever poker book he read on the can. She walked down the hall and went upstairs to her bedroom. Changed into a pair of blue jeans, a gray tank top, and a white blouse over it.

This was her idea of slumming it up for the grocery store and picking up pizza in the drive through window. She put her hair in a ponytail, tied it with a black scrunchy and went back downstairs after slipping into white sandals. She looked down at worn pink toenails. She thought she would have to get that fixed. Tomorrow, she would go to Becca's Nail place, maybe. Unless Harold needed something.

And he always needed something.

She grabbed her purse, stepped out the door, Got into her Lexus, and started down the street. She went out of the complex, past all of the white, gray, and tan colonial homes that all looked the same and had the same floor plans. had bikes and big wheels littered the front lawns of a few homes. Old Mrs. Killebrew still had her Christmas lights hanging up. This always caused friction between Killebrew and Gertrude Herberts, the HOA president. But nobody was going to do anything about it because when you tussled with old lady Killebrew and her demon of a chihuahua, you didn't want to confront old lady Killebrew ever again. So the Christmas lights stayed up all year around.

Minutes later she pulled into the Foodway. It was one of two grocery stores close to White Pines, in the small town of Newton's Crossing. The other was a German place that didn't have anyone working there and you had to check yourself out. She hated that because she had read somewhere they killed jobs.

She went in and grabbed a cart. She started shopping, wandering aimlessly down the aisles, looking for something for herself, and then remembered why she had come in the first place. The king of the castle needed toilet paper.

She found the paper aisle, looked at the quilted stuff with the four ply and the red and yellow packaging that said one roll was equal to sixteen and put it in the cart. God forbid mister all day poker scratched his delicate derriere. She then headed to the frozen section. She didn't want pizza again. She had her figure to look out for, and the Chicken parm had exceeded her calorie count for the day..

She wheeled her buggy down the frozen section and stopped. "Shit," she thought. "Oh shit. Shit shit shit!"

Joe stood in an open door of the frozen section, looking at the chicken nugget packs. She looked down at herself. Jeans and a tank top? She looked so underdressed. Why didn't I think about that? Oh my God, I'm so embarrassed.

She started to turn around, thinking she could come back around later, but he looked up and saw her standing there, mouth agape.

"Mrs Colston?" He said, "What a surprise. How are you?" He started to walk towards her.

She smiled, a caged rabbit to a wolf. "Hi," she said meekly. Brushing her blouse as straight as she could. "Joe, how are you?" Was she blushing?

"So good to see you," he smiled. "Small world, huh?"

"Well when we live a few streets away from each other in a small town, that's bound to happen, us meeting like this," she laughed. "And please, do call me Maxine."

"Maxine it is then," he chuckled. "I guess I'm still in salesman mode, huh?"

"Just getting off the job?"

"Yes. Gotta get the kids dinner. Why is it every ten year old always wants to eat chicken nuggets??"

"It's not just ten year olds," she explained. She couldn't stop looking at him, his blue eyes shining at her, each a brilliant sky. "My Harold still eats them like a kid and he's forty five."

"I guess it's just a guy thing then."

"It must be," she started to walk toward the display cases where frozen fruits and vegetables sat in frozen silence behind frosted glass. She opened the door. The cool air blessed her with relief. What was it about this man that made her warmer than usual?

"Well, don't let me keep you," he said. "I'm looking forward to seeing you in a few days for the assessment."

She turned after grabbing a random bag of carrots, put them in the cart, and said, "Yes, I'm looking forward to it. It'll be nice to get a new look started."

"I'm sure it will," he said as he stepped toward her. She could smell something on him. The hardware store smell, a vague hint of wood, the musky scent of warehouse dust. She stuck out her hand to shake his. He held it, and shook.

Maxine felt a warm vibration when he took her hand, like a low grade electric taser had shot through her palm and wrist. She held his hand a few seconds longer than she should have, felt the coldness of his palm in hers, blinked a couple of times and pulled away.

"Wow," she said with a smile, "Your hands are cold."

"They were in the freezer a couple of minutes ago," he explained with a grin. "But you know what they say."

"No," she questioned. "What do they say?"

"Cold hands, warm heart."

"Yeah," she agreed. "I guess they do." His momentary touch had her heart beating rapidly. She gulped.

"Well it was nice meeting you again," he smiled and started by her. "Maxine."

"You too," she watched him walk around the corner of the aisle, his ass cheeks tight in his khaki work slacks. "You too, mister man." she whispered to herself. "Jesus Christ..."

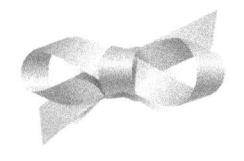

CHAPTER 5
Joe

HE PULLED INTO THE driveway of the white neocolonial box he called home and parked next to Arlene's silver-gray minivan. He noticed a thin layer of yellow pollen coating the van, and said to himself, "Gonna have to wash it this weekend." Then he looked at his white car and vowed to do them both on the same day. It'll give him something to do before he had to mow the lawn and go to the grocery store.

He took out his briefcase, why, he didn't know, and walked to the door. "Shit!" He looked down and noticed he lacked something else. He went back to the car, grabbed the groceries and the brown bag that held her vodka, and then went back to the door. He had been scattered. He felt like his brain wasn't functioning as it had on normal days.

It was that Maxine woman. She had distracted him. He had tried to ignore the thoughts of her and think about something else on the way home but there was something about her. It was that handshake. That cold handshake. That electric current he felt and ignored in the moment. But it was there. He couldn't deny it. That shock of touching someone that gave you a static burst. What the fuck was that about? It must have been a combination of a bunch of different things. The slacks he wore, maybe. Her outfit, the tank top showing just a bit of cleavage, her cute white sandals, and those pink delicate toenails.

You need to stop thinking what you're thinking, boyo, his logical brain told him. Just stop it. Go in the house. Don't think about the way she smiled at you, the way she blushed when she said your name, the way she stared into your eyes. Don't think about any of that. There's a blond in that house that needs you. There are kids, a job, and obligations. That's your life now, sucker. Deal with it.

He sighed, opened the door, and entered the chaos of wedded bliss.

The first thing that happened was the Lego blocks he stepped on that crunched underfoot. He pulled back and saw the car made of red and yellow bricks that had snapped in half. He picked it up, snapped it back together, and said, "Hon? I'm home."

He stepped down into the living room. There was a laundry hamper in front of the gray plush couch, where Arlene sat, folding his underwear. He looked at the farmhouse-style coffee table and there were several envelopes, mostly with windows, a Style magazine with the latest hot actor on the cover, and a glass half full with ice cubes swimming in clear fluid.

She looked up, said, "Hey." and returned to the folding. The TV blared some show involving tigers and drama and he paid it no attention. He bent down and went to kiss her, and she turned her head gently. His kiss, aimed at her lips, landed on her cheek.

"How you doing today?" he asked as he stood back up. He put down the brown paper-wrapped bottle on the table and started for the kitchen to drop the bags on the white subway-tiled island counter.

"Ok, I guess," she said lazily. There was a bit of a slur in the word 'guess'. He knew immediately she had had at least three shots already today. And it was only four PM. "Hey, you got a call from some real estate company? I told them I'd tell you to call when you got home." She paused in thought. "Why would they call, Joe?"

"I'll call and find out," he returned to the living room. "Where's the number?"

"It's on your office desk," she answered. "Some place in New Mexico? Whatever, it's in there." She pointed down the hall to his office. She went back to folding. This time picking up a green kids shirt that said "Bazinga" and folded it while watching her show about lions and tigers or whatever.

"Where are the kids?"

"Oh, Cath is at her friend's house and Joey is back in his room playing kill of duty or whatever. They're fine."

I'm sure they are, he thought. "Is Catherine coming home for dinner?"

"No, she's staying at Meghan's. They have a paper they're working on together. And she says Meghan's mom makes a great mac and cheese."

"Good, one less mouth to feed tonight." He went back into the kitchen and opened the door to the fridge. Takeout containers from Angelo's, a half-eaten cheeseburger in a McDonald's wrapper and a pitcher of Kool-Aid greeted him. It was a well-stocked refrigerator with takeout containers from places like Angelo's, fast food places, and Subway. "Order from Doordash again?" he asked.

"Yeah," she slurred. She stood up to go to the kitchen. "Got Subway today." She reached for the other half of the sandwich she had saved. "I'll just eat this."

"Okay, I'll fix the nuggets in a minute. Let me go do this phone call."

Arlene got the sandwich from the fridge, opened it, and returned to the couch to watch the animal drama. "Whatever."

He said nothing. He just watched as she picked up the sandwich, opened the wrapper, and started eating. Then she picked up her drink, took a sip, and went back to ignoring him.

He walked to his office, sat at the gray farmhouse desk, and looked around. He started his laptop, entered the password protection, and visited the Mojave Express Real Estate website. There was a white sheet of paper, ripped in half, sitting on his keyboard. So he would find it, he thought. She does that. She puts things right in front of my face like I can't find it. She could have put it on the desk right next to it, but she went the whole way and put it down so I'd have to see it and move it.

There was a number scrawled on the paper. He dialed it. After a few rings, a cheery woman's voice answered.

"Mojave Express Real Estate, how may I direct your call?" the woman said in vibrant secretary speak.

"Hello," Joe said. "This is Joe Guillaume, I was told to call this number?"

"Yes, sir, this is Brenda Hartman, we received your offer for the Cactus Road property and I was just following up on that."

"Yes," he said, hopefully. He had seen it last week on the website during his browsing for desert land. It was a weekly thing for him, sort of a hobby. But it was also a desire since he had been a kid, owning a horse farm in the desert, being a real cowboy and not just watching them every few days on Netflix. "What can I do for you?"

"Unfortunately, we can't go ahead with the sale at this time," she said with a salesman's air of feigned disappointment. "We had another buyer come in with a better offer."

"I thought my offer was pretty solid. I can offer more than twenty percent of the down payment."

"It's not about that, and your offer was very generous, I can tell you. But the owner went with someone he knew and they worked out a cash sale," she said sadly, trying to let him down gently.

"Okay," he said. Damn. "I thought it was a good offer, the best I could do. Maybe there's another property in the same price range?"

"I have a few things I can send you, but the one I think would be better and fit your price range is a two-acre lot in a new housing development near Albuquerque. If you get in on the ground floor, the owner will give you a twenty per cent reduction in the price as a signing bonus."

"Is that the Garden Palms property?" he asked. He had seen those. And had looked at the spec house and saw it was a three-bedroom one story adobe brick ranch home. Next to a one-story adobe brick ranch home. And on the other side, there was another adobe brick ranch home, this one painted white.

"Yes," she said in vibrant real estate speak. "If you want, I could submit the same paperwork to the seller, and get back to you tomorrow."

"Let me think about it," he put his hand over his forehead dejectedly, and then said, "Thank you for your time."

"My pleasure," she answered. "Is there anything else I can do for you?"

Go fuck yourself, lady, he thought. "No, you've been very helpful. I'll let you know what I decide."

They said their goodbyes and he hit the red hangup button on his phone. "Fuck!"

Arlene knocked on the door and opened it, saying, "Hey, Joey's ready to eat. You cooking?"

"Yes," he said, standing up. He wadded up the paper with the phone number on it and threw it into a black net trash can by his desk. "I'll be right there."

"What was that all about, anyway?" she asked as he left the office and went down to the kitchen, with Arlene following close behind.

"If you must know," he explained flatly, "That was a real estate company in New Mexico. I put an offer on a seventeen-acre ranch outside of Albuquerque. They didn't accept it."

"Joe," she said. "I'm not moving to New Mexico."

"Neither am I." He took out the box of nuggets, lifted the lid and put it in the microwave. He pressed the two-minute button. "So you don't have to worry."

"When were you going to tell me?" Her hands were on her hips now, her anger rising.

"If the offer went through then I would have talked with you about it."

"You could have said you were putting an offer on a house seven states away."

"It was late at night, you were asleep. It was more of an inquiry than anything else," he explained. "I didn't expect it to go through anyway, so what's the harm?

"What's the harm?" she asked, her voice rising. "You want to move the family across the country and you don't tell your wife about it first, that's the harm."

"It's no big deal," he said. "Besides, that's where we were going to talk about it. It's not like I sent them any money."

"It's not about the money, Joe."

He looked at the microwave timer. The nuggets had one minute left. She stepped close to him. "If you think for one minute I'm going to move to someplace hot and dry and shitty, you've got another thing coming, mister."

"But I thought you wanted this," he said. He had remembered early on in their relationship how they had talked about his dream once. "You said once it would be cool. I thought you were on board with this."

"Since when?" she said harshly. "Since when, Joe?"

"When we were dating, I brought it up once, and you said it would be fun."

"We were dating, asshole. I was willing to tell you anything. Jesus, you may be the stupidest guy I've ever met."

"Hey," he pointed at her. "Don't call me stupid!"

"Whatever," she started walking away from him. The microwave timer was at thirty seconds now. "But if you think I'm moving across the country to shovel horse shit again, think again." She turned. "You don't know the first thing about farms. I grew up on one, remember? I've shoveled my fair share of horseshit in my life and I'm not doing it anymore. If you want to go to New Mexico and work your fingers to the bone for nothing, go ahead. I'm not stopping you."

"It's something we could have as a family, don't you want that?"

"I want what we have now. A place where I don't have to shovel shit, do chores, weed gardens, milk cows, or stand in the dry-ass heat for hours on end harvesting plants. Oh, and you're forgetting all the stuff you have to do with horses, Joe."

"And that is?" he asked, already knowing the answer. "If you think I haven't done my research on farm maintenance, think again."

"There's hoof care, shedding, cleaning, putting a shoe on, there's bits and bridles and all the saddles you have to have, all that. You don't know the first thing about doing any of that, Joe. What makes you think you can learn now?" She put a finger up with every item.

Fifteen seconds now.

"I know all this!" he said. "And we can hire hands for all of it. After I take my retirement out, we'll have enough to do everything we need."

"Retirement to buy a horse farm in the desert?" she screamed. "No. I'm putting my foot down. That is for the kid's college fund. That's to pay off this house. That's to do everything in this fucking world besides whatever you want to do." she turned and walked away, saying. "And the last thing on the list is a horse ranch in the middle of the fucking desert. So give it up!"

The microwave dinged. Nuggets were done. And so was his dream, as long as he stayed here in White Pines. As long as he stayed with Arlene.

He took the nuggets up the stairs to Joey's room and knocked on the door. All he could hear from behind it was a clicking of buttons on a video game controller. He knocked again. No answer.

He opened the door. His ten-year-old son was in a console chair, in front of a large screen television, headphones over his black-haired head, and he was talking to someone, saying, "Roger, that. Tango down. I repeat, "Tango down!"

"Hey, soldier," Joe said as loudly as he could. "Dinner!"

Joey looked up and smiled at his dad. "Hang on guys, the breadwinner just brought me grub." He pressed pause on the controller.

"Hey Dad," he beamed. He had the same bright blue eyes as his father. If Joe did not know it, he's a spitting image of me. God, I wish I was ten again. The boy pulled off his headset. "Thanks for the nuggets."

He dug in immediately, pushing a nugget into the ketchup and biting into it. "Kinda hot," he said, making ooh-ooh noises with his mouth.

"Watch it, kiddo," Joe said. "I just pulled it out of the nuke."

"Hey, what were you and mom fighting about?"

"We weren't fighting," Joe said. "Just a loud discussion."

Another nugget went into the kid's mouth. "Sounded like a fight to me." he wiped his hand across his mouth and smeared ketchup on his cheek. Joe instinctively went to wipe it off.

"Whoah, daddy-o," his son shied away. "I got it." He picked up a dirty tee shirt off the floor and wiped his face.

"Joey," he sighed exasperated. "Give me that." he took the tee shirt and balled it up. "You stained it, you know how your mother gets with stains."

"Yeah," he said. "But she'll get over it. What's she gonna do, kick me out?"

"She just might." Joe laughed.

"I'll take my chances," his son laughed.

"God I love you, kid." Joe admired his son, with so much maturity than most ten-year-olds had.

"Love you too, Dad," he said, as he swallowed another ketchup-dipped nugget. "So really, what was this discussion about?"

"I put an offer on a ranch in New Mexico," Joe explained.

"Awesome!" Joey said. "Like Red Dead Redemption." He equated everything to video games and characters.

"Yes, but set in the twenty-first century." Joe sat down on the bed. "Your mom isn't keen on the idea, though."

"What's not to like?" Joey asked. "Horses, sun, sand, rootin' tootin' cowboys, put 'em up!" he made finger guns and went "Pew pew!" with them at his father. Joe went back on the bed, shot, laughing.

He sat back up. "So it's off the table anyway. You kids need a college fund more than I need to play in the desert."

"I don't need to go to college," Joey said. "If that helps your case."

"It's more about not wanting to shovel shit," Joe explained. "You know, like she did at the farm upstate."

"I like grandma's farm. It's fun. And I got to ride on the tractor with Grandpa." he stopped. Lowered his head and said, "When he was alive anyway."

Thomas had died three years ago when Joey was seven. The kid had a rough time. He looked up to his grandfather. Hell, everyone did, even Joe.

"I know kiddo," Joe said, patting his son on the head. "We all miss him."

"Can we go out there again soon?" Joey asked.

"I'll talk to your mom about it," he said. "Maybe you can ride on the tractor with Uncle Tommy. Would you like that?"

"Yeah," Joey said excitedly. "That would be cool as hell."

"Okay," Joe said. "I'll talk to your mom. Go ahead and finish dinner. I'll let you get back to your game."

"Okay," said his son, putting the headset back on. "Hey, Dad."

"Yeah, buddy?"

"We got any more of that fudge ice cream left?"

"Not unless your sister finished it. You want some?"

"Yes, please."

"You got it, kiddo. Have fun." Joe closed the door behind him. God, that kid is going to ruin me, he thought. He could hear little Joey spouting military lingo and went down the hall. Then downstairs.

Where Arlene sat on the couch, the television still on to a drama involving zoos and tigers. She was asleep. Passed out, more like it. He went to her, picked her up, noticed the new bottle with a few shots of it gone, and picked up her lifeless body.

"Hey," he said. "Arlene, baby?"

She stirred, and said, "Maybe I should take a nap." Her words were slow and slurry.

"Yeah," he agreed. "Let's go." He stood her up on shaky legs and walked her to the stairs. Then he led her up to the bedroom, a ramshackle mess of clothes, books, magazines on nightstands and dressers, clothes on the floor, and a water bottle half full of coins by an open closet full of clothes on hangers. He laid her on the bed, and gently kissed her forehead, she moaned, her eyes closed.

"I'll wake you in a couple of hours," he said with an exasperated sigh.

"No, I'll just lay here a minute," she complained. "Gotta make dinner..."

"It's okay," he said. She closed her eyes and didn't open them back up the rest of the night.

He went back downstairs, shut off the television, and headed to the kitchen. He took out the fudge ripple ice cream, put a dollop in a bowl for his son, ate a bite, and thought about the frozen section of the grocery store.

"This is your life now, buddy," said his logical mind. Wife, kids, house, mortgage, job, PTA meetings, two cars in the driveway. All you need is a dog named Sparky and you've got the middle-aged, trapped-in-suburbia starter kit.

He took the bowl of ice cream up to his son's room, handed it to him without interrupting his shooting game, where Nazis were coming through the wall of a French chateau, and went back to his office.

He browsed the website again, looking at property after property—green cacti, large houses made of adobe with curved slate roofs, ranches, arroyos, and buttes—and reminisced about his cowboy dreams of childhood.

The day in the desert, looking at the pretty flowers, cacti, and round prickly plants, feeling the sun beating down, feeling the heat. Watching his parents kiss, it was a good day. It was seven months before the accident that put his dad in a wheelchair. One of those days where everything was perfect. He longed to stay there, to stay in that perfect day. And all his life, he yearned to go back, to have that perfect day again, only now, to have it every day.

But then mom and dad had an accident. Coming home from work one day, like he had every day. And there was an impatient driver behind him who wanted to go faster, tried to pull around, and pulled into oncoming traffic without looking. That accident had killed the driver of the car instantly, the other driver he had collided with, and led to an eleven-car pileup where nine people died. His father's legs had been crushed and he had to have them amputated.

His mother was one of the nine who died. Joe was sixteen when this happened. His father was still alive, living in a home in the city. He went to visit now and then, and his father was amiable, non-committal in their conversations, and had just wanted to stare out the window for hours on end. So Joe had gone less and less now. And lately only visited on his dad's birthday.

Charley Guillaume was seventy-two, alive, but made living dead when a reckless driver decided he needed to get somewhere faster than Charley did.

Joe wished, like most days, he could go back in time to when he had the perfect day. That perfect day in the desert, in the before times.

When the world was happy, warm, filled with beauty, and he had his parents alive and whole.

He opened up Netflix, turned on the Movie High Plains Drifter, watched it again, for probably the seventeenth time, and ate leftover tacos. He made sure Joey went to sleep, went to bed himself a few hours later, after finishing up details about sales for the next day, and went to sleep.

He dreamed of a hot sun in a blazing Arizona sky, and a flaming red-haired saloon girl on a white horse, riding off into the sunset.

CHAPTER 6
Maxine

TUESDAY MORNING, THE day of the measurement, Maxine went downstairs, humming to herself. Something about feeling like a woman. She fixed coffee, a whole pot this time, not just enough for two cups and one for Harold, she filled the carafe up to the top. She was going to have company today. Good company. Lovely company. The kind of company that she could flirt with and maybe made her feel wanted.

Carrie had told her a few days ago not to do anything stupid, but having a fling with a hot married floor salesman down the street didn't seem stupid at all. It felt right. It felt fun, it felt like a decision that would rock her world and make her feel again. Feel what? Something. Anything, but this.

This long slow drudgery, this descent into madness, she would be damned if she allowed herself to just go down that path anymore. She had lived that way for several years, a never-ending drudge that took her down the depths of depression. No fear, Maxine, just do it. Like Nike says.

There was a knock at the door and she went to it, expecting the first of her company that day. Carrie stood there, a white Stanley cup full of coffee in her hand, "Hey girl," she said, pushing into the house like she always did. "Where's hunkalicious?" she laughed

"Oh, stop," said Max jokingly. "Maybe I got a little overboard the other day. He's just a floor salesman."

Then why are you dressed like that?" Carrie asked. She looked at Maxine, dressed in white denim shorts that held her curves, and a white cotton blouse with a v-neck that showed more curves. "You want to put on a bra?"

"Oh, come on," Max said. "It's still early. Of course, I will. Want some coffee?"

Carrie shook her cup. Ice clattered around the mug's metal insides. "Got plenty, hon." She looked around at the house. "What happened here?" she asked.

Maxine looked at her questioning. "What do you mean? I always keep it this clean."

"Max, there's clean, and then there's this. It looks like a museum in here. Geez, you even dusted."

The house which normally had a lived-in look with glasses on coffee tables, plates on end tables, magazines typically strewn about furniture and floor, and a host of unfolded laundry on the easy chair in the corner, was now a spotless room that an Army drill sergeant would be proud of.

Gone were the magazines, replaced by a couple of coffee table books about sailing, and the Moon. In place of the clothes on the easy chair, there was a throw blanket hanging over the back like something out of a good housekeeping book from the eighties. Dishes had been gathered, cup stains had been Cloroxed, and dust that had crept up in the room for years had been wiped away in a fit of cleaning that had taken Maxine most of Monday to finish.

"Well, at least it gave me a reason to tidy up," she said. "Don't even let it be said I'm not Suzy fucking homemaker."

"You sure have gone all out," Carrie said. "Let me guess, you've made him your special sweet tea, too, haven't you?"

Maxine started for the kitchen, and said, "You know it, girlfriend." She went to the refrigerator, a white two-door monstrosity she made Harold buy her a few years and opened it.

She brought out a pitcher of tea and set it on the marble island countertop.

"Who are you?" Carrie asked. "Is he really that cute?" Carrie remembered the iced tea Maxine had made last July fourth. Most of the guests didn't know it was spiced with coconut rum until it was too late. That was a fun night for sure, Carried thought. "Remember he's still on the job."

Maxine huffed, "I didn't put anything in it, here, have a taste."

Carrie said, "No, I'm not in the mood for that. Maybe later. After he's gone we can spice it up then and talk."

Just then, they heard a car door shut out front and Maxine stopped. "Oh my God, he's here. Answer the door. I have to go get presentable. Shit!"

Carrie said, "I guess we lost track of time. Sure, I'll get the door. Go put on some clothes." Maxine sped up the stairs as Carrie went to the door to see what Hunkalicous actually looked like. She had been intrigued by his description during her and Maxine's chat over lunch a couple of days ago. Now she would see if it was all a fantasy in Maxine's head or not.

Carrie stepped to the small entryway and the doorbell rang. She took a few breaths and opened the door. Joe stood there, for a second and then looked at his phone for confirmation, "I'm sorry, I must have the wrong house. Is Maxine here?"

Carrie looked at him, taken aback for a moment. My God, Maxine was right. This guy was handsome, she thought. She took in his wavy black hair with a bit of gray on the temples, the short cropped beard, the blue polo accentuating his blue eyes, and tan slacks that molded to his hips and crotch. "Jesus," she whispered.

"Hello?" he said again. He didn't seem to notice what she had said. "Maxine Colston?" He checked the phone and looked up at the porch railing that had the house number on the post holding up the porch roof. "I may have gotten it wrong, I write too fast sometimes."

Carrie caught herself staring and said quickly. "Max, yes. Maxine. Yes, she's here. Come on in." she waved her arm and invited him in. He went past her, and she looked at his ass. Nice, she thought. Holy shit. He works out.

Joe held a notepad pad and a red tape measure clasped to his belt. He turned as he came in, "Hello, I'm Joseph. I'm here to do the measurement. We haven't met."

Carrie said her name, shook his hand and let him step into the home. "Maxine is upstairs. She'll be down in a minute."

"Well then, since I'm at the right place, let me get started," he said, pulling out the tape measure. "I have a couple more clients to see today so I'd best get busy."

Maxine heard his voice and shook her head. Damn, that voice of his, breathy and deep. She had dressed herself in a white cotton blouse, white bra, and tan slacks that melded to her figure. She had touched up her lipstick and make-up quickly as she heard him come into the house and gathered herself before coming down the stairs. "Hello, is that Joe?"

Carrie said, "Yes, it is, he just started."

Maxine was at the bottom of the stairs now, and looked over at him. Her breath hitched at the sight of him. Holy hell, she thought. I am going to be no good. He went to her and shook her hand. The electricity of his touch warmed her flesh momentarily as she held his hand, shook it, and let it go slowly. She looked into his blue eyes, God I could swim there, she thought. "Hello," she said. "Good to see you again. Welcome to my home."

If he noticed the flirtatious handshake, he didn't say anything. "Nice place you've got here. The place is like a museum, does anyone live here?" he joked.

"I wanted to make sure it looked nice. Wouldn't want the company to see how much of a slob I am," she answered.

"Oh, you'd be surprised. I've seen some doozies," he said. "So where do I start?"

She pointed him to the kitchen, a large open space with an island, marble counters, and white appliances. "So," she said. "I've decided to do you in the whole house," she stopped. "Do the whole house," she laughed.

Carried looked at her. Maxine mouthed, "What?"

He didn't seem to notice her Freudian slip. "Good, I was hoping I could talk you into doing that. We offer whole house deals. Our installer gives twenty percent off installs if you go that way."

"Yes," Maxine said. "That sounds great. Did you want some coffee? Tea?"

"No, I've had two cups already. I'll just get started." He walked away into the dining room, and the women followed. They watched as he took the tape measure, pulled it out expertly, and measured the whole room. He made notations on the notepad, then went to the living room. There, he encountered a problem. "Hey, Maxine?" he said loudly to let her hear in the kitchen. "Mind if I move the couch just a bit. I have to get up against the wall."

She whispered under her breath, "You can get me up against the wall." Carrie slapped her arm playfully, a scowl on her face.

"Yes, Joe, I'll be right there." she came into the opulent living room and saw him standing next to the arm of the couch. "Here, let me help you," she said.

"No, that's okay, I could use the workout." And he lifted the couch a few inches and moved one side, then proceeded to the other side. He pulled out his tape and got down on the floor, kneeling as he went to the wall behind the couch and measured. She looked at his butt, and marveled at the muscularity of it, wondering what his dimples looked like under those khakis.

Carrie noticed this and said, "So Max says you live down the street. Small world, huh?"

He stood back up. "Yes, he said. "Just down a few blocks. Funny we've never met." But then he added, "I don't get out much, you know with the job and all that. Plus, my wife keeps me pretty busy."

"Oh," said Carrie, looking pointedly at Maxine. "You're married, how nice. Any kids?" She continued to look at Maxine squarely.

"Yes, he said, not looking up. "Cathy is twelve, and my son Joey is ten."

"I bet they're precious," said Carrie.

"They're the best," he said. "Well, Joey is. All he does is talk to friends on video chat while he's playing Call of Duty. My daughter is a handful. She's starting to talk about boys and make-up and all that. That's my wife's job, navigating her through that. I wouldn't know the first thing about what to do with makeup and boys. It's tough having a daughter, you never know what they're going to talk about next."

"Yes," Maxine said, "Girls can be quite the handful."

"Yes they can," Carrie agreed, looking at Maxine again, who had made cupping motions with her hands as she looked at Joe on the ground bent over on his knees. In front of them.

He stood back up with a grunt, went to the couch, and moved it back. "Okay, what's next?" he asked. Maxine sighed quickly at the grunt.

Then she took him around the house, showing him the different rooms, the bedrooms, and bathrooms upstairs and downstairs. When she got to the master bedroom she paused, "Don't mind the mess, I wasn't able to tidy this up as well as the rest of the house."

"I've been in plenty of master bedrooms, Hell if you saw mine, you'd think I was the worst husband in the world. Piles of clothes everywhere." He looked sad at this thought, and Maxine opened the door.

There was the four-poster bed, made up with silk sheets, down pillows, and multi-colored bedspread and throw pillows. There were a few items of clothing on the floor, mostly women's, but he turned his head respectfully at seeing the sight of a white silk bra on an easy chair in the corner. There was a long short dresser, probably made by Ikea, he thought, or Wayfair. Those things were all over the place in White Pines, it seemed to come with the house. He went to work, after saying, "No, this is nice. That's a pretty bed. I've always wanted one like that, but Arlene thinks they're' ugly and outdated,"

"Why don't you sit on it, it's comfortable," Maxine said. Carrie nudged her with her elbow. Maxine chuffed and shot her a nasty look.

"Oh no," he said and looked at her. His eyebrow looked questioningly at her for a second and he chuckled, "I would like it too much and that'd be all I thought about. Then I'd have to get one myself," he added.

She watched as he turned and measured the room just as expertly as he had the other rooms in the house. Then he went to the bathroom. It was large, with a white subway tiled shower with tan accents behind a sliding glass door. In the corner was a toilet, and across from that a large two-person tub. "That's nice," he said, pointing at it.

"I had Harold buy it for us a few years ago," she said. "I was hoping we'd use it but it's only been in operation a couple of times. Mostly by myself. It's got jets and everything."

"Cool," he said. "Arlene would never go for one of those. She'd say it uses up too much electricity."

"You could always come down and use mine," she jested playfully. "You know, if you ever wanted to relax." Once again, Carrie eyed her maliciously.

He laughed. "Thanks for the invite, but I don't really think my wife would approve." He smiled at her, relaxing. "No, that would be no good at all."

"Well, a girl can try, I guess." Maxine jested. Joe moved to measure the bathroom and stood up after he finished. He had drawn complex measurements of all of the rooms, and had asked her questions all during the measurement of what type of flooring she wanted in each room, and by the time they went back downstairs, he had already figured out how much square footage there was in the home.

"So with all of your selections, it should be fairly easy to come up with a figure. I'll go back to the office in a few hours and have everything ready to email you by tomorrow."

"That would be fine. Or you could call me with the estimate," she said.

"Yes," he said. "I'll call you later, but I always send an email anyway, just to make sure there's a paper trail."

"Of course," she said. "So that's it?"

"Yep," he buckled the tape measure back on his belt. "All done. Any questions?"

"Do you install it too?" she asked.

"Oh, no, that's another job for an installation company. We use Virginia and Tidewater Services. They're a great company to work with. Five-star service and everything. The warranty for a year, if anything goes bad with your floor or the installation they fix it with no problems."

"That's good," she said. "Did you want anything for the road?" Like me, she thought.

"No, I'm fine. I have a Coke in the car." He put the pen into his breast pocket of the blue polo shirt and started for the door. If you have anything else you need, just give me a ring. I'm available any time."

"I will, I've got your number, remember?"

"Sure," he looked, another questioning flick of the eyebrow. "But not my cell phone after five. Arlene gets upset when anyone calls me after work. You understand."

"Got it. Working hours only." She shook his hand again, her eyes lingered on his. "If you need anything from me, let me know," she purred. "Anything at all."

Carrie said, "Maybe I'll get my floors done too. I rent apartments so I may need you down the line."

He laughed, "Yes, that would be great. I hope you keep me in mind" He turned and went to the entryway. Maxine opened the door for him, and he turned, and said "Goodbye, I'll talk to you again soon."

"Good," she smiled. "That's wonderful. The sooner we can get this started, the better."

"Fine," he said and shook Carrie's hand. "Nice to meet you."

Carrie couldn't help but be enchanted momentarily by his genuine warmth. "Yes. Nice to meet you too." They followed him out into the driveway, where Carrie and Max stayed under the awning of her front porch.

He opened the door and got in the car, "Bye!" Maxine said loudly, but he had already gotten in and started the white Sonata. "See you soon... I hope," the last came as a whisper.

"Maxine," Carrie said. They both waved as he backed out of the driveway, he held up four fingers as a goodbye wave to them as he put the car in drive.

Maxine waved one last time as the car sped off down the street. "Dear God, that man is beautiful," she said. There was a silence between them as they watched him pull down the street.

"You're going to fuck that guy, aren't you?" Carrie said finally.

Maxine watched the white car turn a corner and go out of sight. "Oh, God yes."

"Jesus Christ."

Diamonds on the Soles of Her Shoes—Paul Simon

CHAPTER 7

Joe

ANOTHER DAY, ANOTHER dollar. He walked into Bennet's Hardware and was greeted by Barb, the head cashier. "Hello, sunshine!" she said with a beaming smile. Barb was one of those women who had morning energy. Always positive, was she. Always ready with a joke or a friendly greeting. She had been at Bennet's for over twenty-five years, and she loved it.

Barb and Joe exchanged pleasantries. He talked about his boring weekend doing chores for the wife and kids, and she talked about her grandbabies and a Sunday picnic in the park. There were few customers, being taken care of by other workers.

He walked past shelves laden with product, down the wide aisle that ran through the center of the store. On the left were household goods, nuts and bolts, plumbing supplies, and home hardware. On the right were fans, tools, gardening implements, and a door leading to the garden center—Jodi's domain.

He saw Jodi standing among hoes, picks, and shovels, stocking products from the overnight truck delivery. When she saw him, she greeted him with her usual, "Hey, Joe, what do ya know?" It had been her greeting for the twelve years he'd worked at Bennets. Jodi was a short, pudgy woman with bleach-blond, graying hair pulled into a ponytail. The tattoo of a flower on her arm had once been a vibrant, multicolored rose, but decades later, time had turned it into an unidentifiable black and blue scrawl. She had other tattoos, some hidden by her clothing and apron, and Joe often joked she'd outlived a lifetime of bad decisions.

"Hey, Jodi, whatcha working on today?" Joe asked politely. They worked together as two people who tolerated each other—not enemies, but not friends either. It was rumored Jodi had wanted the flooring job before Joe applied, but Jamie kept her in Gardening, a role she loved. She knew everyone in town, was good at sales, and excelled at her job. She had even helped Joe with his azaleas and other flowers around his house, so there was mutual respect.

One thing you didn't do, though, was tell her any secrets. People always joked, "Telephone, telegraph, and teleJodi." If you wanted something blabbed all over town, you told her.

"Gotta get the stuff up from last night," she answered. "Then I got Morrison's coming with a truck of fresh inventory. Wanna help out?"

"Maybe later," he said. "Hit me up after I talk to this flooring customer and get her paperwork done."

"I'll hold you to that, mister," she said as she went back to putting up hoes. "Once you get in the door, there's a truck to help put up."

"Hold your horses," he joked. "I've got to do some work, then I'll help out."

"Well get to it, cowboy," she joked back. It was friendly banter between coworkers. But there was one thing he didn't do, and that was to trust Jodi Parker. So he kept it friendly between the two of them, because if you get on her bad side, you don't last at Bennet's. He had seen that several times. She was on good terms with the boss, having worked for Jamie for over twenty years. So you respected her, and kept things you wanted kept secret very tight to the chest.

"Gimme a minute," he smiled reassuringly at her. "I'll be right there." She gave him a thumbs up and he walked into his office.

Office was a generous term. It was more of a cubicle than anything else. He had a satchel full of measurements, designs, and numbers. Always numbers in his head about what he needed to work up for a certain house.

Maxine's. Last week was tough for him. In between other quotes, he had to work up, he had to go to her place. The first thing he had noticed was her, the smell of her, sweet and vibrant. I wonder what she was wearing, He'd have to give some to Arlene on their anniversary which was coming up when? He thought. Oh yeah, October. He kept thinking about her hair, auburn, pretty, curls he'd like to wrap his fingers in and tug.

Nope. don't think about that, you need to stop thinking what you're thinking. You go down that road, it's a disaster waiting to happen..

But it didn't help that she was coming in today, to pick out the final items on her quote and pay for it. He wondered what she would look like. He wondered what she would wear. He pulled out the quote he had finished and looked at the clock. It was nine-fifteen. Good enough, he thought. He picked up the phone, dialed her number and after a few rings, he heard her melodious voice, a southern drawl barely imperceptible but there in a cute way.

"Hello?" she said sweetly, "Colston residence."

"Hello," he said and cleared his throat. Why did that voice do something to him? "Ms, Colston, this is Joe, from Bennet's, I wanted to go over your quote if you had a minute."

"Joe, yes, hello," she seemed to purr into the phone. "I'm delighted to hear from you. But please, I've told you to call me Maxine."

"Maxine, yes, I forgot. Just trying to be professional. But yes, I was confirming our ten-thirty appointment for you to come in and finish up this quote. I have some initial numbers for you, but it all depends on what extras you want."

She answered, "Yes, I can't wait! It'll be good to get this process started." Joe noticed a little bit of excitement in her voice. He liked that, an excited customer always meant a sale and always meant a higher monthly bonus.

"Good," he smiled, "I'll see you then. I'll have everything ready when you get here."

"Okay, great. Well, I have to get breakfast ready for Harold, so let me go and I'll see you soon."

"Sure, don't let me keep you. Thanks again."

They said their goodbyes, and he turned back to the desk in his office. It was actually a cubicle in the corner of the store, behind housewares, near the public bathrooms so there was always sort of an unpleasant smell, and right next to Derrick's cubicle.

Joe went about his morning, answering emails, working out the numbers for another quote he would have to call after Maxine's appointment, and trying to feel excited about the rest of the day. Yep, it was a Monday, but he was glad he was at work.

It had become his peaceful place. Far away from home, from the household chores, and far from her. Arlene had been sulking and sullen all weekend. He could never tell why. He would ask, but she just said, "I'm fine," and walked away from him. He would try to give her a reassuring hug, but when he touched her she bristled, so he had given up. It almost seemed to him like she didn't even want him around. So when he got a chance to go to work, to be out in public with normal people and coworkers who seemed to like his company, he was in his happy place. Work was peaceful for him. A refuge from the anxiety-inducing feeling he got when he had to pull into the driveway.

They say home is where the heart is, but lately, there'd been no heart, and his house was a distant place full of admonishment, arguments, and angst.

He took a sip of coffee, got up and went around the store, helping customers where needed, checking on the shelves to make sure the night crew did their jobs, arranging shelves, and making sure the inventory was right. He was filled with nervous anticipation, waiting for this woman, needing this sale as much as he needed her.

"Joe?" said a sweet southern voice behind him. There was an electric shock in his back when he heard it, and he looked up to see her. Maxine.

She was dressed in pale blue jeans, with a light pink tank top over which she had an open pink blouse that flowed over the smooth curve of her breasts and the slight hint of cleavage. A pretty gold necklace and a clutch she carried completed the ensemble. His heart skipped a beat and something else farther below his waist jumped at the sight of her. "Dear God," he thought. "This is going to be impossible. What the fuck?"

"Hello, Maxine," he went to her, shook her hand. "Thanks for coming."

She said, "I couldn't wait," She held it for a beat longer than she should have and looked him in his eyes with a smile. "Let's get started, shall we?"

He had been drawn into those big brown eyes of hers, warm and enthusiastic.

"Yes," he cleared his throat. "Yes, let's go back to my office. I have all the figures there. Don't mind the smell, though, it's next to the bathrooms. I've got some air fresheners so it should be fine."

"Oh, never mind that," she said sweetly, "I just want to get this over with. I have a lunch appointment with a friend at noon, so I just wanted to get in and out."

"Sure, shouldn't take a few minutes." He led her back to his cubicle. Derrick was there, running numbers on the inventory he had just taken.

"Hey, Joe," he said. Then he saw Maxine, looked at her longer than he should have, and said, "Hi! How are you?" and reached out to shake her hand.

Maxine took his hand quickly, shook it, and then let go. "Hi, nice to meet you."

"Pleasure's all mine," said Derrick in the overtly flirty voice he used with the lady customers. He thought he was being smooth, but Maxine had seen a million of his type and just smiled politely.

Joe said, "Derrick, do you mind? I'm trying to make a sale here, and I don't need you trying to pick up my customers."

"Hey," Derrick shrugged, "Just being polite, you know me."

"I do know you," Joe said. "Don't you have work to do?"

"Yeah, sure," Derrick sat back down in his black office chair. "Nice to meet you, Maxine. If you need any help with lumber or anything let me know."

"I will," she said as Joe pulled up a chair for her to sit on. She sat, and Joe noticed she bent over as she sat and he could see down her tank top. No bra. What the shit?

She looked up at him, put her purse on the desk and said, "So where do we start?"

He pulled out the file he had on her, with all the details. "Okay," he began, "You picked out the Chancellorsville Oak hardwood, which is good, it's got a great color to it, and the coating on it is warranted for fifteen years."

"The coating?" she asked.

"Yes, the veneer is a thick resin polyurethane that keeps its hardness for fifteen years, guaranteed."

"Fifteen years, wow," she smiled. "That's a long time for something to stay hard."

"Yes, well, it's got a lifetime warranty, but I like to tell people fifteen years so they don't get their hopes too high. It all depends on how much you use the floor." He heard Derrick clear his throat and chuckle from the other cubicle.

"What do you mean?" she asked.

"Well, it depends on how much use the floor gets. How much you walk on it, moving furniture, that sort of thing."

"I don't see myself moving furniture a lot," Maxine smiled. "My husband is a bit of a sedentary creature. We haven't moved the furniture in years."

"Just letting you know," said Joe, oblivious. He turned another sheet and said, "Now about the carpet. You wanted Cotton Club White, right?"

"Yes," she said. "It's so pretty, I really like bright carpet, it'll make my bedroom brighter when the sun comes through the window."

"Well, that's one room it's going in, that, the living room, den, and office and the other bedrooms," Joe explained as he pointed to the floor plan. "I notice there are two bedrooms, is this one a guest room?" He pointed to a room on the large floorplan.

"Oh no," Maxine answered. "That's Harold's room when he decides to leave his office and go to bed. It started as a guest room, but now it's just his room." She looked at him with a fierce look in her eye. "He and I haven't slept in the same room together for several years. He snores and it keeps me awake at night."

Joe couldn't comprehend the idea of a married couple staying in different rooms at night. He had always slept with Arlene and all that came with it.

Joe noticed the silence from the neighboring cubicle. He knew Derrick was listening. He could hear the chuckle coming from the other side of the thin partition.

After a beat to gather his thoughts, he said, "I'm sure that'll make a fine choice of carpet. And good luck. It's in stock."

"Good," Maxine said, twirling a long finger in her curly hair. "Is there anything else?"

"Just the transitions from the carpet to the hardwood flooring. Did you want it a paler color for the carpet or to match the flooring?"

"Oh, let's match the carpet," she said. "It should be the same color. How would that look, do you think?"

"It's your house, I'm sure that would look just fine if they matched," Joe answered with a frown. "But yes, we have the transition color for both. He made a note in the computer on his quote screen for the style choice.

He continued, "Now the plush pile height of the carpet is pretty soft, with a pet guard and stain guard lifetime guarantee, so you won't have any problems. And since there are no pets and children, I don't really see it getting dirty or stained with just you and your husband there."

"Does that also depend on how much usage the carpet gets?" she asked.

"Well unless you're running back and forth on it constantly or spilling fluids on it all the time, I don't think you'll ever have a problem," he explained.

"Then it won't be a problem," she said. "Hasn't been any fluids on the carpet since my daughter's toddler days, so it should last a lifetime."

Joe heard Derrick snigger again. He ignored it.

Just then, his ringtone, "The good, the bad, and the ugly" played on his phone. He blushed, embarrassed. "Sorry," he said, reaching for it. "I should have had it on mute. Guess I wasn't paying attention this morning." He went to put it on silent and saw a text from Arlene. Shit.

"It's no problem," she said. "If you have to answer, go ahead. I'll just look over these figures and start the check."

He looked at the text.

Arlene:

You coming home for lunch?

Cath wants gogurt and Joey wants a happy meal.

Pick up OJ and bread at the store too.

He texted back:

   i wasn't planning on
   Going to Macronalds, but sure.

"Wedded bliss, am I right?" he said, putting the phone down.

"I wouldn't know," she answered, putting a loose strand of hair behind her ear. She looked away, back to the quote on the desk, but not paying attention to the figures, lost in thought.

"What do you mean by that?"

"Hmm?" she said, looking at him. "Oh.. nothing. It's just." she chuckled. "Never mind."

He tried to ignore the lost feeling in her eyes, the momentary intake of breath when she looked at him. However, ignoring didn't make the idea of her go away.

"Listen," he said after a few seconds of silence. She looked up and he went on. "If you ever need to talk, you have my number, okay?"

"That's sweet, Joe," she said. "But let's just get this done, and I'll go on my way."

"Okay," he said. His phone pulsed again. Dammit, Arlene, I'm working here. On what he didn't know.

Arlene:

   and go to the LS. i'm almost out of absolut

Joe simply texted back, "ok"

He put the phone down and sighed. "Yeah," he looked at her profile. She had pretty cheekbones, and that long auburn hair curving that face didn't do her any harm. She's a pretty woman, and for a split second he imagined what she would look like naked, but then he pushed that aside. He looked at her eyes again and saw they were watery. "You okay?"

She wiped her eyes, looked at him with a beaming smile. "Yes," she smiled at him. Everything is great." But it didn't sound great. Then he did something he couldn't explain. Something that he would think about on the way home for lunch. Something that he would probably think about for years.

He reached out and put a warm and gentle hand on hers. He squeezed, and said, "Really, if you need to talk. Anytime. Just call."

She looked down at his hand on hers, looked back up into his blue soulful eyes, looked back down. He took his hand away.

"Jesus," he was embarrassed now. "Oh, I'm sorry, I shouldn't have–" She stopped him.

"It was nice," she said in a low voice. "You're a really nice guy, Joe. Thank you."

There was an awkward moment between them, like something was shifting in both of their minds. Something neither one could explain. She smiled big then, her teeth showing bright and pure.

"Great!," she said. "This is perfect." she directed her attention back to the quote on the desk. "How do I pay?"

Sensing the shift back to business, he stood up, and said "Follow me, Barb would love to finish the transaction."

They went up to the front of the store, introductions were made between Barb and Maxine, and in the end, Jamie came downstairs to congratulate all of them and try to get a group picture with the receipt that was as long as Joe's arm, totalling over fourteen thousand dollars. He was going to make his bonus for sure this month.

After all the hype died down, he brought her outside. He wanted to explain to her, say something, anything that would explain what happened.

"Hey," he said, "I just wanted to apologize, for earlier."

She looked at him, questioningly. "What was that?"

"How I held your hand back then, I didn't mean to–I mean, I meant to, but I don't know why. It's just.." He babbled, trying to find words.

She said, "Joe," and that seemed to stop him. "It was nice. I liked it."

He sighed. "Okay," he put his hand behind his neck, shrugged, and said, "But I just wanted to let you know, I don't do things like that. It's just at that moment, you looked kind of sad. And there was something in me that wanted to make you feel better for a second. That's all."

"You're very nice," she said. "But really, don't worry about it. It was a nice gesture between friends."

"So we're friends now, huh?"

"I would think so. After all, I just gave you a check for a lot of money. I'd like to be able to call you a friend."

"Then friends it is," he said. He reached out a hand and she shook it. It was a business-like handshake. Except for the end when she pulled away and he felt the trail of her red tipped middle finger drag along his palm.

Then she said, "I have to go. Lunch plans, remember?"

He thought about his own plans. "Yes. Gotta run errands. See you later. I'll let you know when the product comes in and we can start the show."

"Okey dokey, pardner." She shot finger guns at him and he stepped back, his hands over his heart.

"Enjoy lunch."

"You too." She smiled and went to her car. He turned and walked back into the store, his mind on handshakes, a gentle squeeze, and a red fingernail trailing across his palm.

CHAPTER 8
Maxine

WATCHING JOE WALK BACK into the store, her heart fluttered more than it should have for a simple transaction. There was something magnetic about him—something in the way he held himself, the kindness in his eyes, and the quiet strength that radiated from him. She found herself replaying their interactions in her mind, savoring every word. And every touch.

The days that followed were a test of her patience. She kept busy with the usual tasks—tending to Harold's needs, running errands, and maintaining the house. Harold was increasingly demanding, needing more assistance with even the simplest of tasks. Each time she helped him, she couldn't help but think of Joe, of how different life might be if she were with someone like him.

The flooring shipment was delayed, adding to her frustration. Every time the phone rang, she hoped it was Joe calling with good news. She found herself daydreaming about their brief touches—the way his hand had lingered on hers during the final moments of the sale, the jolt of electricity from his touch. She thought about the set of his jaw, the way his hair fell slightly into his eyes, and those piercing blue eyes that seemed to see right through her.

Her nights were the hardest. She lay in bed, staring at the ceiling and thinking about Joe. She imagined his strong arms around her, his warm body next to hers. She pictured his smile and the way his eyes lit up when he talked about something he was passionate about. The longing was almost unbearable.

Finally, the day came when everything was in place. The installers had delivered the carpet and the flooring. They were scheduled for the next day. Joe had called her a few days ago to confirm that he was going to be coming by to make the final inspection and sign the paperwork that would finalize the install.

As she prepared for his visit, she felt a mix of excitement and anxiety. She wanted everything to be perfect, but more than that, she wanted to see him again, to feel that spark and connection that had been missing from her life for so long. As she tidied the house and waited for his arrival, she couldn't help but wonder what the future held and if Joe might be a part of it.

CHAPTER 9
Joe

AFTER MORE THAN TWO weeks, the product had finally come in, Joe decided to check on how things were going. He didn't have to go to Maxine's to see the installation, but he wanted to. It had taken two weeks to get all the product in, and for some reason, he had thought about her almost nonstop since their last interaction.

His hand on hers. The heat in her eyes that had blazed him to his stomach. He hadn't wanted to think about her. He hadn't wanted to even imagine a life with her. But every time he thought about something else, his mind came back to her hair, her skin, the way her hand felt hot in his.

It was as if the stars, moon and sun had all gathered together in that one moment and were pushing them together. Joe was never this lucky. Oh, sure, there were times in his life when things worked out for the best, but this wasn't going to be one of those times, and he knew it.

If he kept going down that road, the road to Maxine's house, he would be going to the land of Ruin. He knew that. Everyone knew that. Derrick had even commented to him one day a few days after she had paid.

"That woman is going to get you in trouble, Joe," he had said. "Trouble with a capital T and that rhymes with P and that stands for pool." Derrick was the king of musical one-liners like that. Some people called his ability to throw musical and movie quotes around "Musical Tourettes." But the truth was, he was right.

"I haven't done anything with her," Joe had answered. But he flushed when he said it, and Derrick picked up on it.

"Listen, I'm only telling this to you as a friend and coworker. As much as I joke, it's something that can't happen between you two, okay?"

"You don't think I know that?" Joe said wistfully.

"Yeah, I know you know that," said Derrick. "But knowing and doing are two different things. And I get the feeling you're going to be doing pretty soon."

"What do you mean by that?"

"Because I know what I look like when I want a woman and you, my brother, have all the symptoms."

"Such as?"

"The way you look at her when she comes in the door," Derrick explained. "Like you've seen an angel, all halos and moonbeams." He popped a peanut in his mouth. Derrick always had peanuts next to his phone on the desk. The shells made a mess on his desk that Jamie was constantly harassing him about.

"Oh, come on," Joe defended himself. "I don't do that."

"Sure," Derrick said. "Pull the other one, it's got bells on." he crunched another peanut. "Oh, and the way you talk to her on the phone. Like your voice gets all Mr. Seductive and shit."

"Please," Joe laughed. "I do not!"

"You totally do," Then Derrick mocked Joe's voice but made it gravelly and seductive sounding, "Maxine, this is Joe. Your product is in, and we'll be able to get the installation started next week. What day works best for you? Oh, Monday? Great, I'll see you then, I'll come over and lay down my hardwood all over your house." They both laughed.

"Listen," Joe said. "I'm trying to help a customer. That's all."

"You're helping yourself into her bed, my man."

"I'm married, remember?" Joe held up the hand with his wedding band on it.

"Married men cheat all the time, Joe."

"Not this married man."

"Keep it that way," Derrick said. "You know that woman is into you, don't you?"

"Yes," he said. "I've picked up on it, for sure."

"So, be careful," Derrick ate another peanut. "Because if it did in some way happen, and Jamie found out? You wouldn't just be losing a wife and kids, you'd be losing a job. He's very particular about that kind of thing."

"Noted," Joe said. He filed a stack of paperwork in a file and finished. "But it's not going to happen. Trust me."

"Good," Derrick said. "Because I like working with you. However, if she has a hot friend, maybe you can hook me up."

"She does, but the lady I'm thinking of has been married three times, is unlucky in love, and is one of those older cougar broads just going from man to man like notches in a belt."

"Sounds like just my style," Derrick was intrigued. "What does she look like?"

Joe thought for a minute. "You know that politics show about the president from about twenty years ago? The press secretary woman. She looks like that."

Derrick closed his eyes, "Oh, yeah. She was hot. Does she need exhusband number four?"

"You're impossible," said Joe. "Get back to work."

Derrick popped another peanut, and said, "Just sayin' is all." He went back to work, putting the finishing numbers on a lumber inventory for one of his larger clients.

Joe went back to his work on one particular client, the one with auburn hair, the one that made him think about halos and moonbeams.

He pulled his white Hyundai in the cul-de-sac right behind a blue and red van that said "Virginia and Tidewater Services" in bold black letters on the side and back of the van. The company was run by Chris Gorman, a regular stand-up guy who did flooring on an industrial level. He serviced the city with a fleet of trucks and vans, doing everything from air conditioner maintenance and installation to flooring installs and everything in between. If you needed a handyman, VATS was your go-to.

Chris was at the back of the van, an elderly gentleman with graying blond hair pulled into a ponytail, wearing a brown polo shirt with VATS in white on the front breast. He was wearing white cargo shorts, and a handyman's belt with all manner of equipment from squares to measuring tapes attached to it.

"Hey, Chris," said Joe as he walked over to him and they shook hands.

"Hey, man, how's it hanging?" Chris said. He had that Marlboro man voice, gravely, but melodious. It made him sound like Tommy Lee Jones at times. "Checking up on me, huh?"

"You know it," Joe joked. "Gotta make sure you're taking care of my client and doing a good job. Don't need any complaints."

"Right," said Chris with a tone of disbelief. "You just wanted to get another look at that number inside." He pointed to the house with his thumb.

"I had some more paperwork for her to sign," Joe explained. "If you must know."

"Sure," said Chris. "Go on in, she's out back." He went back to cutting a piece of hardwood with a circular saw but looked back up. "Oh, hey, just a warning!" he said loudly as the saw wound down from his last cut.

"What's that?"

"She's by the pool."

"And?" Joe asked, intrigued.

"And I've had a hell of a time keeping my guys on task."

"I don't understand," said Joe, clueless as ever.

"You will in a minute," Chris said, and went back to cutting and measuring the wood, shaking his head.

Joe walked through the house, seeing the sawdust, the couch and all other furniture moved out of the way. The kitchen was almost done and looking nice, except for the tools and construction debris scattered over most of the room.

He saw the glass doors to the patio closed and went to them. The backyard he had only briefly seen was nice, as large as his, and had a large pool on the patio, circular with stairs at the short end. He looked out and saw a bunch of blue lounge chairs and folding chairs, the plastic kind that gets molten hot in the summer sun. And speaking of molten hot...

He saw Maxine sitting on one of the chairs, reading a book. A white beach hat shaded her head, and sunglasses framed her eyes. One leg, shimmering with sunscreen oil, was propped up. She wore a bright yellow bikini top and bottoms, covered only by a white, flowy lace sarong. A pair of white flip-flops completed the ensemble.

"Jesus," he breathed. "Christ."

She hadn't noticed him. Yet. He took a breath in, let it out, did it again to steady his nerves, and looked around to see if anyone had seen him. It didn't help. He heard movement from behind him and saw two of Chris's workers coming from down the hall. He waved, they waved, and he opened the door.

She saw him coming out on the patio and gave him a big smile. "Joe!" She seemed excited to see him. The closer he got, her presence seemed to draw him in like a tractor beam. "It's good to see you!"

"Hello," he said. She stood up, her tanned skin shimmering in the sun, and he coughed. They shook hands. "How's it going?" He motioned back to the house.

"Good, so far," she said. "You want anything to drink?"

"No," he said. "I'm just here for a few minutes. I wanted to check on the installation, and see if you had any questions."

"You're a dear," she said. "Chris is really good, and his men are doing a great job. Have you seen the kitchen?"

"Yes, I noticed. It's nice."

"They're in the bathroom now. I'm so happy with my selections," she said, going to the patio door. He watched her, the thong bikini showing a bit more of her ass than he wanted to see. Or did he?

"Where's Harold?" he asked, trying to keep himself grounded in the situation. Sure, she's pretty and all, but severely taken, man so don't go there.

"He had to go sign some papers and get some security stuff done for his trip this week," she said. "So he took this opportunity to run errands. He'll be gone most of the day, so I said, hey, why not get some sun." she twirled around, making the white lace sarong billow out seductively. Joe took another calming breath.

"Very nice," he said politely. He blinked several times, almost like taking a picture to use for later.

She looked at him, "Is everything okay?"

"Yes," he said quickly. "Everything is fine. I should be going. I don't want to be in the way." Remembering why he was there, he added, "I have some paperwork for you to sign, finalizing the install."

"Oh, posh," she said. She came and grabbed him around the arm. "Let me get you some lemonade." She drew him inside. And the Air Conditioning cooled him. He hadn't realized he was sweating. And knew it wasn't from the heat.

"No, really," he demurred. "I have to get going. I have another client I have to go take care of."

She pouted, "Not even one glass?" He hated to say no to her when she gave him that face. And he could stare at those pouty lips all day.

"Sure, You've talked me into it," he said, relenting. "If I'm not going to be in the way."

She smiled happily and said "Good." As she walked into the kitchen and proceeded to fix him a glass from a pitcher. She handed him the lemonade.

He looked around, fumbling for something to say. Finally, he looked at the house and said, "Looks like the carpet went down okay."

"Yes. I love it. The color fits just right with the walls, don't you think?"

He looked at the walls, painted a light gray color, probably with a name like Satin Sheet or Sky Gray. "It's nice." He took a sip. He recognized the taste immediately. It was powdered Country Time.

The thought of his wife steeled him for a few moments. "This is good," he said. "My wife makes this all the time for the kids."

"How is she these days?" Maxine deflated at the mention of his wife. "Arlene, right?"

"Yes," he said. "It's okay. You know, like what we talked about before, wedded bliss." This was a code word for 'My marriage is in a four-alarm fire and the trucks don't seem to be on the way at all.'

She sighed wistfully, "Yeah, same here." She looked around at the house, and he noticed a touch of sadness in that look.

In his mind at that moment he grabbed her, held her tight, kissed her as if it were the last time he'd ever kiss a woman and pulled her to the floor. He closed his eyes, opened them back up and said, "Yeah..."

They looked at each other awkwardly, wondering what had just happened between them. Then, without knowing why, without even controlling his body, he reached behind her neck, pulled her to his face, and kissed her. Their lips met, he opened them with a gentle moan, pressed his lips to hers. His tongue found hers, and danced with it for a few seconds before pulling back, seeing her face, shocked and surprised.

"Shit," he said quickly. "Maxi–" She broke his sentence with a kiss of her own. It was quick, wanton, and their tongues entangled for a moment before they realized what was happening, and he pulled back. She paused with a wicked smile on her face.

"I liked it, Joe," she said, her brown eyes beaming at him.

"Problem is," he said. "I did too."

And there it was. The decision had been made. Not now, not tomorrow, but one day soon, we are going to fuck like a couple of rabbits. And he was not going to be able to get enough of her.

"Maxine?" called out a voice behind them. They froze. Chris walked in the door and started coming into the house. The handyman hadn't seen them yet. They parted quickly. He put the lemonade down on the counter, a bit harder than he would have. It sploshed a bit and she went to the paper towel rack behind her and drew one out to wipe up the spill.

Chris came around the corner, "Everything alright?" he asked.

"Just spilled a bit," Joe said, recovering. Chris looked dubious. Joe and Maxine were standing close to each other in the kitchen, she was wiping up the spill and Joe standing there with a dumbfounded look on his face, wondering what to say, wondering if they'd been caught so early on in this liaison.

"Oh, okay," said Chris, looking at the floor. "Don't spill anything there, haven't put the sealer down yet." he laughed.

"Right," Joe agreed. "Got it!" He breathed then, finished drinking the lemonade in one nervous gulp, and said "Thanks, that was good."

"You're welcome," she said. "Come by any time."

"Sure," he said. "You'll have to invite me over when they get finished. I'd love to see the result." He turned to leave, feeling relaxed and at peace now for some strange reason.

She walked him to the door, following a bit too close behind. He turned. "Thank you, Maxine," he said. "It's been a pleasure working with you." he shook her hand.

She shook it back, held it longer than a normal handshake, and then let go, looking him in the eyes. "It's been a pleasure working with you too, Joe."

He turned, walked out of the house, and went to his car. On the way out of the house, Chris said "Take care now," to Joe as he walked by.

"And you take care of her," said Joe. "I don't want to have any complaints," he joked.

"Give you another excuse to come out and see her though, so..." Chris chuckled and trailed off. He winked.

"Yeah," said Joe, looking back at the house. "Go ahead and fuck it up then," he said.

Chris laughed. "Go on. We got this."

Joe saluted, "Carry on soldier." and went to his car. Maxine was still at the door. She waved.

He waved back, started the car, and drove out of the cul-de-sac. "Oh, I'm in fucking trouble now," he said to himself.

Bad Medicine—Bon Jovi

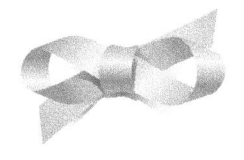

CHAPTER 10
Maxine

MAXINE TURNED BACK into the house to go outside to the patio. She sighed sadly, with the hopes he could have stuck around for a few more minutes. She picked up her book and leafed through it, her mind on anything but the book. She put it back down. Chris asked her something, which drew her back to the present. She was going to miss Joe.

She couldn't keep her mind off of that kiss. She had turned into a giddy schoolgirl who couldn't stop kissing the school quarterback. She hated that he had to leave today.

He looked so nice in his tight khaki pants and blue polo shirt that made his eyes grow bluer than normal. She felt the electric fire in her lips dwindling.

"God, why did you have to do that, Joe?" she whispered to herself. And why did I like it so much? She tried to think of Harold. Tried to think of anything besides that press of lips against hers. She would have to put it out of her mind. Try to reconnect with Harold. Try to do anything that would take her mind off of this man.

But at the end of the day, when the reality of their shared situation pressed into their lives, she had to let his car go down the road and out of sight.

She knew he had to go, but she didn't want him to leave. As hard as she tried to think of what to do next with Harold, she knew he would be unable to compete with Joe.

CHAPTER 11
Joe

IT WAS SATURDAY MORNING. White clouds filled the summer blue sky outside the window as he stood in the kitchen looking out the window to his backyard. Arlene was outside playing with the kids, helping little Joey climb up the ramshackle wooden ladder to the treehouse that Joe built last Christmas. Of course, he had help from Sam at work, but it was stable, functional, and fun. Joey looked out the open door to the four-foot square structure, a water gun in his hand. He shot his mother with a spray of cold water. She screamed with a laugh and fell dramatically, "Ya got me," and the boy laughed heartily..

Cowboys and Indians, a fun game he used to play with his brothers and neighbors. So long ago. When his life wasn't stressed about what bill to pay or what to do for dinner. Every decision had been made for him in childhood. Every person who loved him took care to make sure Joseph didn't have to do anything. It was idyllic. Up until the time his mother died and dad had lost his legs and the medical costs had taken the house, the two cars, and the college fund.

He sipped his coffee. Thought of Maxine.

He looked out at the white Hyundai in the driveway, the silver van next to it, and looked down at the expensive spray attachment of the faucet. Looked at the trappings of life, and sighed. Where did he go? Who were those people in the backyard? The young girl preening in a toy mirror thinking about boys and perfume and fashion. Who was that kid climbing a tree and shooting people with a water gun? Who was that blonde woman who fell, acting like she had been slain by a cowboy defending the fort?

And why didn't he love her anymore?

That's the big question, right there. Why? He had no right not to love her. She took care of his kids and kept the house as best she could. Did the laundry, and the groceries, fixed dinner, stayed home and took care of him and his children. Had been doing it for twelve years since the accidental pregnancy of Catherine, named after her grandmother.

But why don't I like her?

The toilet paper roll. That's why. That one stuck in his craw, as they say.

Joe tried to help around the house. He picked up when he remembered, avoided leaving books and magazines scattered, and changed the toilet paper roll when needed. No different from any modern husband helping around the house. He had heard many husbands didn't even do that. So when he put the toilet paper roll on the holder, he did it because it had to be done. A simple process, nothing stressful about it, one would think.

Only today it wasn't. This morning, he was in the bathroom, washing his hands after the morning constitutional, and was at the sink when Arlene had come in, said "God, I thought you'd never finish," She hurriedly did her thing in the toilet. Then, as if in slow motion, she looked at the toilet paper roll that he had just replaced, took a few sheets off of it, wiped herself, and then without saying a word pulled it off the holder, turned it over, and put it so the paper was on the top instead of the bottom.

Then she sighed with an annoyed grunt, took a look at him, not saying anything. But a look that said, "Can't you do anything right?"

Just like the glass be put in the dishwasher She walked by him and said, "Hey, put that in the back, it'll get cleaner faster." Then walked away. The same directive she had given him many times over. But that one added up.

Or the time when she went back to the kitchen sink rack and rewashed a plate he had just used to make a sandwich. He had left crumbs, and that had gotten on her nerves enough to tell him, "If you're going to wash a dish, do it right." as she walked away.

Thousands of those small incidents. Combined with the fact she hadn't made love to him in years, adding to their utter lack of communication. Divide that by the number of times he went to kiss her and she looked the other way, and subtract the fact that she had been hitting the bottle a bit more than usual and he had mentioned something about it, she had shot back, "Well, you drink too," as she took another sip of vodka.

Do the math, and it doesn't lie. The numbers add up to the fact that up until this morning, there were a million straws on that camel's back, but the toilet paper roll had been the final one that made the whole animal of their marriage come to a screeching halt.

That fucking toilet paper roll. That had been it.

Joe had right then and there checked out and decided it was no longer worth it. He chose that moment to stop trying to love her anymore. And he had kissed another woman. Maxine.

Lost in his oblivion, he didn't notice her come into the kitchen. "Hey, Earth to Joe," she said. He turned.

"Sorry," he said. "Just thinking is all."

"What were you thinking about?"

"Oh, nothing. Just looking at the cars in the drive, seeing you and the kids playing."

"Something wrong with the cars?" she asked, getting a bottle of water out of the refrigerator. "I thought you just had them serviced."

"Bills coming due," he said. "Feels like I just paid them." His voice was flat, uninterested.

"Hey," she asked, "Is everything okay?"

"Yeah," he chuckled as warmly as he could. "Just tired. Jamie's been running us through the wringer lately because it's slow at the store again. Mid-summer blues. You know how he gets. He had asked me to come in today, but I said I had plans with you and the kids." He couldn't tell her where he really wanted to be.

"You wanted to go to work today, didn't you?" she said, an accusation of his propensity to go to work even on his days off.

"No," he lied. "Not at all. I have stuff to do here. I noticed the lawn is getting a bit high. I was going to do that."

"Oh, okay. Good," she said. She closed the refrigerator, noticed him standing there with a coffee mug half full and said, "Make sure you clean that all the way when you get done," and walked out of the kitchen. "And the garage still needs to be cleaned up, too."

He heard the back door shut and watched her go to the tree house. "Fuck you," he said.

Joe went to the garage, noticed how cluttered it was and thought he would do it when hell froze over, fussed with the lawn mower and made sure it would start. Got the gas tank full, started it up, and absentmindedly mowed both the front and back lawns. Then he edged the lawn with his Stihl edger. He lost himself in the act of lawn maintenance.

He spent the afternoon working on the home and all the while thinking he was done with this, he didn't want to do it anymore. He got wet and sticky from his perspiration the entire afternoon. The grass clung to his shorts and shins, he could smell the fresh-cut sweetness of it.

Put simply, he was bored. He couldn't care less about what he was doing here anymore. The thoughts of that auburn haired woman down the street invaded his mind at seemingly every opportunity.

Twelve years, and what did he have to show for it? Two kids and a house and a wife he had no interest in loving anymore.

Arlene had gone to the grocery store. She had taken the kids, and he was alone. He needed a shower. He needed to clean the grass stains, the cobweb junk that he picked up when he went through the web under the oak tree holding up that damned tree house. So he went into the bathroom, shed his clothes, and looked at himself in the mirror. Average chest, not exactly well muscled, but not in bad shape. He was still in his forties, after all. A bit of dad flab from too many hot dogs, hamburgers, pizza and beer. He could change his diet, but he was okay looking. A bit of gray in his beard that he thought looked distinguished, salt and pepper hair with a bit of white at the temples.

He looked down, he could still see his penis so he guessed that walking three days a week had done something to keep the middle age weight off after all. He stroked it, calmly, like men do. Huh, he thought as it jumped to attention. He looked in the mirror and smiled as a thought came to him.

He started the shower, made sure it was hot, and got in the tub, letting the water cascade around him, down his back, in his hair. The tension left him, and he soaped up his hair, playing with himself all the while, letting the suds from the shampoo spill down his chest to his stomach, around his cock and balls, and down his thighs.

It had been a while since he had done anything like this. So long, that he couldn't remember. He held himself in his hands, stroking it harder, the girth growing in his palm. He closed his eyes and thought of random women he had made love to in the past. Thought of them there in the shower with him, one by one. The brunettes, the blondes, and the redhead.

Maxine, he thought. Her smile, the way her hair came down around her neck just so, the way she filled out that blouse and red skirt, the way her ass looked tight against the slacks during the measurement several days ago. Her smile, her laugh, her lips.

And she was there, wearing that yellow bikini. He loved the way it held her curves, the bright sun of it against her white flesh. He longed for those rosy lips against his again. He remembered the redness of her chest and neck after he kissed her. That kiss. The forbidden lust of it. The way she had kissed him back.

In his fantasy she knelt in front of him in the shower. His mind had placed her in front of him saying, "Let me handle that for you, my darling," as she put it in her mouth and the walls of her mouth pushed and pulled against his cock. He stroked harder, the sensations coming on him quickly, the tug of his balls, the feel of his engorged head, pulsing with desire. For her. In his mind, she stood up, and he said, "Oh God, yes," and then he was imagining himself pushing her against the tile wall face first, and he was inside her. His hand clamped harder around his manhood as he stroked faster and he was lost in the fantasy. Hot mist, hot water, hot feelings in his groin, the heat of impending release. His leg spasmed and shook as the flow of blood and need made him weak.

He dreamily pushed into her imaginary body, dreaming of what it would feel like as his balls slapped into her heart-shaped rump, the roundness of her cheeks, and the feel of her hips as he held them tight. His hand finally finished as he grunted and shook, said, "Oh God, Jesus, oh my God," and his body trembled hard as orgasm flowed rapidly through him. His legs went weak, and he held himself up by the new grab bar he had installed months ago. "Jesus Christ," he said, bending slightly forward to catch his breath. There was a sunlit mote in his tightly clenched eyes.

His voice was hoarse, and he coughed. He breathed rapidly, in short gasps as he milked the last of his come out to flow on his hand and get washed away by the scalding water. His legs wobbled and he stood up straight again, trying to catch his breath. He looked down, his cock was still hard and red, but the explosion had made it begin to recede, and he breathed deep and long, steadying himself, then stood, feeling like a new man.

"Holy shit," he said. "Wow. God. Damn. It."

He finished showering and stepped out, The hot water still clung to his body, and he took a terry cloth towel off one of the racks without thinking, starting to dry himself off.

He looked down at the pink towel with the frilly edges and looked at the embroidery on the end. "HERS," it said in baby pink flowing script.

"Fuck," was all he could say. He finished drying himself with it anyway before throwing it in the hamper and walking naked out to the bedroom to get dressed.

JEAN-PAUL PARE

I Want you to Want Me—Cheap Trick

CHAPTER 12
Maxine

•• ✥ ••

IT WAS A SUNNY TUESDAY, a normal day for her as she got home from the grocery store with a bag of goods she had just picked up. She thought for a second at the complaints from the woman behind her in the market, complaining about the cost of things nowadays, and Maxine just smiled at the blonde youngster and said, "Yes, it's a shame, really." She kept her mouth shut after that. She paid the money and left in her car with a couple of bags of stuff for the dinner she was planning tonight. She wanted to make Harold dinner. A proper dinner with roast chicken, celery, broccoli, and mashed potatoes. Today was going to be a test. Today, a decision would be made, and damn the consequences.

 She started the oven, put the chicken in, and made dinner with the practiced skill of a woman who had done this so many times before. Without effort, knowing how long things would take, and how many preparations needed to be made for the correct serving size. It was subconscious. But all the while she thought, "If this doesn't pan out like I hope it will, I think my decision will be made, and damn the consequences."

 When she felt like it was a point where she could leave the kitchen unattended for a little bit, she went upstairs to the bedroom. She looked over at the bed. White down comforter, white sheets, and four large white pillows. The four wooden newel posts reached almost to the ceiling. How it hadn't been used in over seven years for anything other than sleep. She sighed with a mix of sadness and hope. Then she went into the bathroom, she took off the tan slacks and white blouse she wore to the store and then the white conservative bra and panties she had worn. She was sure people could see the panty lines during her shopping trip and she may have been gawked at by lonely men in the aisles, but she didn't care. She liked the eyes on her, delighted at it.

She felt her breasts, how the large pink nipples hardened slightly in her hands, middle-aged breasts, sagging slightly, but still firm enough not to have to worry about how men would look at them. Thin lines of her daughter's birth on her stomach and a bit of extra flab she had tried to get rid of but never would go away, a relic of motherhood. She fell down to her pubic mound, a line of auburn hair with a couple of gray strands here and there she would have to pluck later.

She wasn't a hag. She ran her hands down her hips, full, and supple. "I'm hot," she told herself, a veritable milf at this point. "Why wouldn't he want me?"

She was on the fence as to who the "he" she was talking about but it was about eighty-twenty for that flooring salesman over the man who sat in the office downstairs, totally unfazed as to the growing divide between the two.

She went back into the bedroom and got out an outfit that was sure to seduce him. She pulled out a pair of black boy shorts, pulled them up over the fullness of her ass cheeks and turned to look at herself in the full-length mirror hanging on the door.

The undies rode up the crack of her ass perfectly. She remembered this was one of Harold's favorite undies. She took a sundress out of her wardrobe, a pink and yellow affair with blue and white flowers. She hung it over her bare breasts and let it fall over her body, where it clung to all the right curves and stopped a few inches above her knees.

She twirled around, preening, and let the loose dress fold and mold in all the right places. White stiletto heels finished the outfit. This was it, she thought. Here goes nothing.

She went downstairs, elegant, graceful, seductive. She turned at the base of the stairs and went into the office where Harold sat at the computer, a bag of cheese poofs next to him on the desk, a game of online poker on the screen.

"That's it, fish," he said with a satisfied grunt. "Go all in against my kings." She walked over to him, put her hand on his shoulder and he jerked back to reality. "Jesus, Maxie, you scared me." he scolded.

"Shhh..." she said, as she kissed his forehead. She went to his side. He turned his head.

"What?" She stopped him with a kiss, long and soulful. He jumped back. "What the fuck, Maxie, what are you doing?"

"What does it look like?" she asked, incredulous at the reaction. "Do you like?" She showed off the outfit.

"Yeah, but I'm in the middle of something here. I got trip kings against some dude that probably has shit."

She let the boyshorts fall to the floor, "Your favorites," she said, "Maybe you can take a break a minute?" She walked over and straddled him on the office chair, put her hands in between his legs, and felt for his cock.

"Dammit, Maxie, not now!" he yelled as he tried to push her off. She reached between his legs, looked him in the eyes, and her expression became downcast.

She felt between his meaty thighs and felt a flaccid uninterested bulge. "Seriously?" she asked.

"What?!" he exclaimed, "I'm not in the mood. Jesus, hon, you pick the damnedest times!"

She sighed. "Yeah, you're right." She lifted off of him. Resignedly, she said. "I always pick the wrong times."

"Hey, that's awesome. Yes, all in, bitch!" Harold yelled at the screen. He looked back over his shoulder as she started walking out of the room. He looked at the floor. "You left your underwear."

"Oh, right," her voice was flat and uninterested now. "How could I forget?" She went over, bent down to show her unfettered cleavage to him one last time, the last time he would ever see it again, and stood up, the black fabric in her hands. She looked down at them and thought, he'll never see these again, either.

"Hey," he said, looking at her again, clueless as to the dynamic that just happened between them. "Maybe later, huh?" he winked.

"Sure," she said. "Dinner'll be ready in a few minutes. I got a roast chicken and all the fixin's, your favorite."

"Good, bring it in here when it gets done, will ya? Thanks." he turned back to the computer. "Here fishy, here little fishy, gimme all that money!"

She shut the door behind her, letting his cries of triumph become muffled by the wooden barrier. "Fuck." she said. She went into the kitchen, turned off the oven, slowed the vegetables in a saucepan to the off position on the countertop and went upstairs.

He had done it. He had failed. She had hoped that he would have taken the opportunity to take her on that desk right there, say to hell with the game. To hell with making a few bucks. Maybe even lose a hand, take a momentary setback to save the last possible shred of the existence of whatever this marriage was. What was she to him? A hanger-on, a waste of time. Nothing. A woman who hung around and spent his money on stupid flooring and appliances every few years.

She shook a moment and thought of Joe, the flooring guy, the handsome guy with those eyes as blue as an ocean that made her melt when he looked at her. His hair was dark brown, with glimmers of gray along the sides, the way his beard tugged at a square chiseled jaw, his lips, his laugh, his body.

She laid back down on the bed, ignoring everything but the chirping of robins outside the bedroom window, and the way a light breeze from the overhead ceiling fan swept her skin lazily. She laid back, pulled her dress up to expose her thighs, and her hand went to the folds of her pussy and she started stroking, thinking of Joe.

About the way his body would feel when she seduced him, how he would kiss her like he did only days ago. One hand went up to the low neckline and pulled it down. She tweaked her nipple and felt the shock of pleasure. What if he did that to her? What if he took them in her mouth? What if he took all of her with his mouth?

She pushed two fingers inside her molten core and rubbed that spot she knew would send her over the edge. Her palm rubbed her clit, and she jerked in and out with her fingers, feeling the walls of her muscles inside pushing tighter and tighter.

Her breath came in rapid gasps, as her pleasure mounted, and she lost herself in the feelings, the sensations of her fingers thrusting, her hands probing, tugging her breasts, her nipples, hard, on fire, her back arched, and she was liquid now, her body shooting full with her orgasm as the thought of Joe on top of her, inside of her, feeling her, licking her, kissing her, and she moaned a loud and ferocious moan of letting go and following her bliss to the end, wetness spilling over the fingers still inside of her, easing her down from the mountaintop she just climbed and then jumping off in a frantic release.

She let her body relax, hands at her sides, breathless and relaxed. She felt her skin, her heart, her body, all sensations of climax and release. She lay there a few moments, letting her body calm and her breath come back to her, slow and sure.

She sat up on the pillows, reached over to the nightstand, and looked at her phone. There was a text a few days ago from the flooring salesman. It was all business. Asking if there was anything else he could do for her. Their playful hint of coffee and the start of a possible mutual desire.

"Joe," she said. A thought came to her then. A thought that would change both of them forever.

She texted Joe.

Hey. i was wondering since you live
In the neighborhood you could do
Me a favor

Minutes later, he texted back:

Sure. what's up?

Since harold is going out of town

This weekend for a poker thing i
Need a hand with the lawn

Ok but can't you call some people?

The people the HOA wants to use
Are too expensive and they're
Busy this week.
I totally understand if you can't do it.

It's not a question if i can do it. I have to
Check with the boss and see if this is
okay

. . ⚜ . .

SHE PUT THE PHONE BACK on the nightstand, stood up, satisfied with what her week would look like, and walked down the stairs to the kitchen, a new woman. A free woman. After this, in her mind and deeds, an unmarried woman.

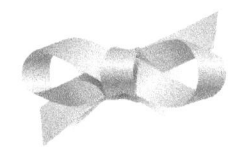

CHAPTER 13
Joe

HE PUT THE PHONE DOWN, thought briefly about deleting the texts Maxine had just sent and stopped himself. There was nothing suspicious in that thread, he thought. Just a neighbor asking for help. His heart raced like it hadn't done in many years. Anticipation, anxiety, and nervous jitters hit him as he thought of her, remembering that yellow bikini, remembered her touch, and the kiss that followed. He thought of that pearlescent skin glowing in the sunlight. He started to become hard and thought that later he would have a really good time in the shower. Then the front door opened and Arlene came onto the foyer holding a couple of bags of groceries and it brought him back to the present.

"Hey," he said, going to the door. "Let me help you." He reached for the bags and she handed them over.

"There's more in the car," she said. She turned to go back out.

"I got it," he said and went out to the car to see the white and blue grocery bags piled high in the back of the minivan, the tailgate open wide.

He grabbed all of them with two hands full and hefted them. They were heavy with fruits, snacks, gogurt for Cathy, corn pops for Joey, meats, cheeses and all manner of food. He Carried them in, put them on the floor, and before he could go back out, Arlene said, "Hey, did you close the tailgate?"

"I'm going out to do just that," he said flatly, wanting to add, "Do you think I wasn't going to?" but didn't.

"They didn't have your creamer," she explained. "So I got the French vanilla. I hope that was okay."

"Fine," he said. He hated French vanilla. And why wouldn't the store have caramel macchiato when they had it every other day was beyond him. He asked, "They didn't have my kind?"

"No," she opened the refrigerator and said, "They must have sold out. Anyway, where are the kids?"

"Joey's upstairs, and Cathy is out with her friend."

"I wish she didn't have that stupid project," she said. Cathi had picked up a summer project for school, some graduation to seventh-grade thing for the private school for which they had just paid an arm and a leg. That request by Arlene and Cathi had been one that made him work a few extra hours a day for the past month. Good thing he got the Maxine job because that bonus was going to help with that expense, even though he had other plans for it.

"She wants to make a good impression," he said. "Besides, it'll help her get into a better school if she gets a good GPA."

"I guess," Arlene sighed. "I just wish she was here more. I need help with the house."

Joe looked around at the piles of washed laundry on the couch, Lego toys scattered around, drink cups on end tables and a few of Joey's crumby plates when he watched a show still on the coffee table. Arlene saw this and said, "What did you do today?"

"I was at work," he said. "I had to check on the Sydney job again. So it took a few extra minutes. I just got home."

"Is that bitch complaining again?" she asked.

"Yep," he answered, sighing. "It's those stupid transitions again. Can't get it through her thick head that the things are the same color even if they are a shade different."

"Whatever. She'll get over it. What, have you been working on this job for the past six months trying to keep her happy?"

"Yes, just around that," Joe put more stuff in the fridge. He moved a few things out of the way, put the creamer in, then opened the drawer and put some green grapes in it on top of carrots and a half-used bunch of celery.

"What are you doing?" she demanded.

He looked up, "What?"

She went over to the fridge, looked down, and pointed at the vegetables. "Joe," she explained in her 'Arlene is the boss' voice. "The grapes go in the fruit drawer. This is the vegetable crisper. God, do you not pay attention to anything?"

"A drawer is a drawer, Arlene." he walked to get some more groceries as she went to correct his mistake.

"It's like you don't even try," she said. "Never mind." She shook her head, went and took the stuff out of his hands, grabbed the gogurt and the slim Jim packets Joey liked. "I'll put stuff away. At least then I'll be able to find what I'm looking for."

He raised his hands, saying, "Okay," and walked away from her.

"That's your answer to everything," she said. She went to the counter, grabbed a shot glass and poured some vodka. She chugged it quickly, then filled it again.

"And that's your answer to everything," he jabbed. It was out of his mouth before he could get it back in and oh boy here's where the fight starts, he thought.

She drank the second shot, pounded it on the counter and shot him a look. He'd seen that look too many times to know he had just fucked up somehow. "And what does that mean?" She demanded, arms tight across her chest.

"Nothing," he said. "Forget I said anything."

"No, Joe," there was a calm anger in her tone. "You had something on your mind, why don't you spill it?"

"Like I said, forget I said anything." He went to hug her but she pushed him away. "I'm sorry."

"Whatever," she said, but continued, not wanting to let the matter go. "You know, if you had to put up with all the stuff I had to, you'd drink just as much."

"What stuff do you have to put up with?" he shot back at her.

"What stuff?" she waved an arm at the kitchen, the dirty living room, the plates on the coffee table. "This, Joe. All of this!"

"So we'll clean it up in a few minutes, it's no big deal." he went toward the living room to start getting stuff off the tables and floor.

"God, you don't listen at all, do you?"

He turned to her. "What do you mean I don't listen?"

"I've told you a number of times that I don't like you to put the fruits with the vegetables. But you do it. It's like you want to make me upset. Like you want me angry all the time. Why don't you just follow a few simple instructions?"

"We're back to that all the sudden?"

"Yes!" she said. "I've told you time and again where stuff goes, how to do the dishwasher, how to fold the clothes, and yet you do it your way. And I have to go back and do it all over again, wasting my time."

"Hon," he said, as calmly as possible. "It's not a big deal, why are you making it a big deal?"

She kept on ranting, "And then when I want to drink a couple of shots to calm myself down and make it easier to live in this place, you go and complain about that too."

He sighed, "Like I said, never mind. Forget I said anything. I'm sorry. I just–" he stopped himself from going any further. He didn't need another four hours of her drinking and sulking around him tonight. He went to her, trying to calm her down. She leaned up against the sink.

"You know it's been hard for me since dad died," she seemed to calm. The vodka was working its magic on her. "I don't need you to make my life any harder than it already is."

He went in for a hug. She let him. "I know, it's been hard on the kids too."

"Joey used to like riding on that tractor with him, didn't he?" Arlene said, and Joe could sense her brain sloshing a little bit now. She broke the hug, went to the counter and poured another shot. This one was her sipping shot. He went back to putting the groceries away.

"It's okay," she said. "I'll put them away. I'm sorry I got bent out of shape. Traffic was a bear, the house was a mess, and I lost my temper."

"It's fine," he said. "I understand." he didn't, though. He could get through many days without drinking or doing anything and have all the stress in the world on him. It didn't make him pick up a drink at the earliest opportunity. One day, he'd have to have a frank discussion with her about it, but today was not that day.

He let her put the groceries away, watched her finish her third shot, and said, "By the way, I have some stuff to do this weekend that shouldn't take a couple of hours to do. Do you have plans?"

She waved a hand in the direction of the clothing-draped sofa. "Just that, and grocery shopping. Why does a ten-year-old have to eat so much? Hasn't he heard of inflation?"

"I'm sure he has, I just don't know if he understands. Plus he's going through another growth spurt." Joe explained.

"So what do you have to do?"

"One of my clients, an older woman down the street, needs her lawn mowed. So she asked me and I told her I would."

"You mow the lawns for your clients now?" she chided. "Sounds a bit above and beyond the call of duty, don't you think?"

"It's community outreach, and Jamie likes that kind of thing. The workers of his store, helping out people in the neighborhood."

"Can't she get her husband to do it?"

"He's going to Vegas this weekend," Joe said. "He's some hot shot poker star."

"Can't she use the one that the HOA uses?" Arlene asked, a hint of suspicion in her voice.

"I asked the same thing. They're all booked up this weekend. It'll only take an hour or so. And she's giving me fifty bucks." That was a lie, but he pulled it off and she turned to him.

"Okay," she said. "No big deal, then. Every bit helps."

"I'll let her know then," he said. He pulled out his phone to text Maxine but she stopped him with a question he wasn't expecting.

"How old tho?" Arlene said after a beat.

"What?" Joe said distractedly.

"How old is this woman? This client of yours?"

"Married 24 years to a rich poker star old, hon," Joe said. "Fifties or something, I don't know. She's got a kid in college. And the job she bought paid for my latest bonus, so that's how old."

"Whatever," Arlene said. "It doesn't matter anyway, I'm going to be cleaning, shopping and running around to hobby stores for Cath. So if it gets you out of the house for a few minutes, so much the better."

"Okay," Joe said. "Good. I'm off Saturday anyway, I'll do hers after I get done with our lawn. And if you need help around the house, I can do that too."

"I think I can manage, Joe. Maybe you could do the garage like I've been asking for weeks?"

"Okay, I'll see what I can manage," he said. "Maybe get Joey to help out." He walked away, saying he had to go to the bathroom and she just waved him dismissively like the boss waving away the help.

On his way there, he texted Maxine:

Ok. it's cool i can spare a couple

> Hours saturday morning. Is 9 too
> Early? Shouldn't take a few hours
> Anyway. The yards are pretty
> small here.

> Great. But come at eleven. I need to
> Wake up and get coffee and stuff
> Done around the house. It's a mess.

> It's just the lawn Maxine. I don't
> Plan on going inside.

> Great :) 11 it is then. I'll make
> Lemonade and we can chat
> Like neighbors do.

> Sure. 11 it is then.

He put the phone down with nervous anticipation. His body shook a moment as he went into the bathroom. He looked at himself in the mirror, flexed a second, and then settled down. Was he going to do this?

If the opportunity presented itself, he had decided, yes, he most certainly would. Full speed ahead and damn the torpedoes.

JEAN-PAUL PARE

I Want you—The Beatles

CHAPTER 14
Maxine

SATURDAY MORNING SHE woke up and went through the first hour doing the things she had to do every day, tidying herself, getting coffee, looking at her phone to find out news, weather, sports, fashion, and watching untold amounts of cat videos. All the while, her body and brain hummed at the thought of him. The man who was coming over to mow the lawn. She ate, showered, and got dressed in the same sundress as she wore for her failed seduction a week ago with Harold. If this didn't work on a hunkalicious flooring salesman, she didn't know what she would do.

She called Carrie, at around ten thirty to help calm her nerves.

Her best friend answered, "Hey girl."

"Hello," Maxine said, twirling her hair. She felt like a schoolgirl with her first crush waiting for the prom date. "How's your day going?"

"What's going on, M?" Carrie sounded dubious.

"Nothing," Maxine lied, then said, "Only I have a very neighborly gentleman coming over to mow my lawn today."

"Is that what they're calling it these days?" Carrie laughed. "You little tramp."

"Hush. It's just the hot flooring guy, that's all."

"Maxie," Carrie got serious. "Be careful. Don't do anything stupid. Wait, who am I talking to? Of course, you're going to do something stupid."

"I'm not going to do anything," Maxine gave a disgruntled retort.

"Tell that lie to someone else," Carrie chided. "Not your best friend."

"Ok," Maxine surrendered. "You know me too well. Let's just say I'm going to flirt very heavily with the man and see what happens."

"You're going to get pregnant," Carrie laughed. "That's what's going to happen."

"I am not," Maxine said defensively. "I've been on the pill again for the last month. I'll be fine."

"Whatever you say," Carrie said. "I hope you're right. I'm also hoping you don't have to test it out."

"I'm hoping we do," Maxine said with a tone of seduction.

"Maxine," Carrie was serious again. "Just... Just think about it. About this. It's all okay to flirt and be dressed pretty and make advances, but you're dealing with a married man here."

"I know he's married, and so am I." Maxine scolded. "But it's just an adventure, something to think about. Something to make myself feel sexy again, like a woman. God knows the other day, I should tell you I felt like a piece of trash." Maxine told her what she did with Harold a few nights ago, and what happened.

"He didn't," Carrie said, disappointed. "He actually said that?"

"Yeah," Maxine said. She mocked his voice, "'Maybe later huh babe? Oh and bring my dinner in here.' Like I'm his fucking slave."

"Oh, Maxie, I'm so sorry." Carrie's voice had an air of sympathy to it. "Why didn't you call me?"

"I didn't want to talk to anyone. I just went upstairs after dinner and went to bed."

"Okay, I understand, then," Carrie said. "So flirt with a hunkalicious floor guy, but don't go any further. And don't do something stupid like kiss him or anything."

"I assure you, that isn't on the agenda," Maxine said, thinking, there's more than that on the agenda. I assure you, girlfriend.

"Let's hope not," Carrie sighed. There was a knock on the door and three soft raps.

"Oh shit, he's here. He's early. What should I do?" Maxine said hurriedly.

"First, you hang up the phone, and then answer the door," Carrie said helpfully. "And then you talk to him and tell him where to mow, and let him do his job." She was saying all of this matter of factly like a teacher to a student.

"Fine, let me go get the door," she said, going to the foyer and opening the door, the phone still in her ear. "Jesus, Christ," she said uncontrollably, regretting having said it before it was even possible to take it back.

Joe stood there in a white tee shirt that hugged his torso, gray cargo shorts, and black sneakers. He smiled at her, expectantly as she stood there taking in his form. "Carrie," she said, "I have to go."

"Hello?" Joe said, looking around, "I'm sorry I'm early, but I kind of wanted to get started before the heat of the day."

Maxine stood still looking at him. "Maxine?" Carrie said. "Are you there?"

"Yes," she said into the phone as she tried to regain her composure and raised her finger in the international, 'Just a minute' pose and then motioned him in. "Yes, I'm here. He just distracted me," she whispered. "I'll let you go. I have a business to discuss with the lawnmower man."

Carrie chuckled. "You're incorrigible, darling. I love you. Be careful. Bye."

"Love you too," she said, and pressed the button to hang up. She whirled around, looking at him. "Hey!" she said, excitedly. "Come in."

Joe smiled, and said, "Yeah, sure. But don't you think I should get started?"

"Yes," Maxine said. "I just wanted to show you the great job the flooring guys did."

He looked at the kitchen floor, the golden brown hardwood shining mirrors like in the sun coming from the front window. "Yes, that's nice." He came into the house, looking at the flooring, the carpet, and as she glanced over her shoulder, she caught him taking a glimpse at her ass in the sundress that flowed tightly over her body.

"Isn't it though?" she said. She twirled around too quickly and he stopped. He looked at her.

"Yes," he answered. "They did a good job."

Looking at him, she said, "Yes they did." She walked past him and went to the open kitchen, "Did you need anything before you started? I've got lemonade and beer."

"No, I've got water outside. I brought my push mower because it's not that big of a lawn."

"Okay," she said. "Best get on with it, huh?" she went outside with him. She saw the red and back lawnmower, cleaned and maintained. She walked him around the house, telling him where to cut, and what not to cut, showing him her flowers, the hydrangeas, the azalea bushes and a small garden bed she had made Harold build and put dirt in but never used. "I wanted to put something in there like herbs and stuff, but I never got that far," she explained. "Have you ever done that? Started something you knew with certainty you'd finish and just lost interest?"

Joe stopped for a second in thought, "Yes, quite recently, in fact."

Maxine asked, "What was that?"

He just looked at her, saying nothing. He brooded for a second, as if to say something, but then just said, "Let me just get started."

She pouted momentarily but understood. "That's fine. Go ahead and do what you need to. I shouldn't have asked."

He reached out to her, held her shoulder in a gentle hand, "Sorry, I shouldn't have been short with you. It's just that, well, I don't know, maybe after a beer I'll let you know. Right now, I just want to do this and then we can talk, how's that?"

"Perfect," she smiled. Tender, yet bold, I like that. And you can keep your hand on my shoulder, boyo. That's doing you a lot of favors, she thought.

He turned and walked to the front door where he had parked his mower. He took it to the driveway and knelt, looking in the gas tank, checking the filter, and then standing up to yank the power cord a couple of times.

She watched as he pulled the cord, his forearm pulling the cord with a tight grip. I am going to be no good if he does that to my hair, she mused. After two more pulls and a grunt, Joe started the lawnmower, and it growled to life.

The grunt hit her in the solar plexus in a visceral desirous way and she said, "mfff" but he didn't hear it over the sound of the mower. "I'll just be going in, now. Let me know when you've finished!" She said loudly, hoping he would hear.

He gave her a thumbs up and started down the lawn, making one perfect row, then another, and then another as he pushed up and down the lawn with practiced ease. She went inside and into the kitchen. She looked out the window and watched him go back and forth. Watched his powerful leg muscles push the mower with the force of a man bending the machine to his will.

After a few minutes, she decided she couldn't sit here and eye fuck him anymore and decided to tidy the house and make him a snack of apples into chunks, bananas, and an assortment of nuts in a bowl on a charcuterie board. She went to see how far he had gotten, and he was in the backyard.

"Oh dear God," was all she could say. The man stood in the middle of the backyard, sunbeams casting over him through the shade of the large oak tree, his torso bathed in light and sweat that made his tee shirt cling to him wet with working man sweat. He pulled the bottom up and wiped his face, revealing his toned torso, the thin line of hair going up to his chest and getting obscured by the white sweaty fabric.

She just stood there, staring from the patio doors, and he noticed, looked up, smiled, and waved. She waved weakly back. He mouthed the words, "Almost done" and gave her another thumbs up. She gave him a wave and then walked away slowly, saying, "Lord Jesus, I am no more good."

She finished the snacks and went to the bedroom, took off her undies and stowed them in the top drawer. "Won't be needing these," she said to herself in the mirror. Then she went back downstairs to welcome him into her home.

Within an hour, he was done. And as she heard the final growling bellow of the lawnmower, her excitement grew. She watched him take the mower back to the front yard and leave it there. She went to the front door, opened it invitingly, and said, "Nice job, it looks great!"

He came to the front door, "Thanks," he said. "Mind if I come in? I'm kind of messy, and I need to wash my face."

"Oh, by all means," she ushered him in. "I fixed a snack, and a glass of lemonade for you."

"Just one glass," he said. "I have to go soon. I only wanted to stay here for a few hours."

"Well, don't let me stop you," she said. She handed him a towel and said, "The bathroom is down the hall," and then she laughed. "Of course you know that. Your place probably looks like this inside too." she giggled.

"Yes, it does," he smiled at her. He went down the hall to the bathroom, taking off his shirt as he went through the door. She watched the bare muscles on his back flex as if he were trying to get the soreness out of them. After a few minutes, he came out, his face washed, but his tee shirt still hugging him deliciously, still wet with sweat, only looking like he had pulled it off and tried to wring it out.

"I could throw that in the dryer for you if you wanted." she motioned to the shirt.

"Oh, I couldn't," he said. "It'll dry off in a few minutes. It's one of those new ones that do that. I'll be fine. He grabbed an apple slice and bit it in half, "Good. I like the green ones," he said...

"I like what you've done to the place," he continued, looking around.

"I still need some help with the decor," she explained. "It's still showing, 'Home With Kids' and I kind of want a new vibe. Just haven't discovered what that vibe is yet."

"I'm sure you'll come up with something," he finished the apple slice and picked up an orange slice next. He looked at her, there was an awkward silence. He bit into the orange and then sucked it into his mouth. She had a quick intake of breath and turned around to the refrigerator.

"Lemonade," she said and pulled out a pitcher she had made. "It's only powder stuff, but my daughter liked it growing up so it must be okay."

"Perfectly fine," he said, looking at her. Did she notice a hint of desire in the way he said it?

She poured him a glass of lemonade, He took it from her hand and drank half the glass. She picked it up to give him a refill. He started walking toward her.

"You asked earlier if I've thought of something and been certain about it.," he was next to her, standing only a foot away, She could smell the fresh wet cut grass smell on him, a fragrant summer smell. "I'm certain of two things. One, the sun is going to come up tomorrow, and two," he said as he took her chin in his fingers. "If I don't kiss you again, I'll regret it for the rest of my life."

All she could do was let out a breathless, "Oh..."

And then he kissed her, and the touch of his lips ignited a desire in her chest she had not felt in months, perhaps years. She kissed him back, hungry now for his lips, his body, his soul. His heat for her was a palpable inferno, and seemed to ignite his hunger for her as well. All they could do was kiss, locked in an embrace she never wanted to escape.

She pulled his tee shirt off, and he pulled the sundress top off of her, revealing her breasts with large pink nipples. He put them in his mouth, one after the other, and as his tongue swirled around them, a shock went through her core. She couldn't stop this now. They were in it, and the way his manhood against her pelvis bulged in his shorts, she knew he wouldn't want to stop now either.

She felt herself pressed against the wall, and she brought her legs up around his waist. "Take me, Joe. Take me please, take me now," she whispered in his ear, her breath hot, wanton, and carnal. He smiled at her, his eyes looking into hers with a predatory darkness that made her body weak.

He nodded, and with both hands, lowered her legs, pushed the sundress down to reveal her nakedness. He kissed her again, deeper with longing. Their tongues danced and her pleasure grew. He reached down to feel the wetness in her folds, flowing and wet, and she took in a breath as his fingers found her entrance. He played with her, pushing into her with a finger, then another, rubbing her vigorously with his hand and she felt her first orgasm building, cresting, pounding, and she exhaled with a grunt of desire. "Oh Jesus, keep doing that!" she cried. "Keep doing that!"

She reached down to his belt, pulled it open quickly and reached her hand down his pants. His cock was engorged, full with the power of imminent release. She couldn't have that. No need with all this build up if he were going to be done in seconds. She smiled and unsnapped the button, kept her eyes on him as she lowered the zipper.

His shorts fell to the floor.

Her hand stroked him and he let out a sigh. "Keep that up," he whispered, his hot breath in her ear. "Yes, baby, do it." Then she pulled her hand back, he groaned, and she wet it down with her tongue, keeping an eye on him with a seductive smile. "Let's prime the pump," she whispered. Her hand shot back down to his cock, stroked the meaty head, her hand feeling his girth for the first time, and hopefully not the last.

He moaned and closed his eyes as her hand pushed up and down on him. Soon he cried out as the explosion in his loins pushed her harder into the wall behind her. She could feel the warm wet spray of his flow on her hand and fingers.

Without thinking, she lifted her hand up to her mouth and slipped two fingers in, tasting the salty brine of his ejaculation. She moaned, "mmmm..." as she looked at him in his sea blue eyes.

His breathing slowed, and he kissed her again, came back with a smile, and rubbed her sides. Every sensation in her was on fire now, everything was here. Everything she wanted was here right now, and she wanted more of him.

She kissed him again, wanting nothing more than to feel his lips on her forever. "Joe," she whispered into his ear. "I want you to fuck me now."

He smiled at her, and simply nodded, unable to form a coherent word.

She led him up the stairs now, and turned as she entered the bedroom. He stood on the threshold and she sat up on the bed. She looked at his naked form, his cock solid and rising again, the look on his face of desire and want. He sped to her then, Kissing her quick and hungry.

"Oh, Maxine," he said, kissing her breasts, kissing down her belly, to her thighs and his fingers opened her folds. His tongue found her clit, and the sensations pulsed through her. She arched her hips up to his face, grabbed his hair in her hands, and expelled a hard moan. His tongue went to work on her. His finger entered her, first one then another, and he found her spot, her nub, her secret. The combined pleasure of both soon had her screaming, "Oh my God, I want you, Joe fuck me. Fuck me now, Joe fuck me!" She panted uncontrollably, though gritted teeth, her body hard and needful.

He went to her, his solid body pressing her into the mattress. He was inside her then, the flow of her juices letting him take her all the way. She gasped with the intrusive power of him, and pressed herself into him to make him deeper, wanting his girth to fill her all the way.

They paused, neither one ignoring the significance of this moment. Here they were now, their weeks long flirtation manifested into physical passion. She looked into his stone cold blue eyes, feeling his hardness inside of her, another man filling her fully, and nodded.

"Take me," she whispered into his ear. "Take all of me. I'm yours now," He looked into her eyes, smiling. He agreed with his body, strong and needful. Then she melted into him, and allowed him to be the first man to love her since Harold

He thrust into her, slowly at first, and she urged him on, her legs pressing against his ass, "Take it, faster," she cried into his shoulder, smelling his hot man sweat. He did as commanded. Every thrust filled her, every slap of his pelvis on her left her weak. Every one of his grunts and gasps fueled her own against his, and their music echoed in the room, as the carnal escape rose in power, like a storm.

She couldn't stop saying, "Take me," as he thrust faster and harder into her. This was a carnal desire. There was no lovemaking. There was a primal wanton ache in her core, an ache he was satisfying with each hard thrust. He took her. He filled her.

This man wanted her. She wanted all of him. She felt his pleasure building once again, his cock growing harder with each fierce attack on her. "Give it to me, baby. Give it all to me," she whispered in his ear. Her hands flew out to either side, and she grabbed the bedspread with all her might as the onslaught of his physical attack upon her sped up.

He pulled out, smiling, his breath slowing down. "No," he said. "Not like this."

"Put it back in," she gasped with need. Then he turned her over, and he was inside of her again, from behind. He slapped her ass hard and the sensation shot through her. The pain collided with the pleasure her body already felt. He slapped again and her desire to keep this moment grew. He was in control, and she wanted him to be. She couldn't help it. Everything in her wanted this man. This was a passion she thought she would never have. He took her, and she surrendered to him. She cried out, "Take me, Joe, take me oh God take me, fuck me! Fuck me, baby!"

She buried her face in the pillow, grabbed the sheets again. She could feel her feet and toes curling and the muscles in her body were a tripwire with pending release. She could hold no longer, and with eyes closed felt a surge of release wash through her as her moans stifled in the pillow. She broke into a thousand tiny pieces, and saw a kaleidoscope of color in the darkness of her closed eyes. "Oh, God," she cried, lifting her head from the pillow, "Oh Jesus!"

She could feel his pressure build again, the surge of his release coming quickly. He thrusted faster now, taking her, owning her, filling her.

"Give it to me, Joe. I want to feel it," she said, looking up at him behind her, his powerful chest sweaty with a vigor that made her collapse again into the pillow, every quick thrust took her again to the pinnacle, every moment was lost in the sensations of pleasure, desire, and feeling. Every nerve in her body was afire.

"I want it, Joe!" she cried. "I can feel it, give it to me," She looked back at him, and nodded her head.

He let loose inside of her with a grunting moaning roar, a lion taking his pride queen. His release filled her and mixed with her own lubricating flow. She felt the heat of it spill into her in pulsing liquid jets. He collapsed on top of her, and she let him fall against her sweat hot back, his heaviness relaxing and molding her into the mattress. She felt the slowness of his orgasm recede, the hardness fade with its release, and never wanted this sensation of him inside her to end. She never wanted his body to leave her again.

She couldn't form a solid thought. Emotions collided with each other in her head. Guilt, pleasure, passion, desire, hope, fear, and anxiety fought with each other in her brain. But none of them had the upper hand against the heaviness of Man weighing her down into the comfort of the thick white mattress.

And then she was back inside her body, her breath shifting from rabid gasps to calmer, easier breaths. She liked the way she moved against his body, the way her pendulous breasts felt in his hands, the way her smooth skin felt in his palms, the nipples, and their hardness in his fingers. She breathed and basked in the way her skin felt pressed into his body, her ass cheeks against his cock.

She took a calming breath. Tears flowed then, and she couldn't decide if they were of sadness or joy. He took her face in his hands, kissed her cheek where a tear came down.

"I'm sorry, I've made you cry," he whispered, and she sensed caring there..

"Oh no," she laughed. "This isn't a tear of sadness, darling. You've just made me feel..." her voice trailed off.

"Alive again," Joe completed her sentence. Maxine nodded, and he kissed her deeply, with heart this time. She kissed him back.

"Dear God, I'm in trouble," she said. She looked into his blue eyes, the eyes she first noticed many days ago in the store. Those eyes she could swim in for all eternity.

"Why do you say that?" he asked. "I'm the one in trouble."

She sighed, "So I guess we both are, then." She moved to get up from the bed, and he held her there for a moment more.

"Stay a minute," he said. "I want to say something."

"Listen," she said, "Don't say anything. Not now. I want to feel this right now. No words."

He tried to say something, but she closed his mouth with a kiss. "Don't ruin it, darling. Just... don't ruin it." He noticed another tear running down her cheek. He lay back in the quiet, looking up at the ceiling fan, going in slow lazy circles, white blades whirring. The truth was, she couldn't speak. She didn't know what to say. Didn't even know where to start.

Maxine just wiped away a tear and looked over at him. "I don't know what happens now, where this goes, what we're going to do," she said. The sentence hung in the air for a few moments of silence.

"Mind if I say something now?" he smiled.

"Sure, I just wanted to be quiet and feel everything I was feeling in silence," she said. "I don't know what I'm doing. This is uncharted territory for me."

"Alright, I'll say it." He rested on his side and looked at her.

"So this happened, and there's nothing to do about it," he said. "And if it's the only time then that's fine. I guess. I don't know if I like it being this once, but I can live with it. I won't like it, but I'll live with it and keep it locked away and never speak of it again to anyone, not even you."

"Oh, but it'll be fun, keeping our secret together," she laughed.

"Shh," he said, holding up a finger to her lips. "But if I'm being honest, I don't want it to just be this one time." He stopped, watching her reaction. She smiled expectantly, and he continued. "I don't know what happens next. I don't even know where we go from here. But I do know one thing. This wasn't the last time I'm going to do this to you." He looked into her brown eyes, wet with what he could only hope were the burgeoning tears of happiness. "So however that looks, we'll figure it out." He paused for her reaction, which was only a large grin of agreement. "Okay, now I'm done."

She kissed him long and fiercely, as she had done when she had first kissed him. "I want that too," she admitted.

"Okay then, it's settled." he sat up on the bed, then looked around for his clothes. "Uhoh," he said. He couldn't find his clothes. She stifled a laugh with her hand over her mouth. She found joy in this moment then, an awkward loving embarrassment shared between lovers.

"Downstairs," she smiled. "Remember?"

He grinned, "Oh yeah." He went to her. She stood up, and they embraced. She buried her face in his shoulder. She thought, smelling the sweat of their passion on him, "Don't make me fall in love with you, mister man." But felt that would be impossible.

They went downstairs, finding their shedded clothes on the hardwood floor of the kitchen. They dressed in silence, exchanging furtive glances, wanting to see each other's nakedness, catch glimpses of bodies half dressed, the color of skin, comfortable in the act of simply putting clothes on in front of each other. She noticed something that hadn't occurred to her before.

He didn't wear underwear when he came to mow the lawn. She smiled deliriously with the idea that he was looking forward to this afternoon just as much as she.

Maxine went to him after he dressed. She gave him a hug. "Thanks for coming over and mowing my lawn." She escorted him down the hall and to the front door. He turned before the door opened and kissed her. She gazed into his blue eyes, those eyes that made her weak.

"If you need anything else done around the house, you let me know," he said. She opened the door quickly and said, "Yes, I'll do that." maybe a little louder than she should have, but none of the neighbors noticed, and wouldn't have said or done anything about it if they had.

He went to the front yard where the lawnmower stood a silent sentinel as it had been for the last hour he'd been in the house. He grabbed it, and pushed it down the yard, to the sidewalk, and down the street. She closed the door behind her, leaned against it and sighed breathlessly, smiling. "Don't fall in love with this guy, Maxine," she said to herself in the empty home. Somehow she knew it was already too late for that. Her body screamed with the passion they had just shared. Her heart pumped with the desire of wanting more.

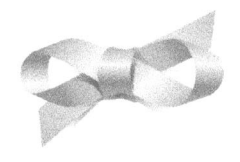

CHAPTER 15
Joe

HIS THOUGHTS WERE LOST and scattered. It was as if she had scrambled his brain. Snippets of their encounter hit him in momentary jolts as he remembered her. The way his manhood looked inside her, her hair splayed on the pillow, the way her legs grabbed his hips, the way her red fingernails grasped the sheets as he drove into her. He stopped and went to his phone.

He opened his messages and saw that Maxine was the first one. He deleted the conversation.

There was a text from Arlene explaining that she had gone grocery shopping anyway, and that she would bring him beer.

Joseph pushed the lawnmower the three blocks home. "What am I doing?" he whispered to himself. He couldn't be falling in love with her, could he? For the first time in several years he wasn't nervous, wasn't filled with this anxious feeling of not knowing what was around the other corner. He wasn't wondering when the other shoe was going to drop. At the same time, he didn't know where to go from here.

Where does it go? We'll see, he thought. "What the fuck am I doing?" For the first time in his life, he had an answer, and it was an answer he liked.

Yes, he thought. He would see her again, and hopefully soon. This was an answer he liked. And it was an answer that would destroy homes.

CHAPTER 16
Harold

• • ⚘ • •

HE SAT AT THE HOTEL bar, thinking of the tournament he had just almost won. If he had just gotten to the final table it would have been all she wrote. Sure, it was just a minor tournament, but he was in the circuit, and it would be a matter of time before he was at the world poker tour again, playing with the big boys, the celebrities like Helmuth, Negreanu, and Ivey. He had been there once, several years ago. He had come in seventh place in '15, kicked out by an all in raise with a ten four suited and a flush of aces on the board. His opponent, some kid with sunglasses and a hoodie, had a higher spade, a king, and won the hand. The payout was over forty grand. It was enough to finally pay off the house with a bit extra to put in savings for his daughter to go off to college.

But it had ignited his desire for more. That's when he had discovered online poker, and what had grown from a hobby quickly turned to an obsession. He thought nothing of playing for eight to twelve hours a day, cashing out every big pot, staying in just long enough to not go on tilt. Which was another way of saying losing too much and getting pissed off to the point of making mistakes. He would play til he felt his lucky streak start going downhill and then cash out. Sometimes he would take a break from the game, watch videos for an hour, walk around the house, maybe watch some porn and jerk off. Because Maxine certainly wasn't helping in that arena.

Sure, they had tried, but the more he lived with her, the more he listened to her, the more he was around her, the less he could stand her. She was always spending his money on stupid things like jewelry or clothes. Or Target gewgaws to decorate the house. One year it had been a whole suite of furniture. And he hated that stupid four poster bed she put in her room. He tried to sleep on it with her one night and couldn't get comfortable. He always felt like he was being sucked into a hole. So he decided he would stay in his own room, the guest room from then on. She didn't argue with him, because after twenty plus years of marriage, you just get comfortable doing your own thing and letting the other person do theirs.

He took another sip of his Crown Royal and his phone rang. His ring tone sounded like a guitar riff from Freebird, his favorite song. He picked it up, looked at the sender. "Well, I gotta take this," he said, when he saw it was Maxine.

"Hey, babe," he said as he put it to his ear. "What's up?"

"Heyyy," she said, trying to sound flirty. "Just calling to check up on ya. How you holding up out there in sin city?"

"Good," he said, wanting this conversation to go quickly. "Won a few thousand so far. Going to try to get a streak going this afternoon."

"But it's Wednesday, I thought you were coming back today," she said, disappointed.

"Yeah, so guess what happened," he explained. "Some guys saw me in the tournament and said they wanted me to come play with them. Sunday night there's this big game at this millionaire's house. I was thinking of staying here till then."

"Sunday?" she sounded surprised. "But i thought-"

"Maxie," he said. "Listen, these guys are rich, this could be a big game for me. There's a promoter and everything's gonna be there."

"I get that, but-"

"No buts," he interrupted again. "Listen, this could be huge for me. Some guy from poker stars, and another from the world tour are going to be there. There's even a dude that won the watch a few years ago. I can skin them alive."

"Okay, but I miss you," she said. "That's an extra week."

"I know," he agreed. He drank another sip. He looked up as there was movement to his right. He saw a young brunette girl in a gold dress plastered to her plastic frame. He smiled. She smiled back, her plastic lips in a demure grin.

"Okay," Maxine said. "If you want to do that, who's to stop you?"

"Exactly," he said. He lifted the glass to her in salute. "Trust me, I know what I'm doing. I'm going to take these suckers for everything. You'll see."

"Maybe when you get back we can talk about new appliances," he heard her say. He was looking at the brunette, her curly black hair cradling her shoulders, the thin straps of her dress barely holding plastic tits.

"Appliances?" he asked. "What the hell, Maxie, we just got some, didn't we?"

"Yes, ten years ago."

"They still work right?"

"Yes, they do, but I was just hoping to get new ones that would match the floor and be more contemporary. The white ones don't match the kitchen any more. I was thinking stainless."

"Shit, you're going to make me stay out here for a year at this rate."

"Okay, whatever," she said petulantly. "We can talk about it when you get home."

"Okay, I'll think about it," he said. He motioned for the young bartender girl behind the counter to get him another drink. "Listen, I gotta go, hon. Talk to you later?"

"Yes," she said. "Go ahead and go play your games. I'll start looking around for prices."

"Okay, whatever. If it makes you happy. Jesus. I'll talk to you later, okay?"

"Okay," she said. "Love you."

"You too," he said. He hung up. He looked at the girl in the gold dress and said, "Hi, how are you? I'm harry."

"Hello Harry," the girl purred. "I'm Toni." she smiled. "Buy a pretty girl a drink?"

"Of course," he said. "Put whatever she wants on my tab." he told the bartender.

"I'm flattered," Toni said. She pointed to the phone after her drink came, a double bourbon on the rocks. "So, marital bliss?"

"Oh, that?" he said. He put the phone in his pocket. "No, that's not bliss, I can assure you."

"Oh no," she feigned sadness for him and took a sip of her drink. "Is everything alright?"

"Not exactly," he said. He looked down at the gold band on his wedding finger. "I should have taken this off a few months ago." And he slipped it into the pocket of his slacks. "We've been separated since the spring."

"That must make you sad," she said. Putting a finger on his shoulder in mock sympathy.

"Yeah," he smiled at her touch. "It does. But I have an idea."

"What's that, sugar?" she said, suggestively.

"I have a room here," he pulled out a handful of cash, and paid the tab with a hundred dollar bill. "Why don't you come up with me and maybe for a while you can relieve that sadness."

Toni beamed, "That sounds like a fine idea." and after seeing the stack of bills thought that was a fine idea indeed.

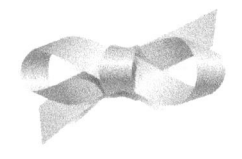

CHAPTER 17
Joe

HE CAME HOME FROM WORK Wednesday, ready for another night of the same routine. He walked in the house and noticed that Arlene had cleaned up a bit. At least the Legos weren't lying all over the living room anymore, and the dishes in the sink were gone. Arlene was at the kitchen table, finishing up a phone call. She looked at him and gave a half hearted wave. He went to the refrigerator and got out a bottle of soda.

"Yeah, mom," he heard her say. "That'll be fun. Joey is going to love it." She paused, listening. "I don't know, maybe I should leave her here? You know how much she hates getting dirty. Girls, right?" Another pause. "Okay," She said in resignation. "I'll bring her along. Maybe we can take her shopping. I'm sure she'll love that. But don't spend too much on her, would you? I know she's going to be a teenager, I just don't want her to be one of those girls." Arlene shook her head. "Okay, mom. Thanks. I'll see you Friday night. Love you. Joe's home. Let me tell him. Okay, bye."

Joe opened the bottle of soda, chugged the dark brown fluid back, and said, "So how's mom doing?"

"She's good," Arlene got up, went to the counter, took out the Absolut from the freezer, and filled her tumbler that still had a bit left from an earlier pour. Joe looked at the clock. Five thirty.

"What's going on with you and the kids?" he motioned to the phone in her hand.

"Oh, Mom invited us up to the farm this weekend," she said. "Tommy is gone to a farming symposium in Durham and she's going to be lonely. Wanted the company."

"Well, that'll be fun for y'all," he said. He went to give her a hug and kissed her on the forehead. She pulled away.

"Wanting us to get out of the house, huh?" she asked.

"What do you mean?" he asked in return.

"It's just you sounded a bit excited, that's all."

Joe thought, here we go. "No, hon." He said. "I just said it'll be fun for you to go." He tried to soothe her.

"Did you want to come with us?" she asked.

"Sure," he said. "If I didn't have to work this weekend."

"It's always work with you, isn't it?" she spat.

"Yes," he answered. "It is." He tried to be calm, but it came out as being shorter than he had wanted. "Jamie's got me going through old accounts, and this weekend I'm going to probably have to go to Raleigh anyway to find those transitions for the Sydney job."

"Fine," she said, walking away. "Go to work. Do what Jamie wants." She knocked back the glass and went to pour another. "Just help me pack up the kids. And the house better be cleaned when we get back. I'm sure he won't work you forty eight hours straight." She walked away, and Joe took that as his cue to shut up and let her go. He was too tired to argue with her. He knew it would be the silent treatment tonight and maybe into tomorrow.

He would be fine with that. He would have to hide his excitement for the next few days. He was cheating after all, and he knew he should feel bad about his indiscretion, knew deep down he shouldn't be doing any of this. But why did it feel so right? He wasn't attracted to his wife anymore. Not that she wasn't attractive, it was so much more he was turned off by.

The judgments, the anger, the drinking. The way she turned her head when he wanted to kiss her. Her constant complaints about him working too much. It all led to him being annoyed with her more than loving her. He had to face the fact that he just didn't like her anymore and he was going through the motions of a marriage at this point.

Maybe when the kids grew up and moved out they would get a divorce. But until then, he had decided he was going to have fun. And that fun started with Maxine.

He was in the shower, thinking of their first time together, remembering her, the way he felt inside of her, strong and powerful, and her underneath him calling his name, urging him on to take her, fuck her, fill her.

Soon, he was taking care of himself, rubbing one out in the shower as his body went hard and then soft in his climax. Imagining what he would do to Maxine this coming weekend, hoping she would be available.

He would have to share the good news with her, but not yet. Now was the time for secrecy. Now was the time for him to be a good father for the night, to keep Arlene calm, let her drink. Let her pass out. Tomorrow, he would contact his love. But until then, he had to be a husband and a father, and be present for his family.

So that's what he did. During the night he kept his mouth shut, Fixed pork chops for the kids, and listened while Arlene complained they were hard. He made mashed potatoes out of a box and forced a smile when she bitched that they were too runny. He talked to the kids about their day over dinner. Listened to Joey talk about how he sniped a guy from a thousand yards away, a trick shot. Looked at Cathy reading some book about games of kids killing each other for scraps in a post apocalyptic world. Told her to put the book down. That it wasn't for kids her age. Saw her look at him like he was the biggest idiot in the world. Watched Arlene look at him like he was the biggest idiot in the world. And watched her take sip after sip of vodka, thinking she was the biggest idiot in the world.

The next day, he went to work. Derrick told him about a guy in Raleigh that called a few minutes before Joe came in, that he had good news.

"What kind of good news?" Joe asked.

"I don't know, all he said was that he looked around his warehouse, and found what you were looking for," Derrick said. "He said he had good news."

"Cool," Joe said, sitting his coffee down on the desk and picking up the phone. "It better be what I'm looking for. This Sydney job has gone on long enough." He dialed the number for Carolina Flooring Solutions in Raleigh. A minute later, he heard a man on the other end pick up and say, "Hello, Jake Stratton's office," in a deep southern drawl.

"Hey, Jake," he said. "This is Joe from Bennet's, we spoke yesterday."

"Yeah," said Jake. Hey, buddy, I got what you're looking for. Seven transition strips in mahogany brown, all with the same batch number. Found 'em yesterday after we got off the phone."

"Is it the batch number ending in oh nine oh four?" Joe said hopefully.

"One and the same, buddy," Jake answered.

"Dear God, you're a lifesaver. I owe you a drink," Joe said, relieved. "Thank God. Can you hold them for me? I'll be there this afternoon."

"Sure thing. They've been here for a few years. Almost was going to throw them away but figured someone would want them eventually. Funny how that works, huh?"

"It's amazing how that works," Joe said, happier than he had been in a few days. Things were looking up for Joe Guillaume this week for sure. "I'll be there in a few hours. Let me take care of some business here, get my client happy, and I'll be there around one, is that okay?"

"Perfect, I'll be back from lunch then. See you then."

"Thanks again, man," Joe said. "You're the best!"

They said their goodbyes, and Joe fist pumped the air. "Thank Jesus and all the saints!"

"Good news, then," Derrick said. "You've been working on that Sydney job for a while now, haven't you?"

"Too long," Joe answered. He picked up the phone, said, "Now I can call and give her the good news."

Feeling Good—Michael Buble

After a couple of brief calls to the client and Chris the installer, plans had been made for the job to be completed in the following weeks. His day was looking up already. Things just seemed to keep coming up fine for Joe.

He was on the road a half hour later, alone in his car, with the radio tuned to an oldies station. The Beatles were singing "She loves you yeah yeah yeah" and he relaxed into the drive. Raleigh was an hour and a half away up interstate forty. He dialed Maxine's number.

"Hey, Joe," she said happily. "This is a surprise, you called me first."

"It's been a good day," he said. He loved hearing her voice. Since he had it on Bluetooth pairing with his phone, she came through every speaker.

"What's the occasion?" she asked.

"Seems my wife is going out of town this weekend with the kids, and i was wondering, hoping maybe, we could get together?" he paused. "If you want to, of course."

"Wow," was the only way to respond. He quickly became disheartened. Maybe it was just a one time thing.

"Wow?" he asked. "What's 'wow'?"

She said, "Wow is that Harold decided to stay in Vegas another weekend, that's what wow is."

"Wait," he put two and two together and came up with an idea. "Does that mean we both are free the whole weekend?"

"That does, Joe."

He noticed a bit of joy in that answer.

"So," he said. "What do you think?"

He could hear the smile in her voice as she said, "I think it's going to be a very good weekend. For both of us."

He sighed in relief. "I was hoping you'd say something like that."

"Whatever shall we do?"

"I think we'll come up with some ideas."

"I think so too," she said. "When are you free?"

"She's leaving Friday night, probably after I get home from work so the kids can say their goodbyes."

"Good," Maxine said. "My place or yours?"

"Yours?" he asked hopefully. He didn't want her to see the disheveled house, and there was a matter of another woman's scent in the bed.

"Sounds like a fine idea," she agreed. "Text me when they're gone. I'll leave the back door unlocked."

"Okay. sounds great!"

"Yes, it does. I can't wait."

"Neither can I," he said. "Neither can i."

They said their goodbyes and he continued down the road with the Beatles still shouting about how she loves you yeah yeah yeah, and things were definitely coming up good for Joe Guillaume. Plenty good, indeed.

A BRIGHT AND HOPEFUL PLACE

Love on the Brain—Rhianna

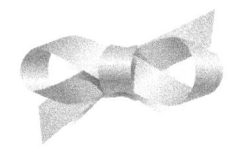

CHAPTER 18
Maxine

FRIDAY NIGHT WAS HERE. Their time alone would start soon. To say she was excited was an understatement. All week she had envisioned how this weekend would go. Their time together, their alone time. They would have time now, to explore each other. Fully, without interruption. She had picked out her outfit, the blue sundress was the only thing she wore. She had told him in texts to come in the back way, through the woods to her backyard. So he did. It was amazing the hold this man had over her. She felt it completely, never having this feeling of anticipation in seeing a man ever before in her life. She had never felt this way with Harold. She had never been allowed to feel sultry, full of want for a man. Sure, she had "Wanted" Harold, but not in that aching way, that hungry way.

Joe was different. There was a scent about him, a smell of man that made her insides weak, desirous, feral. After their first coupling several days ago, that is all she felt. Whenever she thought of him, her cheeks blazed, and her skin felt hot, burning for him. Uncontrollable lust, unquenchable fire. How had he done this to her? How had he made her addicted to him so badly? How had he become the drug she couldn't get enough of?

The way he looked at her, the way he touched her, the way he turned her on in so many ways she had never felt before when she thought of a man.

He was at his back patio door, the pool behind him sparkling in the summer sun, blue and white like the heat between her loins. He knocked softly on the glass. She saw he was clad in tight gray shorts and a white tee shirt. He came to the door, and she smiled as she slid it open.

"Hey," he said. She gestured for him to enter, and poked her head out to look around, but no one could see. It may have been instinctual, knowing that what they were about to do and what they were about to share was an illicit act. He came in.

She stood before him, looking at his chest rising with anxious anticipation. Her body went warm, her skin prickled with her goosebumps at what was about to occur.

He kissed her, taking her face in his hands, a soft kiss, warm, at first and then hunger filled. She wanted to eat his lips, and soon she was devouring them, and he devoured hers. They embraced each other, bodies close, so close, pressed tight, heat rising now. She lost herself in the sunlight burning him.

He lifted her legs around his back and pushed her against the wall behind her. She felt nothing but the solid press of him on her, the solid press of her back to the wall. She buried her face in his shoulder and said, "Oh, yes,"

His face went to her breasts, licking them through the cotton fabric. She reached up to pull it down and exposed them for him to get a better taste. He moaned in them, the fire of his lips cascaded over her, and she gasped again. She was uncontrollable now, grabbing at his shirt. She wanted to feel his hard flesh pressed against her own. She frantically dropped her top around her waist, he pulled down his shorts, revealing hardness, his meat wanting her.

"Put it in," she gasped and he did as she wanted. He filled her quickly, the moisture between her legs letting him go in deep and hard. She hummed into his chest as he held her wrapped around his body, taking her, wanting her, loving her.

His thrusts were powerful, and she came quickly, the feel of him inside her burning and melting her in a way she had never felt before. Bliss. Heat. Wanting. She broke into pieces at his touch. The strength of him pushed her further to breaking point.

Her moans echoed in the room, she collapsed into him as he was inside collapsing into her. Their want was palpable. She never wanted it to end. And as he came, filling her, she threw her head back and it hit the wall, that momentary pain gone with the explosion of his juices inside her. She could feel nothing but his power, the control he held over her, the passion he held only for her. She broke like glass hammered into a million tiny pieces. She sighed, "Oh Jesus, oh God, oh. Oh. oh."

He smiled a delicious smile. "I guess that was round one," he said finally. His breath was ragged, his face flush, the redness of his desire showing on his neck and chest. He lowered her slowly.

"God, you're amazing," he said.

She collapsed into his chest, held him, and hugged him with all her might. "You too," she said. "Oh, man, I can't get enough of you. I've missed you so much."

"I've missed you, too," he whispered in her ear. He kissed her neck, making her blush.

"I've made dinner. Do you need to clean up?" She asked. He looked over her body, her dress hanging limply around her waist, her skin flushed as pink as his. Her breasts were exposed to the warm air in the house. She looked at his own naked chest again, and ran her hands across the muscled form.

"No," he said. "I want to feel what we just did while I'm eating." She hugged his solid form again with her whole body. "While I'm thinking of eating you."

"I like the sound of that." He smelled her hair, making her melt into him.

She could hold him like this forever. "Let's eat," she said finally. "Then it's on to round two..."

Her words electrified him. "Yes, round two," he said. "Then let's eat. I'm starving for more than just food."

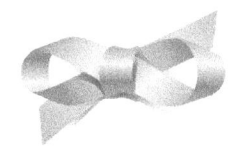

CHAPTER 19
Joe

JOE WOKE UP CRADLED next to her, spooning her back, a hand clasped to her breasts, the heat of her a soothing balm against the cool air from the overhead fan on his naked body. She slept soundless, breathing in a calm steadiness that made him smile. He was lost in the thought of her, the feel of her, her nakedness warm against him. His hand roamed the curves of her body, softly caressing her side, her hips, the soft curve of her ass cheeks and thighs.

She moaned slowly, still asleep. He could stay like this all day, he mused. With her. Away from the world. Away from everything. Away from Arlene.

The name in his mind sent a shock through him and he froze. Lost in the warmth of this beautiful woman nestled in his arms, he hadn't given Arlene a single thought until now. He pulled away from Maxine as if a shot had gone through him, and laid back on the bed. Looking at the ceiling. He caught sight of the fan, the white blades circling slowly, a revolution that made him think of the circle of his life.

The playground of his youth, baseball games in the summer sun, high school. The girls he used to date, meeting Arlene, and being smitten. Wanting her, wanting to be with her. Kissing her the first time in his car after their third date. The coupling in her apartment soon after, the news of her pregnancy, the arguments, the hasty wedding, the birth of his daughter, how he had been happy. The distance growing between them, the eternal distance that came with the separation of emotions, the guilt, trying again with her, a second honeymoon. Her getting drunk, the insane mad cap lovemaking session in the beach cottage in Puerto Rico. The news of the second pregnancy, Joey. And the distance growing. The arguments, the drinking. The blackouts, picking her up off the couch to bring her to bed.

He looked at the sleeping form beside him. Remembering their lovemaking before and after dinner last night, he looked down at himself and realized he was erect. Gotta pee, he thought. He slowly edged out of bed and went to the master bedroom. He managed to finish the necessities and decided to take a shower. Maybe he could just get the thought of what he was doing out of his mind for a minute. Taking a shower had always allowed him to think, to get his day arranged in his head, and to lower his anxiety somewhat. Hot water on his scalp had always managed to do that.

He started the water, and it quickly became as hot as he needed it. He stepped in, grabbed her flowery shampoo and put some on his hair. The hot running water hit his back, causing the muscles in his back to loosen. They were sore from the past week, having not been used for carnal pursuits for so long. He heard the door open and saw her through the glass, picturesque in the rising mist of the shower.

She smiled as she looked at him, admiring his form. She slid the shower door back and said, "You disappeared," as she stepped in to join him.

"Sorry," he said. "You were sleeping, I didn't want to wake you. Had a lot on my mind, and this always helps."

"I know," she said, putting her hands on his chest, feeling the hot water on the tips of her fingers, and looking at the thin line of hair, wet against his chest. She kissed him, slowly, their mouths tangled for a moment in an embrace of desire. "It helps me too."

"Maxine," he started, but she cut him off with a finger to his lips.

"Shh," she breathed, stepping closer to him. Their bodies touched, she pulled him close and kissed him long and deep. He kissed her back, as the water embraced them both.

He kissed her more fervently, and she accepted his tongue into her mouth with a renewed hunger. He couldn't get enough of her, as his hands roamed her wet back, down her sides, and grabbed her ass. He pulled her against his rising manhood. She moaned in agreement as the heat between her legs welcomed his embrace. She reached down and felt him, taking her in a wet hand. "Looks like someone has risen to attention," she smirked.

"Keep doing that," he breathed with a sigh. She stroked him hard, and then with a wink, she said.

"Don't you worry, I have other plans." She knelt before him on the tiled floor, and put him in her mouth. She swirled her tongue around the head of his shaft and his cock bounced with pleasure. "Mmm," She continued.

He involuntarily pushed his hips forward, and she moaned as he went deeper into her mouth. She cradled his balls as her tongue and throat took him to new heights of desire. He could feel his girth growing, the length and power of it pulsing in her mouth. He sighed, "Oh, Maxine, baby."

He looked down at her, the auburn hair now black and water slick. This was heaven, and he never wanted to leave. Soon, he was at a point of no return and he pulled her head back, took a breath and felt the heat rise in his chest both from the mist and his own burgeoning desire.

"Come here," he said and pulled her up to kiss her again. She melded to his body, and he pushed her up against the warm marble tile of the shower wall.

His hand went to her center, rubbed down her folds, and inserted a finger into her waiting warmth. "Two can play at this game," he laughed. She cooed against his shoulder, biting lightly as her pleasure mounted with his finger inside her, then he inserted another, and she pulled back a bit wanting him to go deeper. A shock went through her, "Oh my God," she sighed, and clawed his back as he brought her quickly to release, her nails digging sharply into his back.

He kissed her again, his lips more fervent on hers, and brought her legs up around his waist. With a sharp thrust into her, he pushed her against the tile, entering her deeply. She gasped with alarm and pleasure as he went into her. And then she folded her body around him, feeling his thrusts, welcoming them with gyrating hips, meeting him thrust for thrust. Her heart pounded, and he said, "Oh Jesus Christ, oh my God," and she cried out, "Fuck me, baby oh my God keep fucking me!"

He did, and was about to release, but remembered a former fantasy. He slowed, his desire almost getting the better of him, and he pulled out of her, dropping her feet to the floor.

"Wait," she moaned softly in his ear. "I want you back in, put it back in." he simply laughed, turned her around, lifted one leg and thrust into her from behind. She took it, pushing her hips back into him and getting it as deep as she could. He hit the inner walls with a shock, and as his passion renewed, pushed her against the wall with his body.

Her breasts smashed into the hot marble, making her nipples tingle with delight as he pushed rock hard like a hammer into her. He looked down at her rump, her ass cheeks like a golden heart, and watched himself enter her again and again.

She jumped as another orgasm hit her with the force of a cresting wave and he felt the walls of her pulsing harder on him. He was uncontrollable now, feeling nothing but the sensations of water hitting skin, flesh hitting flesh, and his own orgasm hitting him as he groaned and spilled deep into her. His cock pulsed with release, and her arm reached behind her and held his neck as she moaned, lost in the sensations of his desire.

"Oh my God, so hot, I can feel it, so hot," she sighed breathlessly, feeling everything he had given her as it lubricated her insides.

They stood like that for a few minutes, him kissing her back, her feeling him ebbing a bit inside of her and soon he pulled out. She moaned with disappointment. They had been locked together, bliss overtaking them, and now that sensation of closeness was gone. In that brief moment, she missed him terribly, the feel of him inside her, wanting it there for the rest of her existence.

She turned, melted into his embrace, and they kissed again. "God, you're something else," he said. It had been amazing what she had done to him, how she made him feel.

"So are you, handsome," she said. "Now, let's wash up, shall we? I'm famished."

And they took their time washing each other's bodies, feeling the sponge and washcloth against their skin, getting to know each other's bodies with every touch, kiss, and slow caress.

CHAPTER 20

Joe

THEY HAD BREAKFAST, eggs, bacon, toast, and mixed fruit. They had prepared it together, wearing practically nothing. She wore a white terrycloth robe, nothing underneath, and he had on his briefs. She loved to watch him as he flipped the eggs perfectly in her saucepan while she put the toast in the toaster oven and couldn't help but smile. Her skin was flushed, and she had that post-coital glow, a feeling of relaxation that they both shared.

"What are you smiling for?" he asked.

"Nothing," she said. "Just you. Just, I don't know. I like this."

"What's 'this'?" He put the eggs on a plate and went to her, kissing her forehead.

"This," she folded herself into his chest, letting him embrace her. "I could get used to it."

"I could too," he said. "Breakfast is ready," he kissed her.

"Don't stop," she purred.

"Later," he went to the table, carrying the plates. "But I'm famished, and so are you. Let's eat."

They ate in companionable silence, glancing at each other at times between bites. Joe told stupid dad jokes. She laughed at them, feeling joy she hadn't felt in a long time. Truth be told, he was too. He knew this would be the last day they would spend together so he relished every moment of it. He wanted to feel what a stress-free day felt like, what a day without anxiety at how a woman in his life would react to anything he said but with laughter, hope, and a smile.

When they were done, he picked up the dishes, kissed her again, put them in the sink, and as she finished her coffee, she came to him to embrace again. She put her head on his shoulder, and he kissed her neck. Then ran his fingers through her hair, down her body, and reached under her robe. His hand found her skin, that soft fold between her legs, and she sighed with pleasure. "You need to stop," she said. "Something bad might happen."

"Something bad has already happened," he said, pulling down his briefs, and revealing his hardness.

"That's not bad at all," she looked at it and then stroked it to make it a bit harder. "But I have an idea."

"What's your idea?" he asked, intrigued.

"Come with me." she led him up the steps, to the four-poster bed and pushed him back onto it with a playful smile.

He laid back. She came up to him and straddled him, but didn't put him inside her. "I want to do something to you," she said, kissing him. She pushed the robe off of her shoulders, letting it fall to the bed. Then she started kissing him again, deeply this time, and he felt his arousal grow.

She kissed his chest, the muscles of his stomach, and slid her body down to where her face was right above his cock. "Maxine," he said softly.

She grinned, and said, "Just lay back, I want to try something."

"Okay," he said. "Why am I worried all of a sudden?"

"Oh hush," she said. Then she put her mouth on his cock, and swallowed it halfway into her mouth. She swirled her tongue around it, then pulled up. She grinned, a bit of saliva trickling down the side of her mouth. Looking him in the eyes, she took him in her lips again, kissing the shaft, stroking him. He could feel himself getting harder as she worked his cock in her hand, and he laid back letting the sensations flow through him deliciously.

She put a knuckle on his taint, pushing slightly and a shock went through him. It was pain at first, and then she pulled back her finger and it was pleasure. She sucked him again, her tongue going around his shaft, then tickling the base of his head. The knuckle pushed back into his prostate and he felt a tug of pleasure there as well.

"Oh, God," he said. "Keep doing that..." he let out a pleasure-filled breath. She kept doing that. Pushing her thumb into the fleshy spot below his balls, licking and sucking his penis as he became rigid in her mouth. "Dear God..." was the only thing he could say. "Holy..."

She continued with all three: thumb, knuckle, and mouth for a few more moments and he could feel himself about to explode. But then she stopped. She looked up at him.

"That feels awesome," he breathed. His breath came now in gasps as the pleasure in his whole body seemed to build. She continued.

Thumb.

Knuckle.

Mouth.

Lips.

Teeth.

Tongue.

His rugged breathing was music to her and she got him close to the breaking point and let off. She stroked him with both hands, letting the wetness of her mouth serve as the lubricant. Then she went back to it again. She was building up in him a release he had never had. And she continued with her work on him for a few more minutes.

Mouth. Wet with saliva. Up and down on him. Thumb poking and prodding under his balls, making his body rise magically, he was hers, and he couldn't stand it anymore.

"Please," he breathed, unable to form words. "Oh God, oh Jesus. God," he babbled.

Mouth. Tongue. Thumb. Prodding his prostate. Knuckle. Balls. Stroking. Feeling the fluid in him pulsing.

She stopped. He groaned. He felt like he was about to explode. He had lost track of time. His entire body was on a taut string, vibrating with the threat of release. She kept up the pressure. Thumb. Knuckle. Mouth. Up and down. Tongue. Flicking his head. The sounds of her gargling as his girth filled her mouth.

"Max..." he sighed. He couldn't help it. He couldn't stop, and he moved his hips up and down as her mouth increased the speed at which it made his pleasure climb ever higher.

Mouth. Gargle. Tongue. Flicker. Thumb. Press. Hand. Rub his balls.

And she let him come. Let his fluid fill her mouth, let him scream as his body released in a powerful gasp and a moan that he was sure the neighbors would hear. His body jerked, his hips pushed up into her, and his hand held the back of her head as he flowed into her mouth. She took every drop, swallowing everything he could give her. Everything he had. Everything that was him.

Light came quickly behind his closed eyelids. He realized he had had his eyes closed this entire time, feeling all the sensations, almost in a meditative state as she sucked him dry. He was spent. His body was at the height of its relaxation and he felt supported on the cloud of the bed and he felt nothing but pleasure in his entire body. She had sucked out all of his ability to even process emotions.

He was speechless. She came up to him, she kissed him, he looked at her, he tasted himself, the salty briny love of his come.

This was intoxication. This was desire. He tried to form words but none would come. He was unable to even sutter any kind of words.

"Are you alright?" she asked with a hint of concern. He nodded. He blinked. He reached up to her and kissed her again, tasted her lips, her mouth, her tongue. Wanted to taste her all day. He coughed, trying to find words.

"I can't," he said. He was breathing heavily now, feeling everything his body was doing. The heartbeat is rapid and strong. The skin and goosebumps made his hair stand up and felt the breeze of the fan overhead. The coolness of it. He looked at her again and smiled. "Jesus." was all he could say.

"Mission accomplished," she chuckled.

He laughed. As much as he could. "Wow," he said. "Damn that was.... Damn."

She moved to lie beside him and let him caress her with a weak hand, he could hardly move, his body felt like every muscle had been turned off. "I guess you liked that?" she grinned.

"Yeah," he said. "I guess..." he moved his head to her, to face her as she looked at him with admiration. "Yes, wow."

She grinned satisfactorily. "Tired?"

"Yeah," he said. "But I feel like I need to do that to you now,"

"There's always more time this afternoon," she said. "Right now, you rest. I have to go clean the kitchen. Then maybe later we can watch a movie.

"Okay, sure."

She kissed him again. "Get some sleep. Maybe when I come back I'll be ready for another round."

"You will," he laughed. "But will I?"

"I'm sure we can think of something if you aren't." she turned, and he watched her naked body pick up the robe, pull it on, pull the cord around her waist, and then head downstairs.

Minutes later, he was asleep, lost in a dream world of halos, moonbeams, and red-haired women licking lollipops.

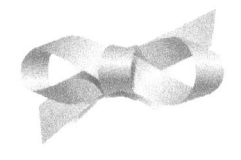

CHAPTER 21
Maxine

HE CAME DOWN AFTER his nap, and she had fixed sandwiches and chips to serve him lunch. This was going to be the best weekend she'd had in many years. While she served him a plate of food, her eyes never left his body, clad now in just his shorts and nothing else. She was still in the robe, naked underneath. They kissed often during lunch, neither able to keep their hands off each other.

They talked over lunch, about simple things, about their lives before and during marriage. It was a conversation to get to know each other. He told her about his story, his mother dying in the accident and how his dad was in a home now, practically dead inside.

"That's so sad," she said sympathetically. "I'd like to meet him one day, your dad."

"He'd like you very much," Joe said sadly. "But enough about my sad life, what about you? It couldn't have been as bad as mine, right?"

She nodded, then looked aside. Memories long held dormant flowed into her mind.

"There's a few things I'd rather not discuss, not this early."

"I totally understand," he said. He held her hand across the white kitchen table and smiled reassuringly.

"Basically," she started. "Long story short, my mother left my dad when I was a kid. We went to live with my aunt and uncle for a few months. They were great. Always happy, always smiling at each other.

If there was a couple of people who loved each other it was my Uncle Dave and Aunt Helen."

"Must have been nice," he said. "Go on."

"They had this thing they would do that I thought was really special. Mind you, I was seven so I couldn't understand it at the time but I always thought it was funny."

She smiled at the memory of her Aunt and Uncle, wishing she could go back to that time before Allen.

"He would come home from working in the oil field, all sweaty and tired. But she would cook him dinner every night. She was one of those housewives that did that sort of thing and enjoyed it, taking care of her man that way. He would come in, kiss her on the neck, and say 'Hey good lookin', what you got cookin'?' and he would pat her on the ass."

Joe laughed. "Cute," he said.

"Helen would then say, 'Chicken, wanna neck?' and then they would kiss each other and hug. It was cute, and it was something that i wanted if i ever got married, had a husband that came home to me like that.

"I told Harold one day, and he tried it for a while, but then he stopped doing it. After Kuwait."

"So he was in the war?" Joe asked.

"He was a supply sergeant in Kuwait, a couple of years there and when he came back he had some PTSD. he didn't want to talk about it, and I didn't pry. I'd heard somewhere that men in war don't want to tell their loved ones about their experiences, and I respected that."

"Understandable. I know my grandfather never talked about his experiences with my grandma either,"Joe said sympathetically. "So you grew up with your aunt and uncle?"

"No," she said, her face went sad. "We stayed with them a few years and then my mom met a guy named Allen." He saw her shudder.

He said, "I'm assuming by that look he wasn't the greatest."

"No," she nodded in agreement. "Far from it." her voice hitched when she remembered the 'Sit on Daddy's Lap' game. "He was a bastard, if I'm being honest.

"How so?"

"I was ten when he and my mom met. She thought he was the greatest guy she'd ever met. He was wealthy, had a house downtown, a big mansion, fancy cars, handsome, charming, what she needed. So far from my drug abusing father, a father I can't remember, actually.

"They got married a few months later. After the honeymoon, he became a different person, or maybe he was that person all along and he just made my mom think he was this good guy who would take care of her and her ten year old daughter. We quickly found out that wasn't the case."

"Sounds like a narcissist."

"That, among other things," she said.

"Hey," he went to her and kissed her. "You don't have to tell me anything you don't want to."

"It's okay, it'll come out eventually, and I'd like to tell it to you now."

She continued, after another kiss. "So one day, we were in the living room. It was bright shiny day, summer, much like this one. He wanted me to sit on his lap and let him read me a story. I was eleven. Mom urged me to do it but he had this look in his eyes I didn't like. Like I had some womanly intuition just starting to form. There was something off about that look and I protested. But mom said just go long, and I did it finally. He sat me on his lap and then he got hard and then he just sat there reading while his dick pulsed between my butt cheeks.

"And then after about five minutes of this he coughed, exhaled with a sigh, and let me get off of him. His white pants were wet where I sat on his lap, and mom looked out the window, sitting on the couch in her designer clothes, looking out at the nice cars in the drive, ignoring it, or maybe knowing what was going on, but just getting along to get along because she had the money and the house and the car now."

"That's horrible," Joe said. He went to hug her. She held him. There was a tear in her eye.

"So this happened a few times a year, until I was about fifteen, but I would always catch him ogling me or my friends when they came to visit. Eventually I just stayed in my room when he was around. I didn't want to see him. He always tried to find ways to see his teen stepdaughter naked, but I kept away from him.

"I was sixteen when I met Harold. He was a nerdy kid in one of those Mensa clubs, but nice. I was a cheerleader because by then I had blossomed into womanhood and got these," she motioned to her breasts. "He helped me with my homework. So we started going out and he had a car so he could take me away from Allen."

"And then we kept seeing each other, we agreed to get married, he joined the Army, and that's it. Pretty boring story, actually."

"Not really boring," Joe said. "The Allen part pissed me off more than anything. Do you still talk to your mom?"

"She and Allen divorced a few years after I got married. She's in California now, living with some B-list actor that does action movies."

"You'll have to go see her one day," Joe said. "Or are you estranged?"

"No," she said. "We talk once or twice a year to catch up."

"What happened to Allen?"

"He got busted talking to some fourteen year old girl by the cops on one of those catch a predator videos a few years later. He's in prison. You ask me, it wasn't soon enough."

"Good," Joe said. "But I'm sad that happened to you. Sounds like Harold took you away from all that."

"Yes, he did," she said. "I mean he was a nice guy, a good guy. Solid, but plain and boring. He was a member of one of those Mensa clubs too, the ones that do the competitions with other Mensa clubs?

"But over time I grew to like him, I guess. The smart nerdy guy who took care of me and had a car."

She looked over at Joe, felt a warmth in her chest just looking at him. She tried to tell herself not to fall for this guy, but it was too late. He made her feel all 'wamey' inside whenever she looked at him.

He picked her up and held her then, holding her tight. He held her face in his hands, gave her a long kiss, then said, "Thanks for sharing. You didn't have to go through that for me."

"I wanted to," she said. "I had this idea that maybe you thought I was a perfect woman."

"You're perfect for me," he said. He kissed her again.

They went back up to bed, settled in, bodies touching. Then they loved each other, slow and languorous. While he rode her from behind she spread her arms wide and grasped the sheets in tight fists and when he took her to the peak of her passion she opened her body like a bright white sky under a hot Arizona Sun.

JEAN-PAUL PARE

More than a feeling—Boston

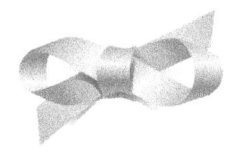

CHAPTER 22
Joe

HE HAD HATED TO LEAVE Maxine on Sunday morning, but it had to be done. They couldn't seem to stop kissing, and at last he had to escape from her embrace, because duties of a husband called more than another possible love making session.

Arlene was coming back to the house later that night, and there was work to be done. He thought it odd that she hadn't at least texted him during the past day, but then thought it wasn't odd after all. She had gone Friday night with the thought he would be working, and he let her believe that. They'd argued some more during the week about shit he couldn't remember, so he decided to leave her alone as much as she did him.

He had gone home, smiling, but wanting more of Maxine. He had wanted to stay another day, and she had wanted him to as well. But their time together was shortened, and they would have to agree to meet at various intervals in the coming weeks.

They had agreed, this was something they'd like to continue, this affair. This deception.

So he had come home, gotten dressed to mow the lawn in a t-shirt and cargo shorts. He finished that task, cleaned the car, went inside, had a lunch of chips and salsa and nachos. Then cleaned up the house as best he could, putting laundry away, picking up half empty containers of take out food, vacuuming the floors, even mopping the kitchen after a deep clean of all the counters.

When he was finished, it looked like a brand new house. He made the bed with new fresh sheets, cleaned the bathroom, but didn't move any of her makeup. Not that she used it a lot anyway, and then took a power nap.

He awoke to the message that she was going to be home in fifteen minutes, she had some stuff to bring in, and he was waiting for her when the minivan pulled up.

He went to kiss her and she allowed him to land on her lips. "Hey," he said. "Did you have fun?"

"The kids did, yeah," she said. "Mom and I took them shopping. You should see the stuff mom bought for them."

Joey stepped out of the car, yawned, and came to give his dad a hug. "Hey, buddy!" Joe said to his son. "Did you have a good time?"

"Yeah, I got to ride with gramma on the tractor," he said. "Then I got to go shopping. I got a lot of Legos and some cool anime guys!"

"Cool," Joe said. "I'll have to see them."

His daughter Catherine, Cathy, came out of the other door and walked past him, focused on a tablet game she played, pink headphones playing some kind of tinkling Korean music. He reached out to her, and she looked at him, "Oh, hi dad." in a voice that was just as disinterested as a person was to an ant.

"Hey, baby," he said. He reached out, they hugged each other.

Then she said, "Hey mom, can I go to my room? I gotta talk to Meghan. There was no cell service at the farm, ugh."

Her mom said that would be okay, and Cathy went inside the house, ignoring her parents as most twelve year old girls do.

They looked at each other, and Arlene said, "The stuff is in the back of the van. Bring it in, would you? I gotta get a drink. That trip was hell, and traffic was a nightmare."

"Sure," he said with a smile. "You go ahead, I'll be right behind. Hey, kiddo, help your dad out, huh?"

"Yeah, I guess," Joey said, stopped midway up the sidewalk to the front door, turned around with a sigh and came back to help his dad lift heavy boxes and groceries out of the back of the van.

They brought stuff in, set it down, and he noticed Arlene was already a couple of tumblers into her vodka. She said, "Place looks nice. Wish you could do this all the time."

"I had time. Took all day. I'm glad you like it," he said.

"I'm sure I'm going to find some stuff wrong, though. But good effort."

Of course she would, he thought. "Glad you're home," he said. He hugged her, and she walked away, into the living room where she picked up the remote, turned it on and started watching a show about a family that was much happier than theirs.

"Wedded bliss…" he said under his breath. Then went to start putting away the boxes of groceries in the pantry, and groceries in the fridge at the appropriate spots.

JEAN-PAUL PARE

The Gambler—Kenny Rogers

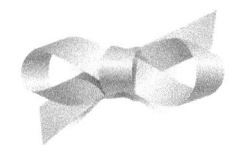

CHAPTER 23

Harold

SUNDAY NIGHT, HE SAT around the table in this million dollar home with four other men around the table. There had been seven when the game had started, and he was about to take down another pot. His opponent was a hot headed guy named Trent who had been on a losing streak for the past few hands and was getting noticeably angry.

The pot was close to half a million dollars, and Harold sat with a monster hand. When the hands were shown, he came up with aces full of threes, a full house. Trent only had two pairs, and this loss made him the short stack at the table. One more, and he would be eliminated.

"Lucky son of a bitch," said Trent angrily. "How this fish can come in here, taking all my money, I don't know. Who invited this asshole?"

Joe said, "Hey, let's all just get along. You won some good hands off of me, you know."

Trent retorted, "Yeah, but who are you, some guy off the street. I've been playing in this town for years, never saw you. I think you're cheating."

One of the other players, Marcus, a Panamanian business executive who owned an airplane factory said, "Hey, i invite him after seeing him play. He's good. Lay off, Trent."

"Good or not, I think he's cheating," Trent said.

"You think I'm cheating how," Harold asked, trying to joke. "I don't control the cards, they just come out where they land, man. Chill out."

"Sure," Trent said, sullenly. "Go ahead and deal the next hand, dealer." He shot the man in the white tuxedo shirt a glare. "How about you give me something besides shit, huh?"

"I'll do my best, sir," said the bald man dealing cards. He dealt.

Harold was in the big blinds, which was twenty thousand. He put in his chips, the dealer dealt, and everyone but Trent went out. Trent called.

"Get to see the flop for free, I guess," Harold said, "Check."

The flop came up an ace of hearts, a deuce of spades, and a six of clubs. Harold looked at his cards. He had a pair of red sixes. Holy shit, trips. He said, "Check."

Trent put in sixty thousand dollars. Most of his ever dwindling stack. Harold called. Trent started looking nervous. Was this kid bluffing? Harold thought.

The turn came out, it was a king of clubs, which didn't help him, but maybe it would help the kid. He felt sorry for Trent. He'd gone through similar losing streaks. So he knew how it felt to be angry about losing hand after hand.

Sometimes you had to walk away from the table when you hit that kind of bad luck. But Trent kept playing. Maybe he has the aces. Let me go ahead and bet and see what happens. Give the kid some of his money back, let him calm down a bit.

Harold said, "What do you have over there?" pointing to Trent's chip stack.

"About seventy thousand," said Trent.

"Cool," said Harold. "I'll bet that. All in."

Trent grinned triumphantly, "Ha!" he said. "Call!" and threw down his hole cards. A pair of aces.

Harold sighed, "Damn, kid, nice hand. Looks like you got this one wrapped up. I got one out."

"Damn right," said Trent. "Let's see that river."

The dealer knocked on the felt, put a card away as was regulation, pulled out the last card, the river, they called it.

It was a six of spades. Harold had gone and hit a quad 6 hand, beating the trip aces Trent had up until that last card, been winning.

"Holy shit!" said the Panamanian. "Whoa, that's a beat if I ever saw one."

Trent just stood there, mouth agape, looking at the hand and seeing how he had lost. "Fucking cheater," he said. "Fat fucking cheater!"

"Whoa," said Harold. "I'm just as amazed as you are, kid." He started gathering up the chips. "What a rush! I thought you had it for sure."

Trent pulled out a snub nosed nine millimeter pistol and pointed it at Harold. "Fucking cheater!"

Harold looked up, "Whoa, calm down kid, whoa now." He held up his hands, trying to be as calm as possible.

"You play it back!" Trent yelled. The other men pulled back from the table, as the two men stood off against each other.

"Listen, kid," said Harold in as soft a voice as possible. "That's the way the game is played. Now put the gun down. How about we do this, I'll split the pot with you, even i agree that was a bad beat. We keep playing and everyone gets back to having fun, how's that?"

"I had my fucking house on this game, man!" Trent yelled. His finger went to the trigger. "You think your scraps are gonna help me get it back?"

Harold said, "Son, this isn't the first time I've had a gun pulled on me, so I'm going to give you two options. One, you can put the gun down, take half this stack, and we play the game and forget the past few minutes."

"What's number two, old man?" Trent's voice was shrill and high pitched with anger.

"Two is, I come across this table, grab that fucking thing out of your hand and shove it down your throat!"

Trent pulled the trigger, the first bullet hit Harold in the stomach. He looked down as the force of what felt like a car hit him, he looked up as the kid pulled the trigger a second time, sending his body flying back, a bright red hole in his chest. This one felt like a truck hammering his chest, and blood flew as Harold's body went flying back out of the chair.

The third bullet fired and hit Harold in the chin, spraying bone matter, skull, and viscera all over the gray carpet. His body came to rest, unmoving, dead.

CHAPTER 24
Maxine

THE PHONE RANG IN THE middle of the night. Maxine was sleeping soundly at four AM when her ringtone, "She's a lady," played and woke her out of a deep and peaceful slumber.

Her eyes still closed in the darkness, she shifted, hearing the ringtone, and wondering who would be calling at this hour. Sleep still kept her in a cocoon of tiredness as she woke fully, reached out for the phone and looked at it as if it were a foreign object she had never held before.

It was an unknown number, with a seven oh two area code. She blinked. "Who is this?" she thought groggily. She hit the answer button, dread in her heart as she knew a phone call at this hour only ever meant bad news. She was almost going to send it to voicemail but thought better of it.

"Hello?" she said with a shaky voice.

There was a man's voice on the other end of the line. "Hello, Maxine Colston?"

Her heart started hammering in her chest, and she coughed, listening to the man. "Hello?" he said again.

"Yes," she said. She was awake now, her mind filled with questions. "Who is this?"

"Ma'am," the man began. "This is Detective Frank Lutz, Las Vegas police department. Is this Maxine Colston? Your Husband is Harold?"

"Yes," she said with a question. "What's wrong?"

"Ma'am," he said and hesitated. "There's been an accident." he paused to let it sink in.

"An accident? Harold's been in an accident?" She sat up and let her legs fall off the side of the bed. All the alarms in her mind started to sound off. "Is he okay?"

There was a pause. Frank cleared his throat. "Ma'am, I'm sorry to be the bearer of bad news, but your husband has been shot."

Her heart stopped. She couldn't think of anything to say. Her mind was suddenly filled with white noise that wouldn't allow her to make a coherent thought.

"Shot?" she found her voice again. "Is he okay?"

"No, ma'am," said the detective. "I'm sorry to have to tell you like this, but he's been murdered. He's dead."

Everything in her body went numb. Her body pulsed with a blood roar and she couldn't hear if he was saying anything at all. Her mind flooded with too many thoughts for anyone to take hold. She was breathing hard, rapid gasps. "What?" is all she could say.

"Yes, ma'am, I'm so sorry." The confirmation from this man had her thinking that everything up to this point had maybe been a joke, a ruse, a bad dream, anything but the cold hard reality of what he was telling her.

She threw the phone across the room, it hit the wall and landed on the floor several feet away from her. She sat, numb, her body cold, and sweat poured out of every pore.

"Hello?" she heard the tinny voice from feet away on the phone. "Hello, ma'am?"

She screamed a keening wail that went for as long as she had breath. Tears streamed down her face. Her blood went cold, and her body shattered into pieces. She just sat, breathed in as much air as her lungs could take and she wailed again, unable to stop the flow of emotion, of fear, of heartbreak.

On legs shaky as water, she finally stood up and went to the phone. She picked it up. The man was still there, trying to get her attention.

She listened, not speaking.

"Ma'am," the detective said sadly, "Are you there?"

She cleared her throat, and in a broken voice said, "Yes, I'm here."

"I'm sorry for your loss," he said. "I'm so sorry."

She breathed again, trying to calm her nerves. She was on autopilot now, and nothing she could do would calm her nerves. She didn't know where she was anymore. Her whole body felt like a million pins and needles had been shoved into her all at once. "I don't know," she started. And her legs gave out.

She tumbled to the floor and collapsed. Blackness started invading her eyes. She shook her head. Lying on the floor, her phone to her ear, she said. "I'm sorry, I seem to have fallen. Oh, Jesus, Harold." At the sound of his name on her lips, she started crying again. "Oh, Jesus, Harold, oh Jesus. What do I do? What did you do? What did I do? Oh, Jesus, Harold!" Tears flowed again. "What do I do?"

"Ma'am," said the detective. "Is there someone you'd like me to call? I can have the paramedics at your house soon if you'd like. Are you okay?"

"Okay?" she screamed. "Okay? You call and tell me my husband has been murdered and you ask if I'm okay? Are you fucking insane?" she wailed.

He waited for her to calm down a bit before answering. "Again, I'm sorry for your loss. If you'd like, I can call back later, after you've had time to process."

"No, motherfucker," she said. Her anger rose like a fever, overtaking rational thought. Adrenaline pumped in her body now and she was feeling sensations and emotions on a level above the normal human experience. "You tell me what happened. NOW!"

"Yes, ma'am," he said and continued. "Turns out he was in a poker game and one of the guys pulled a gun. Name of Trent Wannamaker. We have him in custody. According to witnesses, Trent lost a hand to your husband, started saying things like cheater and lost my house or something, and then shot your husband to death. It was an accident, he said. The gun just went off, he told us. He's upset and confessed. Of course, witnesses will corroborate the whole story."

Maxine was starting to breathe easier, her mind's sharpness coming back into focus, and her emotions leveled off. She looked around at the bedroom. The empty house was dark, as dark as her soul at this moment.

She took another calming breath, "So what happens now?" she said more calmly.

"Well, formalities mostly, we need you to come to the station here in Vegas to fill out paperwork and identify the body. Then arrange for transport back to your home." He explained.

"I have to call my daughter," she said on autopilot. Her brain hadn't fully registered all of this yet. It was too big. The thought of everything this week was too big. She thought of Joe, probably asleep in his own bed, envying the fact he would probably never have to have this type of phone call in his life.

She thought of Joe. Tears flowed in long huffing guffaws. "I have to call some people. I have so much to do."

Frank said, "If there's anything I can do for you, let me know. You have my number. If you need help with the flight, we can take care of that. The host of the party said he would pay for everything. He feels awfully sorry, I assure you."

"Yes, that would be fine," she thought. I'm not paying out of my own pocket for this. "Yes, please have him do that. Let me know the details. It'll be for myself and one other person. My daughter."

"I understand," Frank said. "Noted. Anything else?"

"I don't know yet. Can I call you back?" she asked. "I'm still in shock. I can't think of anything right now. I don't know what to do."

"I understand, ma'am," said Frank. "Let us handle stuff on our end. You go ahead and make some calls. Do what you have to do."

Her breathing still ragged and gasping, even at her insistence on her body to slow down and think rationally, made it impossible to form anything besides basic instinctual thought. "I will. Thank you, officer."

"Yes, ma'am," he said. "And again I'm sorry–"

She hit the red phone button, hanging up before he could offer more empty platitudes. She sat for a few minutes, clutching the phone to her chest. Her body went numb, and she laid back on the floor. Tears gripped her. She sobbed. She sobbed until she couldn't cry anymore and obliviating darkness washed over her.

CHAPTER 25

Joe

HE GOT THE TEXT FROM Maxine when he first woke up and looked at his phone. He had been keeping his phone on 'Do Not Disturb' since their initial meeting, knowing any time his ring tone went off, there would be questions from Arlene. He was still new to the process of having an affair and he would do anything now to avoid suspicions from her.

He didn't like having to go behind her back. There was always the question of how he would tell her, when he would give her the news. And right now, he couldn't risk the timing. How do you tell someone you're in love with another woman? How do you tell someone you want to end their world and start a new one with someone else?

These questions quickly went to the back burner as he saw the text message Maxine sent.

Call me. I need you. Something

Awful has happened. Need to talk.

It had come early that morning. He jumped out of bed and went to the bathroom. He waited a few nervous minutes. His thoughts raced to the possibilities in that text. Had Harold found out? Had they made a mistake? Of course that was always a possibility. Was Harold a violent man? Was she on the street? What was wrong and how would it affect them going forward? These were all the things he thought about as he texted her.

Hey. what's wrong. U ok?

Its Harold. He's gone. Call me. Easier to explain.

Give me a couple minutes

He went to the bedroom, fumbled for his running clothes, and snuck out. Arlene was still asleep and would probably wake up from yet another hangover in a few hours. She had come home from the farm exhausted, drank almost a half of a bottle of vodka, and had summarily passed out a few hours after she had gotten home. Usually when she did that, it would be after ten o'clock when she finally roused herself to wakefulness.

He left the house, noted the time as a bit after six in the morning and walked down the street. His hands fumbled nervously with the phone and he dialed her number.

Two rings went by and she finally answered, a groggy sound in her voice. She had been awake for a few hours, he could tell.

"Hey," she said, and he also noted a hint of sadness in her voice.

"Hey, hon," he said. "What's going on? Is everything alright?" For some reason, he felt fear grip his chest, he walked slower, trying to get his heart rate to slow. This is what anxiety feels like, he thought.

"No," she said, tears in her voice now. "It's Harold, Joe." She paused. "I don't know what to do. Harold's dead."

He stopped. Everything in him wanted to start the day over again. He didn't know what to say or what to do. He said, "Wait, what was that? I don't think I heard you right."

"Harold's dead, Joe," she said a bit louder. "He was shot yesterday, in Las Vegas. He's dead. Oh my God, what am I going to do?"

"Hon," he tried to remain calm. His heart was a trip hammer in his chest. He found a neighbor's white picket fence to lean against and catch his breath, get his bearings. The world suddenly swam around him, and he was unable to grasp a thread of thought. "What?"

"Yes," she said. "He's gone. Apparently there was a fight at the poker game he went to and someone pulled a gun and shot him," she broke down again, sobbing, "Oh my God, what am I going to do?"

"I'm coming over," he said. He started for her house.

"No," she said. "It's okay, I have more phone calls to make and I don't want anyone here. I don't think. I don't know what I'm doing. What do I do?"

"I'll be there in a few minutes."

"No," she said. "I don't want the neighbors to say anything."

"Fuck the neighbors," he shot back. "You need a friend. I'll be there in five minutes."

"You're sure?" she asked. "I don't want to put you out."

"Maxine?"

"What?"

"I'm coming over as a friend. I've been through this before. Just trust me."

"Okay," she acquiesced. "I didn't want to get you in trouble."

"I don't care about any of that. You need a friend. I'll be right there. I can see your house from where I am. I've been walking to you this entire time."

He stepped faster then, and saw her white colonial two story home at the end of the cul-de-sac. The very same home he had left not twenty four hours earlier, hoping he'd be back soon, but never in years thinking it would be for a reason like this..

"Okay, I'll leave the front door open," she said. "Just come in. I'll be waiting."

He said, "Okay," and hung up. He jogged the rest of the way to her house, steeled himself when he got to the front porch, went to the door and opened it.

She stood there, wearing a white cotton robe and they went to each other with the force of two magnets polarized to each other. They embraced tightly, and he let her hold him. Her body shuddered in his grasp, and he walked her to the couch. She nestled into his chest, her hair a matted mess, eyes red and puffy from crying since she heard the news.

He held her, letting her body collapse into him. Let her hold him, and the tears wet his t-shirt. They would go away. Her grief would not.

"Thanks for coming. I didn't know what I would do if I didn't have you," she said, squeezing him tighter. "Or this." She snuffled again and blew her nose. "I'm getting you all messy," she said, looking at his chest.

"You're fine," he said. "I'm here for you. I'm not worried about the messy shirt."

"God, why are you so good to me?" she asked, and looked up. He saw in her face the grief she must have felt since she heard the news. The puffy eyes, the red face, the tiredness in her eyes as their gaze met.

"If you haven't already seen it, I kinda like you, darling," he smiled. He started to get up and asked, "Do you need anything? What can I do?"

"You're doing it now," she sighed. "Just stay here. Let me hold you."

"Okay. you got it." He sat back, let her nuzzle his chest. He put his arms on her back, soothed her, rubbed her back through the robe. "Shhh. it's okay."

"I just don't know what happens next. What should I do?"

"Maxine," he said. "What happened?"

She explained what the police officer had said in her initial conversation, and the one she had with him a few hours later when she was more composed.

"There was a fight at the poker game Harold was involved in. It seems this guy lost a hand and lost everything. He kept saying he lost his house, that he was bankrupt and he was going to lose his wife in the process. So he got desperate, he had a gun, and Harold didn't stand down. So he shot him. Oh God, Joe, he's dead. I can't wrap my head around it. It's too big." She started crying again. "It's too big."

"We'll get through it," he assured her. "Together. IF you want that, that is."

"Oh, God, you know I do," she said. "You're the first person I called after I let my daughter know. That was a conversation, I can tell you. Two blubbering idiots trying to comfort each other. She'll be here later today."

"So you'll have her, at least," his voice was calm with reassurance. "What happens next for you?"

"We have to go to Vegas to view the body, make the arrangements to get him here. It'll take a few days, what with meeting the police officers and all the other paperwork for the body to get cremated."

"And then what?" he asked. He didn't know what to say. He simply tried to keep her talking, to calm down, to grasp something that couldn't be held in a tangible way just yet.

"I'm just numb," she finally admitted. "I don't know what will happen next. Carrie is on her way. She'll walk me through it, since her second husband died suddenly and she had to navigate all that. So she'll be able to help set everything up."

"What can I do for you," he asked, concerned.

"Just be you," she answered. "Just be Joe."

"I can do that," he said.

They heard a door slam in the driveway, and someone coming to the door. Maxine looked out the window at the tall thin brunette stalking quickly to the front porch. "That's Carrie now. Speak of the devil," she laughed. But it was just a chuckle and a wan smile.

"I'll be going," he said. "You two have a lot to discuss."

He stood up, embraced her. The door opened quickly behind them. Carrie stood there, looking at the two. Maxine was wearing just a robe, and Joe in gray sweatpants and a white tee shirt looking like he had just woken up, hugging in the foyer.

She cleared her throat. "Am I interrupting?"

Maxine broke the embrace, said, "Oh, no, you're not, Joe was just leaving."

Carrie went to her, pushing Joe out of the way. She looked at him, said, "Joe."

"Carrie," he nodded.

"I'm so glad you're here," Maxine said to her friend.

"Wild bears couldn't have kept me away, sweetie," she said. "Oh Maxie, I'm so sorry."

Joe stepped back a bit, letting the two friends hold each other. "I'll just be going, then," he said. He wanted to go to her, kiss her, hold her all day, but he knew he couldn't do that, couldn't do anything but pray she would be alright.

Maxine looked over at him and said, "Thanks for coming by Joe. It was nice seeing you again." in a business like manner. He took the hint.

"Any time," he said. "You need anything, I'll be right down the street. Give me a call."

"Thank you," she said. "I'll do that." Joe turned to leave. Carrie shot him a scathing look. It was a look that told him she knew what was going on, or had the suspicion of it nonetheless. It was a look that said, 'I've got my eye on you, mister man'.

He nodded silently, then stepped out the door. He closed it behind him, started walking down the street.

"Well, this changes things," he said. "This changes a lot."

Then he walked home, his mind abuzz in thought of how this would change everything, and realizing it may end up being a good change at the end of it.

CHAPTER 26
Maxine

MARCUS HOLSTEIN SAID, "I appreciate you meeting me like this, Mrs. Colston. However, I can't understand how I can help you."

Maxine sighed, "I don't really know what I'm doing here. I've asked the police if I could see Trent, and since I'm not on the visitor list for the jail, I can't see him." she fiddled with the strap of her purse, nervous, not really knowing what she was doing here either, or how this man could help her. But she had to try.

She had traveled here a few days after finding out the news. Travel arrangements had been made for her, and after an all day plane trip in first class she had arrived to find a driver, a fully stocked limousine and a somber gentleman waiting for her at the airport. Following his lead, they went to the police station, to the morgue, had identified Harold's body, such as it was, and they had arranged to have his body cremated.

Carrie and Maryanne had decided to stay behind in Newton's Crossings to finalize the details for the memorial, what that would look like, and who would be invited. Maxine had wanted to come to Vegas herself.

That was Harold's wish, upon his death. They had discussed it one time, not ever knowing it would ever truly happen. He wanted to have his ashes thrown into the sea, a childhood dream of his because he liked the beach, it was his happy place.

"I came here, hoping you would help me arrange a visit, I suppose," she said at last. "I just want to talk to him. To tell him I'm not angry. Or that I am, but I don't want him to feel bad about what he did." tears were coming to her eyes again, the weight and gravity of the situation starting to wear on her nerves.

"As the defense attorney assigned to the case, I can definitely ask him to meet you, but I would have to be present. What would you have me say to him?"

"I know my husband wasn't the worst guy in the world," she started. "But he wasn't the greatest either. He was my husband, he had his flaws, as we all do I guess." she thought of Joe, what they had done over that weekend. The joy she felt, and now the tremendous guilt.

"I agree," Marcus said. "Human beings are complicated, for sure. And relationships, even marriages, between those people are even more fraught with complications. Naturally."

"Yes," she said. "But I loved my Harold, in some way, or else I wouldn't have stayed with him for twenty four years." She wiped her tears with a tissue and continued. "But I have to move on, to find some closure. That's why I want to talk to Trent. To tell him I don't hate him. That I don't want him to suffer for his mistake."

"That's very nice of you," he said. "He's on suicide watch right now. The day after he was incarcerated, he indicated to a guard he was going to hang himself in his cell. I think it was a cry for help, and most agreed, but he's in lock down for his own safety currently, and is allowed no visitors except myself now anyway. So seeing him is off limits, even to the victim's wife, I hope you understand."

"Can I at least write a note? Can you give it to him?"

"I could, yes," said Marcus. He took out a pen and some paper. He shoved them across the desk to her. "IT would go a long way to helping his mental state, I'm sure."

She wrote a note, a quick flurry of words expressing how she felt and what she wanted Trent to know. About how she wasn't going to hate him, he didn't need that. He didn't need to know that someone else out there, even his victim's wife, bore any ill will toward him. That he knew he was sorry for what he did, that she hoped he got the comfort he needed from this note, and that she forgave him. To live his best life and help others if he ever got out of prison. She signed it, handed it back to the attorney.

He read it, and asked, "Is this what you genuinely mean to tell him?"

"Yes," she said. She wiped away another tear. "Is there any way to know how he's going to be charged?"

"The prosecution will want to give him a plea deal. Since there are witnesses, and he has confessed, they're willing to offer a plea deal, which we will probably take. For the charge of manslaughter, they'll want four years. The gun charge will be dismissed, and they'll ask for probation for a year after that."

"What if I met with them?"

"The DA?" he asked. "What for?"

"To maybe tell them to give him a more lenient sentence, maybe?"

"That's very generous of you," he stood up, went to her and said, "I'll tell you what. Why don't you write a letter, telling them the same thing you put in the note, ask for a more lenient sentence, ask the court to forgive him since it was his first offense, and maybe they'll see what the judge can do. I can't make any promises, and the sentencing hearing isn't for another couple of months, but we can certainly see what can happen."

"Thank you," she said, feeling better. And then she wrote a note to whom it may concern, with the same message that she gave Trent, and also how she wished for leniency from the court for his mistake.

"This will work fine," Marcus said as he finished reading it. "But I have to ask," he paused. "Why?"

"Why what?" she asked.

"I've had wives who want to throw the book at their husband's killers. Sure, it works out sometimes that a member of the family wants to give a lighter sentence, but it's very rare. I'm just curious as to why you want to be so generous and merciful. I'm not used to seeing that in people."

"I guess, she started. "I don't want him to feel responsible for a careless act, or how it will affect me. I don't want him out there thinking that someone hates him. If I forgive him, and I have to, I don't want him to think he's ended two lives instead of just the one."

"I see," he said. "But I get the sense there's another reason. One that you're not telling me."

"That's the only reason," she said. "As much as Harold and I had our disagreements, and there were plenty for sure, he was my husband. He's the father of my daughter. And he would be doing the same thing if the roles were reversed. It's just the way we feel. People make mistakes, and Trent made a big one. We're human. We're all going to make some pretty big doozies in our lifetime. Trent made one of those when he killed my husband in anger. I just don't want it to wreck the rest of his life."

"That's very nice of you," Marcus said. "I commend your kindness. It's rare to see it in the world, and especially this place." he gestured to the window where the Vegas casinos promised every kind of sin.

"Are we done here?" she asked. "I don't want to take up more of your time. And I have a lot to do in the next few days. I really should get back to Carolina."

"Yes," he said. "I'll have these notarized and put in his file. I'll fax them over to the prosecutor's office for their files as well. Is there anything else?"

"You have my phone number, right?"

"Yes," he answered. Showing her to the door.

"Call me when the sentence comes in. I just want to know how it all worked out."

"Of course, I will."

"Thank you. You've been a big help." She shook his hand, and he ushered her past his bubbly blonde secretary to the front doors of his office. "Again," she said. "Nice to meet you. Thanks for all your help. If there's anything else you need to help him, let me know."

"I have a feeling," he said. "There's something else at work here than just kindness for another human being."

"What's that?" she said nervously.

"I feel like Trent maybe did you a favor," he said gravely. "Call it a hunch."

She stopped and looked at him, surprised. "What do you mean by that?" Her heart raced for a few moments, her face flushed.

"Maxine," he said with a smile. "You don't want to play poker here, you don't have the face for it."

"What is that supposed to mean?" She tried to remain calm, but feeling guilty all the same.

"You have a really bad poker face," he said. "But that's okay. It'll be our secret. God knows, I've kept many of those in my time doing this job. I wish you all the best. I'll let you know what happens."

"Thank you," she said, relieved. "You're very helpful."

They said their goodbyes and she went down the steps to the street. She wouldn't be anything in this town, least of all gambling. All she wanted to do was to go to the airport and return home. She vowed never to visit this city again for the rest of her life.

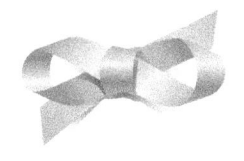

CHAPTER 27
Maxine

A FEW DAYS LATER, SHE received a phone call. Sitting on the couch, browsing the TV, not landing on anything worth watching. Her life had become a miasma of grief. She was lonely, she was in despair. There were bright spots, but those were few and far between in the restless humming of her life without Harold in the other room. It was at least twice a day she would go into his office, expecting him to be there, hoping it was all a nightmare, opening the door, and saying "Harold?" in that hopeful question, only to find the chair empty, the computer off. A room as dead and silent as its former occupant.

She had seen Joe one time, held him as tight as she could, wanting him to stay with her and knowing he couldn't. They barely spoke when he was there, but he held her, and the holding made all the difference for the moment they had been together.

Her daughter had made the trip home and was staying with her, but at this moment she had gone to run errands and getting everything ready for the memorial in a few days.

Harold had wanted a quick funeral. They had discussed it a long time ago, the kind of somber discussion they had had as a married couple one day. He had told her, "Have me cremated and have my ashes dumped in the ocean." It was the one place he loved. He'd grown up in this town, had loved the beach, and had wanted to be in the Navy but didn't make the cut, so joined the army instead and went off to be a supply clerk in Kuwait.

The phone rang and without looking at who it was, she answered. "Hello?"

"Hey, Maxine," said a familiar voice. It was Harold's money manager, lawyer, and keeper of the estate, Jerry Winters. "How ya doin', hon?"

"Okay," she answered. "Considering the circumstances, of course."

"Of course," he said. "My condolences on your loss. When I heard the news I was devastated. Did you need me to do anything for you?"

"No," she said. "My daughter's here, she's handling everything."

"Good. good," there was a pause. "Is this too early to go over the estate?"

"Now is as good a time as any, I suppose."

"Okay, so I've looked into the financials, and it all looks pretty good. One thing about Harry he always kept in touch. Is there any way you can come to the office today or tomorrow? I know it's on short notice but this is something that can't be done over the phone," he explained. "You understand. Paperwork to be signed, checks to be disbursed, that kind of thing."

She didn't think anything he was saying was out of the ordinary. "Yes, does my daughter need to be there? She's running errands right now."

"No," he said. "Just you."

"Okay," she looked at her phone and saw it was twelve-thirty. "Is one thirty too soon? I have to get ready to go outside. I'm not dressed to go out."

"Sure," he answered, being as calm and friendly as possible. "That's fine. I'll have everything ready when you get here."

"Good. I'll see you then."

They said their goodbyes and she got up off the couch. She clicked off the tube, went to the bedroom, took off the white terrycloth robe she had on, revealing her nakedness, and then took a shower, remembering the passion that she had had there with Joe not two weeks ago. Then stood under the hot water and cried until the water went cold.

"So I was looking at everything," said Jerry. "And I made a few phone calls. Harry had a lot of pans in the fire, and lord, it took me a few hours on the phone with insurance folks, banks, and finance companies to get it all sorted."

"Insurance?" she said. She hadn't remembered Harold getting any kind of insurance before. Sure they'd talked about it, but she didn't know he ever had done it. Jerry had been keeping their books since after the first big poker tourney win, and she was out of the financial picture. Let the men take care of the money, I'll take care of spending it, she thought.

"Yes," said Jerry. "So the assets on the house, which is paid for, are here, the value at three hundred seventy-five thousand dollars. I have a real estate agent who can list it for you, and she's a dynamite seller, let me tell you. Probably get four hundred easy."

"I need to sell the house?"

"No," he smiled. "It is all part of the asset list. Like the furniture, his property, and anything in the house. Cars, whatnot. You understand?"

"Yes, I got it," she drank another sip of the cold ice water in front of her on his voluminous desk. Jerry sat back with a pen in his hand and held it out to her.

"So you just need to sign all this paperwork, and then there's the matter of the life insurance check."

"Life insurance?" she asked dumbfounded. "I didn't know he had that. When did that happen?"

"About five years ago, now. I thought you knew. Huh." he looked at her. "I was wondering why you hadn't called me before now."

"He had an insurance policy?"

"Yes. he wanted to take care of you and your daughter if something unfortunate happened. I made all the arrangements with Mutual, he signed it all and made you the sole beneficiary."

"Harry?" she asked. "My Harold had life insurance?"

"Yes," he repeated. "I'm sorry you didn't know that." he reached into Harold's file folder, and pulled out some paperwork, several forms of boilerplate in triplicate. There was a cashier's check attached with a red plastic paperclip.

She gasped at it. She looked up at Jerry. She looked at the check again. She looked back at Jerry, who was smiling now. He nodded.

"Is this right?" She asked. "This can't be right."

"All perfectly legal. All right," he beamed. "All one million dollars of it right."

Tears flowed. She couldn't stop them. She didn't know if it was sadness, despair, or the heavy feeling of guilt that spilled out of her eyes at that moment. "Harry did this?"

He handed her a tissue, and she wiped her eyes. "Harry? My Harold?"

"Yes, Maxine. Your Harold. He put a one million dollar life insurance policy on himself. Figured since he was winning big, he was a commodity. So he had me draw all the paperwork, handle the payments, and get it all worked out. You seem surprised."

"I," she started. "It's just." she dabbed her eyes, "Oh, Harold, you son of a bitch..." and then she cried. It was grief, it was guilt, it was anger she hadn't felt in a few days since she got the call of his death. But not anger at him, anger at herself. Her face grew hot with redness, and she couldn't stop the tears.

"Oh, Harold, you son of a bitch. How could you? How could I?" she kept repeating, "Oh, Harold."

Jerry went to her, put his arm around her shoulder, and let her get it out. When she finished, in guffawing hiccups, he handed her the box of tissues. "You need this more than I do, hon." he joked.

She chuckled with relief, sniffed, grabbed a tissue and blew into it. "What the hell? Harold did this?"

"Yes, Maxine," he said and went back to the desk. He sat down and handed her the pen. She took it with shaking fingers and almost dropped it.

"So with all the assets, cars, house, insurance policy, the total comes to one million, seven hundred eighty-two thousand, and forty-three cents. Give or take."

She looked at him. She stared, unblinking.

"You're a millionaire, Maxine, congratulations."

She signed the papers for the next hour, processing too many emotions for words.

CHAPTER 28

Maxine

•• ⚜ ••

HOW DO YOU LOVE A MAN so hard when the man you were supposed to love had only been dead a few weeks? This had been the question Maxine had on her mind most of the night after the memorial. Joe was tender, gentle, funny in his own way, caring. And hot. Just thinking about the way he touched her made her warm inside. That can't be just menopause, she thought. It can't be. Why was she obsessed with this man?

Carrie came over where Maxine sat at the bar. "How you holding up, kid?"

"I'm okay," Maxine finished her Long Island iced tea, tried to get the bartender's attention again, and pointed to her drink when the young man looked over and nodded.

"You want to slow down there, hon," Carrie said. "Too many of those and you won't be able to walk."

"It's not the walking I'm worried about," Maxine said to her friend. "It's the thinking."

"I get it," Carrie sat down beside her. "I went through the same thing when Frank died. I still wonder what I could have said or done to make him not race that day, but I keep going back to the fact he wanted to and damn the consequences." She finished her wine and put it back on the bar, a bit harder than she should have. "Look at me, I'm getting as tipsy as you."

"It's a good night for it," said Maxine. Two hours earlier she had thrown ashes into the ocean on a beach south of Wilmington, while several people watched on, a young black girl sang Amazing Grace, and an old gray haired preacher gave a homily about ashes to ashes and dust to dust.

It was a standard beachside ceremony. When the news came out that Harold had died, Jamie reached out to Maxine and offered to take care of the ceremony, since Maxine had said they didn't attend a local church. So the memorial had been arranged, several people from the neighborhood were there, along with other members of the store, and friends of the family. Joe was there too, and she found it hard to keep her eyes off of him.

He looked so handsome in his black three piece suit, with gold buttons, a white shirt, and a black tie that she just wanted to eat him up right there.

But she knew she couldn't, obviously, so she would have to wait.

And that was another thing about this whole sordid mess. They would have to wait. The only thing is, she didn't want to. He had done something during their weekend together, something that made this attraction go from a fling to a real actual love.

She had to admit to herself that she was falling for him badly. That her heart was firmly in his hands now, that he had her in the palm of his hands in a way Harold never could.

"The ceremony was nice," Carrie said, breaking the silence. "Don't you think?"

Maxine roused herself and turned to Carrie. "Hmm?" she asked. Then it registered what Carrie had said. "Oh, yes, very nice."

"I know you're not okay, sweetie," Carrie said. "You want to come over here and join your daughter and me to finish out the night?"

It was a Thursday in a downtown bar. They were finishing out the night on a leather couch by a cozy fireplace in which a fake fire burned. It was nearly two in the morning. Closing time.

"Sure," Maxine said, going over to the two drunk women, and now there were three. She had gotten the last Long Island ice tea and sat down on the couch next to her daughter.

Maryanne looked at her lazily and with a slurred voice said, "Glad you could join us, mom?"

Maxine hugged her daughter around the shoulder and tried to come up with something to say. She couldn't think though. After a few sips of her last drink, her mind went numb. Finally, she thought. Nothing there. No Harold, no Joe, no nothing.

Carrie said, "They're about to close. We should call an Uber."

"None out right now," said Maryanne. "I checked."

"Well I can't drive," Carrie said. "I've had too much wine. Man, I'm going to have a headache so bad tomorrow. Why did I let you talk me into this?" she asked Maxine.

"Because I needed my best friend," she said. "And my best daughter." She put her arm around Maryanne again and pulled her tight.

"Well," Carrie said. "What do we do now? How we getting home?"

"I know someone can pick us up," Maxine said, fishing into her clutch for her phone.

"Oh, no," Carrie said, knowing who she was going to call. "You can't, Maxie."

"It's just a call, what's he going to say, no?" The phone was ringing in her ear. Two rings and he answered.

"Hey, what's up?" Joe asked.

"It's two o'clock, Joey," said Maxine in a flirty voice. "What are you doing up? Waiting for my call? You're a dear."

"No, I just happened to get up and go to the bathroom. It's lucky you picked this time to call. What do you need?"

"I have a problem," she said. "There are three women who need to get home and there's no Uber and I just wanted to know if you would like to come and get us from the bar?"

She heard him sigh, exasperated.

"You don't have to if you don't want to," she said. "It's just... you're the only one I thought to call. And I need you, Joe."

"I'll be right there. Give me a few minutes. Where are you?" He said, in a caring tender voice that made Maxine melt.

She told him where they were. Mcgee's Pub was downtown in Newton's Crossing in a revitalized Front street. It was a small Irish pub, built into a renovated hundred and fifty year old bank.

"I'll be right there," he said. "I know the place."

"What about Arlene?" she asked.

"Fuck her," he said. "You need me more. Besides, she won't know. She's been passed out since nine o'clock."

"Okay," Maxine smiled. "You're a gem. We'll be outside. They're about to close up and we're the last people here. I think Johnny wanted to go home a few hours ago."

"Just stay there," Joe said. "I've got my keys in my hand. I'm walking out the door now. I'll be there in ten minutes."

"Okay, we'll be outside," Maxine said. They hung up together, and she said, "Easy peasy. Got him right where he wants me." and she held up a finger to twirl it, and the world swam around her in a circle and she almost passed out. "Wow, what was in that last drink?"

"Everything but the kitchen sink, Maxie," Carrie explained. "And you've had four of them in the last two hours. You'll be feeling that for sure, tomorrow."

Carrie lifted her to her feet, gave her a few light slaps to wake her up, and said, "Hey girl, still with us?"

Maxine felt the slaps, like a far away pain, and said, "Ow, stop it."

She turned to Maryanne, who was just about as drunk as her mother. "She'll be alright, what about you?"

Maryanne tried to stand and fell back down on the couch. "Shit," she said.

"Jesus Christ, " Carrie said exasperated, "You two are hopeless. Johnny!" she cried to the bartender.

He looked up, "What's up?" She had caught him in the process of counting out the night's till.

"Can you help me get these two drunk broads out to the street so you can clean up?"

He laughed, "Yeah, I'll help." He came out from behind the rich mahogany bar and went to them. He lifted Maryanne to her feet, let her stand and get steady, and then Carrie and he walked the two women out to the street. Carrie thanked him for the help, reached into her purse and brought out a twenty. "Here," She attempted to give him the bill.

Johnny pushed it away, "Sorry ma'am, can't take it. You know how rich I'd be if I got paid for every woman I ever helped out of here drunk?"

"A millionaire?" Carrie laughed.

"Exactly," said Johnny.

"Take it anyway," she said, and jammed it into the pocket of his blue jeans.

"Okay," he said. "Y'all going to be alright out here? I can wait a minute til your ride shows up."

"No, that's okay," Carrie said, glancing down at the two drunk girls. She looked up and down the street lined with revitalized, empty buildings, antique stores, art shops, and multi-colored awnings. No one was on the street this late at night. In the distance, rounding a corner, she saw a white Hyundai, its bright headlights flashing under the sodium arc streetlights. "I think that's him now."

"You all have a good night then," he said. "I'm right inside, you need anything."

Carrie said, "Okay, have a good night." Johnny went back inside, locked the bank pub door, and a few seconds later, the interior lights went dim.

Joe pulled up to the side of the curb and he was out of the car faster than any man she had ever seen. Maxine stood up next to the wall, the red brick to her back offering a welcome steadiness to the layers of images swimming in her head. There were at once three Joes, then one, then two. Why was he driving two white cars? We only needed one.

He came to her then, white t-shirt and jeans, and with a deft movement of her hands, said, "I got you," and lifted her off the ground to take her to the passenger side of the car. Carrie opened the door for him, and he slid Maxine's recumbent body in, reached over, pulled the seat belt around her and snapped it tight.

"Hey," she said, reaching up to his face. "You came."

"Yes," he sighed. "I did. I wanted to make sure you were safe. Sit back, relax." He sounded to her like he was exasperated, like he had been put out by this whole scenario.

Carrie and he helped Maryanne into the back seat on the drivers side then. She had passed out, and her slim body was almost lifeless.

"Looks like you've done this before," Carrie said to Joe.

"More than I want to, yes."

"Hey," she said to him, getting into the other open seat. She closed the door.

"Yes?" he said. He made sure they were all safe, checked his surroundings, and pushed the car to start.

"You're a good guy, Joe," she said. "I like you."

"Well," he said as he pulled off down the street. "I'm glad I have your approval."

"No really," she sat back in the warm seat, looking out the window. "I didn't like you at first, but you're a good guy."

"Thanks," was all he could say.

A few minutes into the drive, Carrie had passed out too. Maxine stirred.

"Hey," she said, looking over. "You're here. What are you doing here?"

"I'm taking you home," he said shortly. He sighed. "Dammit, Maxine."

"What's wrong?"

"I'll tell you tomorrow when you sober up. Right now, let me get you to your house, and then we'll talk later, okay?"

"Why not now?"

"Because I'm not in the mood and you're in no condition to hear what I have to say."

"But," she started.

"But nothing," he spat. "Let me get you home, get you into bed and let you sleep off whatever this is."

"Get me into bed," she tried to flirt. "Oh, you're scandalous, darling." She put a hand on his thigh. He took it off abruptly.

"Stop," he said, eyes on the road.

"But darling," she said.

"Maxine," He looked over at her with a look that said in no uncertain terms would he be amenable to any situation involving the physical tonight.

"Okay," she said. She removed her hand, looked at it and saw two there, then three, then the world swam out of focus and went dark.

Minutes later, she felt the car door open and rough strong hands reach across to take off the seat belt. She looked up and saw Joe, her savior. "Hey, we home?"

"Yes," he said. He looked at the car, where three women were passed out on the seats, drunk. She heard him say, "Goddammit." and then he came back to her, lifted her out, and steadied her on the side of the car. "Hey!" he shook her lightly.

"What?" she looked up at him.

"Where's your keys?"

"In my purse," she pointed drowsily back to the car. "In there"

He got out her Louis Vuitton clutch, looked inside and saw her keys, a pretty jewel encrusted wallet, lipstick, makeup, and a few green bills. He pulled out the keys, went to the door, and after finding the right one, opened the door.

Ten minutes of fumbling with drunken women later, and with a little help from Carrie, he managed to get them all into the house. Maxine was in her room, lying on the bed still clad in a white blouse and black skirt.

Maryanne had been deposited in the same room she'd grown up in, and when Joe turned off the light, he saw little fluorescent stars dancing on the ceiling.

Carrie gave him a hug, said, "Thanks, a lot." and promptly passed out on the couch.

He went back to check on Maxine. She sat on the edge of the bed, taking off her blouse, and failing at it.

"Why are there so many sleeves?" she asked him. He went to her, pulled one off, then another. He looked at her white lace bra, decided to leave it on, and then unzipped the skirt along the side. He stood her up, and let it fall to the floor. She still had pantyhose on, and he pulled those down too. He smelled the musk between her bare thighs as he knelt to help her out of them. He put her back down on the bed, and went to pull the covers over her when she laid down to get cozy in the sheets.

She reached behind his neck and brought him in for a kiss. He kissed her back, smelled the liquor on her breath, tasted alcohol. He drew away.

"Joe," she sighed sleepily. "Stay with me, please. I need you to hold me." she pleaded.

"I can't," he said. "And you know it." He went back to the door, turned and said. "Even if I could, I wouldn't Maxine. And you know why."

"Can't take advantage of a drunk woman?" she said. Her eyes were closing again. He turned off the light. A small night light lit up a portion of the room in a steady yellow glow.

"No," he said. "That's one thing I'd never do. God knows I've had plenty of chances."

"You're a good guy, Joe," she said. Her eyes closed. There was a short snore as the weight of sleepiness took her over. Joe leaned on the door frame of her bedroom, watching her sleep.

"Joe?" she said after a minute. "God, I love you."

"I love you too," he said. And he meant it.

She smiled and fell fast asleep. He left the house, after making sure the girls were alright. Then he got into his Hyundai and drove home, the white knight returning to his castle.

High Enough—Damn Yankees

In the morning, the sun shone bright in the bedroom window. The house was silent, and her head bulged with a pain she hadn't felt in years. What is happening? She thought. Where am I? Her eyes shut out the bright light, brighter than it should have been. Hungover, she thought. That's what it was. She's going to pay for last night.

She moved slowly, waking up her numb body, feeling the pain in her arms, her face, her joints. "Well, that's the last time I do that for a long time," she said to the room. She still had her bra on, but her torso was bare. She remembered fleeting moments of the night before. They came in rapid shots, a bar, the memorial, the old preacher, the handsome man in the black suit. The breathless "I love you, Joe."

"Shit," she said. "Oh, shit." she rubbed her face. Downstairs she heard her phone in the clutch, "She's a Lady" playing over and over.

What time is it? She thought. She sat up, felt her head fall to one side feeling heavier than normal, then fell back on the bed. "Fuck!"

She heard someone coming down the hall, and for a minute thought Harold was going to come in. this was all a bad dream, she thought. She would wake up soon, waking from this eternal nightmare of three am phone calls, dead husbands, morgues, funerals, police offices, lawyers, and he would walk in the door, a plate of food for her, serving breakfast in bed.

But it was only Carrie, holding a cup of coffee, and her purse.

"Good morning, sleepyhead," said Carrie with a smile.

"Shit," said Maxine. "What time is it?" She sat up, reached for the coffee and took a sip and gave it a few seconds to let it bring her around. She sat up and took another sip. "Thanks"

"Don't mention it," Carrie laughed. She set the clutch down next to her friend. "I'll have breakfast ready in a few minutes."

"I don't think I can eat," Maxine said. "Ugh, I feel like shit."

"You will all day," Carrie said, the font of knowledge on hangovers. "About seven o'clock tonight you'll feel a bit better. You need water, carbs, and meat. And lots of all three."

"Speaking from experience, I see." Maxine reached for her purse. She took out her phone, looked at it. The time was eleven thirty. "Dammit!" She had one missed call from Joe. It had been him calling a few minutes ago. He didn't leave a voicemail.

He'd also sent a text. "Call me. Need to talk."

She sighed. "Shit."

"What, Darling?" Carrie asked, sitting down next to her. She held her friend with one arm around the shoulder.

"Nothing," Maxine answered. "Just drama. Drama I don't need right fucking now."

I think he's mad," Carrie said. "You should have seen him last night. He picked you and Maryanne up and put you both in the car like he wanted to get it over with."

"He probably did," Maxine looked at the phone. "I better call."

"Eat first," Carrie said. "He can wait."

"No," Maxine said. "I got to get this over with. I won't be able to eat, wondering what he's going to say."

"Don't let a guy tell you how to feel, Maxie," Carrie said angrily.

"I'm not," she said. "I just want to explain, and to say thanks for last night. I'll be okay." she pushed redial on the last phone call. "Go fix breakfast. I'll be down in a minute."

The phone rang. Carrie stood up, rubbed Maxine's tousled auburn locks, and said, "Okay. It'll be ready in a few. Good luck."

The phone rang a second time. Maxine just gave her friend a thumbs up.

"Hey," Joe answered. Maxine could hear traffic on the other end of the line. He had stepped outside to have this talk.

"Hey," she said. "How you doing?"

"I was just about to ask you the same thing," he said. "You feeling alright?"

"Yes," she paused. "Listen, Joe-"

He cut her off. "No," he started. "You listen." His matter of fact voice was straight to the point. She felt her heart jump.

She went silent, then said, "Okay."

"For starters, I love you and I'm glad you're okay. You'll probably be feeling kind of shitty all day, so there's that. I understand. It was a hard day for you." His voice sounded caring now.

"I do feel like shit," she said. "But thanks for your concern."

"Maxine, Goddammit, I love you," he admitted. "More than I should, but it's there all the same. And you said the same thing last night. You may not remember it, but you did. You may have been drunk when you did, but I was stone sober, so there you go."

She felt the same and remembered saying it. "I meant it, Joe."

"Okay," he said after a long breath. "But I have something to say, and I want you to hear it and really take it in. Got me?"

"And what's that?"

"Whatever that was last night was a one time thing."

"What do you mean?"

"I've had too many nights worrying about a drunk woman in bed next to me, I'm not going to have it again. I don't ever want to have to take you to bed and tuck you in drunk ever again. I give you one, you're grieving. I get it. But you get the one. No more. It happens again, we're done. No questions. No ifs, ands, or buts. You got it?"

"Listen to you laying down the law," she joked.

"This isn't a joke, Maxine," he spat. "I've spent too many nights watching a woman drink herself to oblivion over grief. I'm not going to watch another woman I love do the same. You need time to grieve? I'll give you that. But the days of me coming to wherever the fuck you are to pick you pu and put you in bed are over."

"Okay," she said, sensing the gravity in his voice. They had talked about Arlene a few weeks ago during their weekend together. She knew what a bear he had to deal with his wife, and she didn't want to add to the troubles the same way. "Okay, I understand."

"Good," he said. "I don't like to talk to you like this, I really don't. Sorry I had to use my dad voice."

"It was kind of sexy, actually," she smiled. "All authoritative and stuff."

"I'm being serious, darling."

"I know," she said after a breath. Her head hurt still and she was trying to find something to hold on to, even humor, in this situation.

"No more drinking and calling you to tuck me into bed. Got it."

"Good," he said. "God, I hate talking to you like that."

"What are you doing now?" she asked hopefully. Hungover or not, the strength of his convictions made her want him today.

"I'm at work," he said. "And I'm in no mood. Take care of yourself today. Call me if you need anything. But I feel like Carrie will be doing the heavy lifting."

"She's got breakfast going for me and Maryanne," she explained. "I'll be fine."

"Okay," he said. It sounded like he was back in the store now, and he heard Derrick's voice say something about Sydney calling again. Joe said, "Shit," and then to Maxine, "I gotta go, customers and stuff."

"Sounds like you don't want to talk to Miss Sydney," she laughed.

"I'd rather have my testicles pulled off, to be honest," he joked. "I gotta go. Have a good day. Remember what I said."

"I will Joe. Have a good day. And thanks for checking on me."

"No problem," he said. "Bye."

She said the same and they hung up together. She sat on the edge of the bed, drank a big sip of coffee, tried to stand up and fell back down. She noticed her skirt and pantyhose splayed on the floor in front of her and thought, "God, why couldn't he have stayed. Morning sex was so hot."

She remembered the time a few weeks ago when he'd woken her up with a kiss, and their slow lazy lovemaking after that, him behind her on their side, inside of her, holding her breasts, kissing her, the heat of him, the smell of him, the taste of him. She shuddered, stood up slower this time, pulled on some pajama bottoms and a shirt, then headed downstairs to eat, the heat in her loins a warm remembrance of his touch.

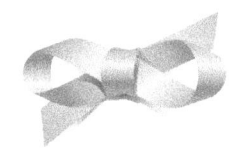

CHAPTER 29
Joe

A WEEK AFTER THE MEMORIAL service, he was at work, doing paperwork for a new flooring install when he got the text from her. Whenever he saw "Max" on his phone his blood pulsed with anticipation at what she would say. This woman had given him new life, and for some reason he couldn't explain he was going down that irresistible road toward loving her. The feeling was almost uncontrollable. What had started out as an experiment in finding a partner full of vibrant lust had gone to a deeper feeling than mere physicality to an area where he could imagine a brighter future with her.

Sure, there were still feelings of guilt, but those were being quickly overshadowed by Arlene's constant disappointment with him in their daily life, her needs, her demands, her constant drinking.

I need to see you.

He could no more resist this type of missive than he could stop eating.

When? Where?

Noon. my place?
ok
:) <3

He finished his paperwork quickly and stood up. Derrick was in his cubicle next to him and he said, "Hey, Derrick, I have to go check on a customer's flooring job. I'll be back in an hour or so."

Derrick only said, "Okay, I'll let people know. Do you have anything the rest of the afternoon?"

"Nah," Joe answered. "Hold down the fort will ya?"

"You got it brother."

"Thanks." Joe went out of the office area, down an aisle where he knew he wouldn't meet Jamie patrolling the aisles and left the store. He got to his car, started it, and sat for a few minutes, thinking of how best to get to the house. "What the hell am I doing?" he sighed. He pulled out of the parking lot and into traffic.

After a few minutes, he was down the street from her house, parked in a different street than his own. He went to the trunk, looked around and pulled out his running sweats, a pair of tennis shoes, and his white tee shirt. He got back into the car, changed as quickly as he could given the cramped space of the Hyundai, and when he was finished, he got out and went to an entrance to the wooded park behind the complex. He started running. If anyone were to see him, he was just another guy out for a mid day jog.

His heart pumped with the exertion of running in the summer humidity but he didn't care. He just wanted to get to her place, to see her. To hold her again would be the highlight of his day. Just to be with her, to kiss her would be everything he needed to get through the rest of the day.

Soon he was at her back yard fence, and he slowed to make sure no one was coming. He stepped through some shrubs to see the freshly mowed lawn he had finished two days ago. It had quickly grown a few inches. He would have to come back Saturday to mow it again. But he only thought about that for a minute when he saw the back patio door open and she was standing there, clad in jean shorts and a pink tank top. She had a kleenex in her hand, and dabbed at her eyes. Her cae was flushed, almost as pink as the pink of her shirt.

He went to her, looking around to make sure no one was looking and she ushered him in. "Hey," she said.

"Hello," he smiled at her. She smiled back and when they were in the house she embraced him, and he wrapped himself around her. She held him for a few minutes in silence. He looked down at her. She dabbed her eyes again and he could tell she had been crying.

"Hey, what's wrong?" he reached up and wiped a tear away with his thumb as he kissed her lightly.

"Nothing," she sighed. "I'm glad you're here."

"I am too." He looked down at her, and for some reason he could tell there was something bothering her. "Really, hon, what's wrong?"

"Let's sit," she said, and led him by the hand to the tan couch in the living room. They sat together, she sidled up to him and nestled her head against his shoulder. He put an arm around her. "This grief shit sucks," She said finally, not looking at him.

"It gets better, you know," Joe said, hugging her tighter to him. "I've been through it, you'll be okay."

"But I just have so many thoughts," she said. "So many regrets. I just feel..."

"Feel what?"

She shook her head. "It just keeps coming up in my head. You're going to think I'm crazy, but I can't escape this feeling that I had something to do with his death. Like I killed Harold or something."

"Wait," he said. "You can't think that. You'll make yourself crazy."

"But what if I did?" she started tearing up again. "He wanted to stay, I could have told him to come home. I could have demanded it. I could have made him get on a plane and come back that day." She broke down in more slow sobs.

"Hey," he took her chin in his hand and looked at her. "Don't think that. He did what he did, and that's that."

"No," she demanded. "You don't understand. He was gone and we had a weekend together coming up and it was our first weekend and I wanted it so bad and he would have been gone and that's all I was thinking about." she said all this quickly, trying to explain. "I told him I wanted new appliances and he got mad and we said we would discuss it when he got home. I could have told him not to bother, to come home anyway. But he wanted to play in that stupid fucking game because i wanted to buy stupid fucking appliances to go with my stupid floor. Oh, God!" she broke down then, her face scrunched into sorrow and sobbed again. "I keep coming back to that. I told him to stay, don't you see? I killed him because of you. because of us!" She buried her face in her hands.

"Hey, hey..." he patted her shoulder, held her to him and nestled her head into his chest. "Whoa.. there you go.. Let it out." and he let her cry because when a woman needs to cry she just needs to get everything out of her system. He imagined there'd been many tears in this empty house in the past few days, and he let her go, soothing her with kind words as she let the sobs come out and wet the tee shirt. She finally slowed, and he said, "Let me tell you a story, and I want you to understand something, okay?"

"Okay," she looked at him with brown tear streaked eyes. "Is it going to make me laugh?"

"No, but it's something you need to hear," he said. Then he began, after taking a long breath.

"When I was a kid, I don't know, ten years old or so, mom and dad sent me to stay with my grandparents for the summer. Grandpa Gus was this solid dad's dad. My grandma Paulette was a true grandma in every sense of the word. Fun, caring, a wrinkled face that had seen a lot of hard years but never lost her compassion. She was love personified. Gus was a fun guy, always quick with a stupid joke like dads are supposed to be. Gus had a big farm, with a couple of horses, CC and Tu Tu, and a lake for us kids to swim. A big forest behind the property we used to run around in, my cousins and I." She sat in rapt attention.

"Well, Gus took us into this big garage on the property. He was a hoarder, stuff like street signs and boxes of toys, metal scraps and all kinds of stuff. There was a corner full of lawn umbrellas he got for pennies from a local hardware store. All pink and yellow and red. He used to do that, buy stuff and sell it in a weekly garage sale.

"One day he shows me and my cousins this toy. It was made in like the sixties or something. Cheap plastic, a novelty item. It was this little guy on a stand holding his junk. We thought it was funny. But if you pulled the trigger on his back, he dick came out and it spewed water and made it look like he was peeing.

"Well, naturally to a ten year old, it was the funniest thing I had ever seen. Then he put it back on the shelf and said not to mess with it."

"And you messed with it, didn't you?" She laughed.

"Of course I did," he answered. "What ten year old who liked fart jokes wouldn't?"

He continued. "So Grampa Gus went back into the house and me and my cousins looked around to play with other stuff in the garage and then went back out to swim in the lake but there was a pull to that toy. I wanted to play with it again. So I snuck into the garage and started playing with it and lo and behold after a few minutes of pulling the trigger and laughing at the whole thing, the trigger broke.

"I was beside myself. I didn't know what to do. I knew I had to tell him, but I didn't know what his reaction would be, so I just said to myself I'll try to fix it on my own. I snuck into the house," he thought for a few seconds. "Gus and Paulette were in the kitchen, talking about stuff that adults talk about, and I snuck past. Only Gus saw me. He said, 'What are you sneaking around for, son?'

"I froze. Heart beating crazy with nervousness, I lifted up the toy and showed him, spouting, 'I'll fix it, I'll fix it, please don't be mad.'"

"Oh no," she said. "Then what?"

"He did get mad. He was furious, saying things like, 'I told you not to touch it!' and 'Now I have to go get some glue at Harvey's!' and then he and my grandma were arguing and he said, 'Stupid kid, keep your hands off my stuff when I tell you!'"

"And he walked out the door.

"Grandma told him to stay home, that he'd been drinking too much and he didn't listen to her. He just grabbed his keys and went to his gold fucking Cadillac and drove away without a word to her or myself. He just grumbled about 'stupid kids not listening,' and 'Gonna have a word with his father when I get back home.'"

He sighed. "This is the first time I've thought about this incident in quite a few years." His eyes were glassy from the remembrance of that day. That stupid kid who wanted to see a pee toy.

"An hour later my grandma got a phone call from the highway patrol. Gus had been in an accident. He swerved to avoid oncoming traffic, went into a ditch and since he wasn't wearing a seat belt got thrown from the car, and the Cadillac landed on him, crushed him, and he died instantly."

"Oh no," she put a hand over her mouth in shock.

"Yeah," he shuddered. "So in this kid's mind, I was responsible for my grandfather's death. I didn't come out of my room for two days. I cried and cried, wishing I could have done things different. Wishing I had left that stupid fucking toy alone. Wishing for my grandpa back."

She stroked his hair and kissed him on the cheek.

"My Grandma came to my room a few days later. She knew what grief looked like and she let me have it. I told her how I felt, how it was all my fault but she just shushed me. 'Honey,' she told me, 'Gus drank, I told him not to go, and he didn't listen. He was a pig headed stubborn old fool. You know how many times he drank and drove? Dozens. Almost every day. Patrol knew it, cops knew it, I knew it. It was a matter of time before what happened would happen. Child, you didn't have any more responsibility for his death than Santa Claus. Gus drank. He drove. He died. That's it.'

"She offered me a glass of milk and some Oreos. She gave me a big hug, 'I love you, I always will, and I don't hold you responsible for anything. So get over it. Just chock it up to shit happens and move on. You hold on to a regret like that, it'll ruin your life. God knows, i speak from experience.'"

He looked down at her. Her tears were gone now. "Later that day she cooked hamburgers on wonder bread and I watched fraggle rock and days went by and more and more days and by the time the funeral was over and I was back to my life with mom and dad, I had forgotten the whole thing. My grandpa drank. He drove. He died. The end."

"So what are you saying, I should forget about what happened? About what I said?" she asked.

"No," he answered. He kissed her nose. "I'm saying, Harold knew what he was doing. He wanted to stay and play poker with those guys. Would he have come home if you begged him?"

She thought for a moment, "No, I guess not."

"You could have begged him, could have said, come home right now and make crazy passionate love to me, and he still would have stayed, right?"

"Probably, yes." she chuckled.

"There you go, then," he said. "Mind you, I'm not trying to negate your feelings here, just trying to get you to understand." He made his voice sound like Mrs. Doubtfire. "You didn't have anything to do with that man's death any more than Santa Claus."

She chuckled at his falsetto voice sounding like a grandmother. She looked at him sweetly. Then she nestled into his shoulder and whispered into it, her face buried in his flesh. "God, it's awful how much I love you," she said.

Then she put her hand down his sweatpants, stroked him hard and as he tried to resist, she kissed him and said, "Stop, I need this."

She stood up, took off her shorts, revealing a red trimmed bush between her thighs. He pulled down his pants a bit and she straddled him.

She rode him with his hands on her hips guiding her gyrations on top of him. And together they climbed the mountain higher and higher til they reached the crest and jumped off, breathless, their combined pleasure drowning out their pain.

Then I saw her Face—The Monkees

CHAPTER 30
Joe

HE WOKE UP EARLY, AND the first thing he noticed was an ache in his legs. He lay in bed, rubbing the knots out of them, wondering what he had done to elicit aching muscles. Then he thought of exercise, the carnal variety. His stomach felt tight, muscles stretched across his midsection, feeling like they were trying to get out of his body. I'm out of shape, he told himself. I have to do something about that.

He looked over at Arlene, still asleep, snoring. A bit of drool came out of her half-open mouth, spilling on the pillow. This is what I married, he thought. How many had she had last night? They had argued about something, he couldn't remember what, but he knew that if he had just shut up about it they would have been ok.

Right, her drinking. Again. It seemed to be the focus of their main arguments, and her saying, "If you had my life and what I had to do all day you'd drink too." he didn't want to argue with her anymore. It wasn't worth the headache. He didn't want to argue with anyone anymore. It was pointless. So recently he had just let it go, said "Okay," and gave up.

Just like most of this marriage. Giving up. Letting her win. Letting her be right. Giving a bit of his soul every time he did to keep the peace.

It was still early, and the sun had just poked over the horizon, filling the room with a shadowed haze of light filtered through the room darkening shades of the picture window in the bedroom. He stood up and figured he would get some coffee. He reached for the phone. There was a text from Maxine that came in a few hours ago.

hey. Can't sleep. Need to talk

It was sent at four-thirty. He smiled at the thought of her thinking of him. He went to the bathroom, sat down on the toilet, and texted back while he finished.

>Ok. i'm up. Thinking of running. Legs
>are sore for some reason

She responded quickly:
Pretty morning for it. Where?

>Around sycamore trail. I'll be going
>Past the tree in fifteen minutes.
>Talk there?

Sure, i'll be there. Can't wait.

Xoxo

. . ⚜ . .

HE FINISHED, WENT TO the dresser and pulled out a ragged pair of black sweatpants, a white tee shirt with a few coffee stains on it, and black socks. Arlene still snored in the bed. The kids were still asleep. He looked at the time on his clock. Six thirty. He thought, get a run in, maybe something more, who knows. Wondered what she wanted to talk about. Probably getting over the grief. It had been a few weeks since Harold had died. She was probably a mess.

And I'm the one who could maybe help her through that mess, he mused. Was this his life now? Living with a woman he disliked and running around with a woman he loved? A consideration entered the back of his mind. *It's going to have to end one day soon, either one or the other. And you're going to have to make a choice, boyo.*

It was a choice he didn't want to make yet, least of all today.

He stepped out of the room slowly, closing the door with barely a snick of the latch, and went to the kitchen. He drank a glass of water, and his daughter came out of the bedroom, glassy-eyed, and sleepy.

"Hey Dad," she said with a smile. "What's up?"

"Going for a jog, sweetie," he said. He walked to her and hugged her. "Did you have a good sleep?"

"Yeah, I guess," she answered automatically. "We got any sugar pops?"

"Sure, they're in the pantry. You want me to make some for you?"

"No, I'm twelve, Dad. Not two," she grinned at him. "I can do it. Go on your run. How long are you going to take?"

"About a half hour. Figured I would go to the sycamore and back. Won't take long. Are you gonna be okay?"

"Sure," she smiled. "Have fun."

"I will, honey. If your mom wakes up, let her know, huh?"

"Okey dokey," she said, walking to the pantry to get out the yellow sugar-laden box. "If she does, that is."

He went to the door, unlocked it and went outside. *Is this where I decide?* He considered. *Is this the life I get? The wife and the two kids and the house and the PTA meetings? Is this really all there is? This can't be all there is.* He started running.

After a few minutes, he stopped, stretched, and went back down the trail toward the sycamore tree that was here before the housing development had been built. Fifty acres around the tree was white pine forest and mixed oak. There was a huge sycamore tree in the center of the woods and the designers had developed a park in the area. There were swing sets and jungle gyms for the kids, picnic tables and barbecue pits for the adults and then a nature preserve with jogging trails and hiking areas for those nature-minded individuals who were going to live in White Pines.

Joe had never been one of those until recently. A few days a week before work he tried to get out and at least jog and walk one of the trails. He had seen the sycamore, with its large green leaves, the thick white trunk with mottled green bark that peeled off white in the winter. During the summer months, it was a vibrant green, then turning to yellow and orange in the fall. God only knew how old it was but it stretched up into the sky hard and strong close to seventy feet.

The trees around him were awash with color. Greens, a few red leaves from late summer had already fallen and dried and scudded across the path, scratching along the asphalt in the cool morning breeze. It was nice, and soon he was padding along, thinking of nothing, reveling in the smells of the morning air, the nature around him, and hearing the sounds of birds singing. Crickets hummed and chirped in the underbrush. He allowed his thoughts to wander to her, their shared passion, their shared affection, their shared bodies. The way she felt in his arms, the way her skin, soft and smooth felt in his hands. He felt himself stiffen slightly at the thought of her on top of him, the shower, the moments after, and then he was slowing, as he saw the tree in the distance, white and commanding, with a woman standing near it wearing pale blue yoga pants and a black sports bra and apparently nothing else.

Yeah, I'm done. She's got me hooked, line, and sinker.
Then I saw her Face—The Monkees

A BRIGHT AND HOPEFUL PLACE

Heaven is a Place on Earth—Belinda Carlsisle

CHAPTER 31
Maxine

.. ⚜ ..

SHE HAD JUST STEPPED out of the shower when she received his morning text. It was a long night, sleepless, dreams coming in fits and starts, tossing in the bed, wishing he were there. She had remembered what it felt like to wake up next to him on their illicit weekend, when Harold had still been alive, playing his last hand of poker in Las Vegas. That had caused her guilt she would eventually have to get over.

Why was she guilty? Because he was gone and she was doing that. With Joe. My God, how he made her body feel, hot with desire, all the time. Flushed, her skin still hot with the shower, she felt along her naked body and caressed her hips. Thighs and buttocks and her hands went to her center, feeling the tidy pubic hair, slipping a finger to her moist center of desire.

Lord, how he makes me feel, she thought. The memory of him pushing into her with all his might shot into her mind and she shook with the memory of it, and what it did to her insides. Here he was getting ready to meet her again, for more, possibly. God, this man made her insatiable.

With a mix of delight and wanting, she got out an outfit that would make him think of nothing but her for the day. She had tight blue yoga shorts and a black sports bra. She put those on, with nothing underneath. Why have one more garment between modesty and what he wants, right? She smiled wickedly in the mirror as she admired herself. Then threw on white sneakers over booty socks and fled out the back door.

A few hundred feet out from the backyard, she found the hiking trail that would lead to Sycamore Trail, a running trail for nature lovers.

A secluded spot for lovers of nature.

Minutes later, she finished her jog around the corner and saw the large white-barked tree. There was no one around but the crickets. A fine slow fog had embraced the forest floor, and the sun had just gotten above the horizon. Soon the place would be humming with joggers, but right now, she was all alone, looking up at the large tree, feeling the huge round trunk with mottled green patches and giant knots. She heard jogging down the path, turned, and saw two people running past. She gave a noncommittal greeting wave and smiled, and they did the same.

He won't come. She thought. She's going to be standing here like an idiot all morning, waiting for him, she considered. I'm going to go home. This is pointless. But she stayed a few more minutes.

She heard more jogging coming from around the corner. Her heart fluttered expectantly, hoping this was him. Her loins began to heat up with the thought of his muscled frame coming around the corner and then a man in blue jogging pants, a flabby gray sweatshirt, and pencil-thin glasses appeared and shot past her. She made it like she was taking a breath and stretching. He admired her, politely, as he rushed past.

Fuck! She thought. Now I look like a—

She heard more jogging, looked up from her bent-over stretching position and saw him.

Dear God that man is beautiful, she said to herself. The sun was to his back, and he floated around the corner like a Roman warrior, golden skin, the sunlight cresting off of his dark hair, and the way his muscles moved under the white tee shirt made her insides tighten with anticipation. Then he saw her, slowed, and looked around for anyone before he smiled and said, "Hey, you."

"Hey, you," she answered back. She looked around and made sure no one was around and then she lept to him and felt his embrace, those arms wrapping around her, cradling her back, his chest powerful and firm. He bent his head and kissed her long and hard. Their tongues swirled an erotic dance before he pulled back.

"So what did you want to talk about?" he asked, looking into her eyes with sincerity.

"Nothing right now, I just want to look at you," she said. "I've missed you."

"I've missed you too," he guided her to the other side of the large tree, making sure they were not seen by anyone. He kissed her again, as her back pushed into the soft bark behind her. "My God I've missed you, darling."

She weakened against the tree, letting him hold her up, as she kissed with a fervent desire, biting his bottom lip a bit too hard wanting to devour him. He wanted her too, she could tell by his kisses, and the way his hands moved to her breasts and took the nipples poking from behind the thin fabric of her bra.

"Want to find a more secluded space?" she sighed, as his hands found the top band of her shorts. He snaked a hand down and rubbed her wetness. She let out a breathy sigh of pleasure as he touched her folds, and parted them, still kissing her neck, breathing fire onto her rosy skin.

"Here is good," he laughed softly. "Besides, I don't have a lot of time."

She moaned as his fingers laced back and forth along her pussy, finding her clit with a thumb, and guiding a finger inside of her. "Ohh," she arched her back as much as she could. He held her tight against the tree, and her body was absolutely his, weak, and collapsing into him as he pushed deeper with his finger. "Keep doing that, I like that, oh my God." She panted.

"I know," he said softly in her ear, barely a whisper. "That's why I'm doing it." He kept up the pressure with his hand as the sensations in her body fired hot and tingling. Her nerve endings made her entire body tremble with delight as his fingers pushed inside of her, the pressure on her hard button a vibrant ache that was soon to burst. Her hips moved with him, and they heard more joggers coming up the trail.

They were in a cleft of the tree, out of sight of the people who ran past. He put a hand on her mouth, gagging her momentarily to shut her up. Her moans had been music to his ears, but she was silenced by his meaty hand as the couple jogged past. He kept up the pressure as they did, and she moaned against his hand as the inner walls tightened with the relentless movement inside her. Her pleasure cries muffled by his hand made the sensation all the more heightened. Would they be discovered? Would they be found out? The danger of the situation made her pleasure grow exponentially as he just said, "Shhh..." in her ear, his hot breath like a shot. Her knees weakened, and she let the tree behind her along with his one arm hold her up.

The joggers had gone, and he let go of her mouth, "Oh my God," she breathed heavily, "That was so hot," and she let go, the orgasm collapsing her into his arms, shaking her body as the tightening sensation of her pelvis broke into a million tiny pieces and she let out a groan of release into his shoulder. "Oh God, Jesus, oh God, unnngg.."

He held her tight against the tree, the bark rubbing her sensitive skin now, kissing her, feeling the moisture on his hands. He looked down, her front was wet, and she thought, "I couldn't have worn dark pants?"

He smiled, brought up his hand and put them in her mouth. She sucked them in greedily, swirled her tongue around them, and moaned with the heady delight of the pleasant tangy taste. He moaned softly.

She pushed her body into him, reached for the tie of his sweatpants, and said, "Your turn, mister man."

"He chuckled warmly at the thought. "No," he said. "This was for you. I have to go to work. But trust me, I'll think of you all day, and the tree." he looked up, and continued. "Hard and strong."

"Oh, no," she gasped. "You can't do that to me."

"I can," he said. "And I will." He kissed her long again, her arms and body almost wrapped around him. She wanted to feel all of him now, on her, in her, his arms cradling her all day.

This man has me hook, line, and sinker, she thought. What the hell am I going to do?

"You sure you can't even give me a few minutes?" she asked with a purr of desire. "It won't take long." she tried to untie the sweats one more time. He held her hand and pushed it away slowly.

"No," he said. "I have to go. How about tonight?"

"Are you going to run again tonight?" she hoped.

"Maybe," he winked. "I'll let you know." And with a kiss, short and sweet, he turned from the tree and jogged away. She watched his ass, his strong back fade into the forest around him and turn a corner out of sight.

"I don't want you to go," she said, "But I love to watch you leave." She went her own way, soft and red hot in the summer sun, but not from the sunlight burning off the morning fog in a relentless red-yellow heat. Humidity is going to be high again, she thought, and felt the pleasure in her groin that was still there, the press of his hand a slowly fading memory she didn't want to let go of.

Yep, she mused. Hook, line, and sinker.

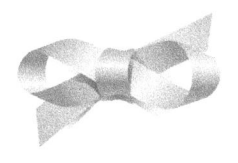

CHAPTER 32

Maxine

A COUPLE OF DAYS LATER, she decided to get him back for leaving her wanting more. The past few days had been a nightmare of wanting for him. So she decided to text him at work, hoping he wouldn't answer his phone while people were around. She got dressed in the yellow bikini. The outfit she wore when they first kissed hung in the closet among other designer clothes and she put it on. Then she went outside and sat on a white towel near the pool. She snapped a picture.

This is delicious, she thought. Joe had made her feel like a teenager again. A hot and horny teenage girl that wanted the hottest guy in class and would do anything to get him.

She texted him:

Hey.. you busy?

I'm with a client. What's up?

I just need you for a few minutes.

I'm busy Maxine. For a few minutes more at least

Too busy for this?
She sent an image of her in the yellow bikini, her skin shining in the midday sun, lounging on a beach chair by the pool.
I believe you liked this number the last time i wore it?

Yes.
That's unfair. Give me twenty minutes.

Ok. but if you're late i start without you.

Then i'll be sure to be late

Now who's being unfair?

Lol. omw

Xoxo

;)

She sent back a ;) emoji.
She knew the picture would bring him over to her house. She knew it as sure as she knew how to breathe. What was it about this man that made her crazy? What had started out as a flirtation in the racks of hardwood flooring samples would go this far? She didn't, obviously or maybe she did.

Maybe this is what she wanted the entire time. Maybe she wanted to be desired. She wasn't getting it from Harold, and would never get it from him. She often wondered why. She asked herself all the time if she was attractive to him anymore. His actions made it appear that he was not. So why shouldn't she have started something with another man? Why shouldn't she have ensnared another man to her bed?

Joe was so easy. He was in the same boat. She sensed it from their first meeting. And he sensed it from her too. It was a match made in the hell of long term marriages to people who didn't seem to love their partners anymore.

This was wrong; she knew it couldn't keep going on. But they had made their decision. They had chosen to get together, to join in an illicit coupling so many weeks ago. Time had made it happen. His wife was out of town. Her husband was out of town. They had a weekend. It was supposed to be fun, romantic, and full of joy for both. Two people who needed physical attraction. Two souls who needed to feel the physical act of love. Why couldn't it have just been that?

But then she woke up one morning and he wasn't there. And she missed him. Missed his warm body next to her in bed. Missed his touch. Missed his kiss. That's when it became bad. Bad for both of them. Because she knew he felt the same way.

Now she was drawn to him like a magnet. She was a four-alarm fire, and he was a firefighter coming to put her out. Only, she couldn't put out this fire she had for him. All the water in the world would never be able to extinguish the burning need she had for him, the fire needing oxygen to survive. And Joe was her oxygen. Whenever she was near him, she couldn't take her eyes off him, couldn't take her body away from him. He had her, mind, body, and soul.

It happened two days ago, after the sycamore tree. When he pleasured her, and the excitement of that act further fueled the flames of her desire for him. She couldn't think anymore. Any fire that may have burned for Harold was gone. Snuffed out in the embers of the ash she had laid at the beach weeks ago.

Then it grew brighter and hotter when Joe had picked her up. She was drunk, and he went to her. He had brought her into the house. He had laid her in bed, tucked her in, made her feel safe. Made sure his daughter was safe.

And he had also made sure that it would never happen again. When he told her he wouldn't do it again, that it would be over forever if he had to pick her up and take her to bed drunk.

And the flame for him burned more after that. His air of protectiveness. His resolute boundary of what he would take from her and what he would put up with. It turned her on even more. He had put his foot down. And she had obeyed. She had been good, and made the vow she would never put him in that position ever again.

And now here he was, jogging up the footpath behind her house. God, she wanted him. She wanted every inch of this man.

He wore a tee shirt and gray sweatpants. He must be hot. She could see the sheen of sweat on his forehead, the sweat stain darkening his t-shirt. The same stain that turned her on when she saw it that first day, mowing her grass, taking it off to wipe the sweat off his brow. And the sweat they both had made a few minutes later in her bedroom. She thought back to that day often. The liquid heat of it. The fire of it. The burning desire they both had and the explosion at the end.

Here he was again, and she stood up to greet him. Thank God she had the oak paneled privacy fence. What the neighbors would say, if they found out. The scandal that would rock the community.

And that was another thing that made this illicit affair even more hot. How bad it was for both of them to be doing this. How wrong it was. But oh, how right it felt. When he looked at her with those eyes, when he kissed her with those lips, when he held her with those arms.

When he fucked her with that cock. She was well and truly insatiable for him.

He came to her, and they kissed. And there it was. The thought of the wrongness of this act was gone. They were together, a couple, a team, a conjoined duo of lust, forgetting the outside world for a few moments of pleasure that made their collective lives more bearable.

"Hi," he said, after breaking the kiss.

"Hi," she breathed into his ear. "God, I've missed you."

"I've missed you too." he embraced her again, looked into her eyes, kissed her deeply again.

Jesus Christ this man knew how to kiss. Firefighter, meet fire. Moth, meet flame. She pushed his sweatpants down, showing his white boxer briefs. She said, "You're overdressed. You must be hot."

"I am," he pulled them down. They landed on the pale tan concrete of the pool deck. He looked her up and down. "How did you know I'd like this?" He reached around with both hands and cupped her ass. She stepped backwards.

Then she took off his shirt, revealing his sweaty torso. She kissed his neck, pulled him closer, and stepped back.

It was a hot August day. The sun bright overhead lengthened their conjoined shadow. He pressed his lips into the cleavage of her breasts, he slid the top aside and nibbled at her large pink nipples. "I've missed these too," he said, and she groaned with pleasure.

She backed up, still holding him. She knew what she was doing, and it would be a fun surprise.

"We keep going, we're going to fall," he said with a devilish smile.

"That's the plan," she said. Still holding him by the waist, she took one last step back and they fell into the water with a loud splash. They went under, bubbles collided against her eyes and her long auburn hair flowed in the wave they had made. She went up and gasped for air. They had parted only for a moment and then they were back together. Like magnets, unable to part.

He reached under the water and pulled a string of her bottoms. They fell off and floated to the top of the water. She lowered her hand to his brief and started to pull them off. He helped her. With one hand he pulled them down, and she felt under water for his erection. She was wet inside and out, and he turned her to the wall. She reached up, holding the side as he put her legs around his waist and entered her with a grunt. She gasped at the intrusion, delirious with his weight inside her. She went up and down with him, rocking back and forth underwater, feeling the liquid going between naked hips and thighs, the coldness on her folds a contrasting pleasure to the heat in her loins.

He rocked her, up and down against the walls. Their cries echoed in the summer air, wind licked at their bodies, cooling them, but not extinguishing the heat between them. She gripped the pool sides as he rammed into her, taking her with meaty thrusts and breathy grunts. He took her, and in that moment she cried out loud in orgasm.

That was quick. He knew how to touch her. How to get her to that pinnacle fast. So fast, she wanted more.

He spied the towel, lying on the side of the deck and the pool. She had been sunning on that white fabric, letting the warm air bask her and the sun to wash over her making her body so much warmer, but not as hot as Joe had made her.

He lifted her up, put her on the towel and still in the pool brought her thighs to either side of his head. She relaxed her legs on his shoulders, and his mouth was on her at once. His tongue was in her seconds later, lapping up the moisture he had caused her to exude from her core. He pushed his fingers in, finding her pulse. Finding her pleasure. He licked her, up and down, swirling his tongue on her pleasure without, as his fingers found her pleasure within.

"Oh, I want you Joe," she exhaled as another orgasm grew quick and fiery inside her. She felt the muscles contract around his fingers, tighter, tighter, and then, it broke, and she folded in on herself.

She gushed into his mouth, and he licked her, trying to get the moisture of her. Trying to get all of her.

He lifted himself out of the pool, bent down and kissed her again. She tasted the sweet evanescence of her juices on his lips, and grabbed his face to keep kissing him. She couldn't get enough of his kiss. The way he nibbled her bottom lip, the way their tongues danced a tango in each other's mouth. He knelt above her body splayed on the white terry cloth towel and she said, "I want you in me," He obliged.

He pushed into her, wetness now lubricating the passion easily he had for her and she felt him solid inside of her, filling her to the back wall, and he pushed harder, deeper than he had ever been before.

"Oh, yes," she cried. "Yes, harder, baby, take me harder, faster, go faster." she gasped, uncontrollable words of passion as his girth pushed into her again and again. Her walls broke down, her body screamed with the fire he gave her. And soon he was coming inside of her, his passion filling her, blazing hot, so hot.

He collapsed on top of her with a throaty growl as his orgasm culminated in gasps and he jerked inside of her. All the while he was inside of her he never took his eyes off of hers, never stopped looking at her as he took her.

"Your knees must be hurting," she laughed.

"No," he smiled. "I didn't notice. I don't feel any pain when I'm loving you."

"I don't either," she sighed. "Oh, Joe, what are we doing?"

"I don't know," he said. He looked at her, kissed her again, longer this time. When he broke the kiss, he said, "But I like it."

"So do I," she admitted. "So do I."

Minutes later, they had to part again. She went to get her wet bikini bottoms from the pool and he watched her half naked body go in the water and draw them out. Meanwhile, he put on his sweats, sans underwear because they were wet.

"I can keep these here," she said, picking them out of the water.

"I better take them," he said. "I don't want any questions."

And there it was. She looked at him sadly. "I know," Was all she could say.

She came out of the pool and put the bottoms back on. "You should go now."

"Maxine, I," he started. But she stopped him with a kiss.

"You don't have to explain," she said. "I know the rules."

"One day there won't need to be rules."

She couldn't say anything to that. She was past the point of wanting rules anymore. She wanted him, all to herself.

And there was the trouble in this whole affair. What had started as a flirtation, a quick liaison, a fiery fling, had quickly become unsatisfying for her. She wanted all of him.

And that was the problem. Because she couldn't have him beyond this. He had someone to go home to. And she wanted it to be her.

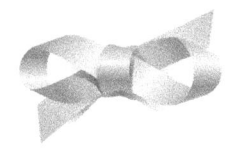

CHAPTER 33
Joe

THAT SATURDAY, AS HE was getting the mower ready to go to Maxines, Arlene came out to the garage and looked around at the mess.

Tools gathered dust on his cluttered workbench. White plastic shelves held all manner of cans full of oil, antifreeze, and other fluids necessary for cars, and she noted the spills and how the white plastic had been stained by grease and grime. Too many boxes for her, and she wondered what was in them.

She asked, "When are you going to get those up in the attic?" She pointed to the brown cardboard packing boxes sitting in the corner of the two car garage.

"When I get a chance," he said dismissively, "probably when I take some time off work."

"When is that, Joe?" she asked. He could tell she was upset about something. His guard went up, like it always had when she started challenging him like this.

"I don't know," he said. "When I get a chance, I told you."

"It's always 'when I get a chance' with you, isn't it?" She locked her arms across her chest. Typical Arlene fighting stance, he thought. Here we go.

"You want me to do it today?" he asked. "I will. After I get back from the Colston's."

"Her again?" she asked. "Why are you still mowing her lawn, Joe?"

"She's just had her husband die, Arlene," he explained to her like she was a child. "I'm doing it to be neighborly."

"When does being neighborly end, though?" Arlene asked, her anger seeming to grow. "It's been a month. Can't she find someone else to do it? Seems she's taking advantage of you at this point."

"I sold her a big flooring job, and you know how Jamie likes us to do things like this for our neighbors."

"But isn't that done now?"

"It is," he said. "But she's still a friend, Arlene. Jesus."

"I just think it's odd that for the past month you've been going down there, doing things for her, when all this needs to be done and you've been putting me off." She waved at the messy garage. "I've been asking you for weeks and you just say 'when I get a chance'. But you've got all the time to mow a neighbor's lawn two hours a week."

That's because she's a better lay than you, he thought. He breathed a calming breath and said, "Listen, if you don't want me to do it, I won't. I'll call her right now, I'll get Dan from the HOA to do it, how's that?"

"It's a start," she said. "Maybe then you can get this shit cleaned up."

"Fine," Joe said. "I'll call him right now and arrange for next week."

"But you're still going today," she said flatly.

"Yes," he said. "I'll let her know I arranged it with someone else. No problem. Happy?"

"Yes," she said. "I guess."

"Fine." Joe took his phone out and started to make a call.

"Just make sure this is the last time," Arlene said, going into the house. She turned. "I have to go to Costco in Wilmington in a few hours. You're going down there, make it quick. I need your help lifting stuff."

He gave her a thumbs up, heard the phone ring his friend Dan, and she walked into the house, slamming the white metal door behind her.

"God damn it," was all he could say.

"Not a way I'd expect a phone call to start, Joe, but whatever," said a voice on the other line. Dan had heard what Joe had said.

"Dan," Joe laughed. "Sorry about that."

"Don't mention it," Dan said. "What can I do you for?"

Joe arranged the mowing job with Dan for Maxine's house starting next week. He fit her into his busy schedule, after Joe agreed to pay half the cost of the lawn mowing.

"That's a generous offer, Joe," Dan said. "What gives?"

Joe explained that she had been a client and bought a big flooring job from him and since she just lost her husband, he was trying to do the lady a favor. Dan said he was a good guy, agreed to the job, and they would arrange for the money issues later.

I'm not a good guy, though, Joe thought. Not a good guy at all. How good could a guy be for carrying on a clandestine love with a woman who had just lost her husband to a murderer's bullet?

Conversely, how good was she for doing the same thing?

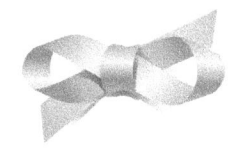

CHAPTER 34
Maxine

CARRIE HAD INVITED her to lunch at Angelo's, their favorite spot. They had come to this place for close to twenty years since it first opened back in '03. It was nice and cozy, the booths were big enough to house a family, and the pizza was true original New York style made by someone who knew how to make pizza the right way.

Max bit into another slice. Pepperoni and red onions flooded her mouth with taste, and she pulled the cheese away from the crust ravenously. Then took another bite, saying, "mmmmhm."

"You want to go easy there, sis," Carrie said. "It'll still be there in a few minutes."

"I'm starving," Maxine said. "I don't know why I'm always eating."

"It's the grief. You're bored," Carrie lifted a slice on her plate and went at it with a knife and fork. "I went through the same thing with Frank."

"He was your second husband, right?" Maxine asked. "The blond guy daredevil?"

"Yes," Carrie took a bite. Between chews she said. "He raced formula vee cars and crashed into a berm, went up in flames. Idiot had disabled his safety devices to make the car speed a few seconds faster."

"That was so sad," Maxine said. "I'm so sorry."

"I'm not. Fucker had a pretty good life insurance policy so I got over that death quick."

Maxine stopped eating, went silent for a few seconds, and then looked at Carrie, her eyes glossy with tears.

Carrie noticed and said, "Oh, baby, I'm sorry." She went to her friend, put an arm around her and hugged her close. "I didn't mean, I was just trying to make you laugh."

Maxine's tears flowed then, she wiped her eyes with her pizza napkin and looked at her friend. "I just miss him sometimes. I don't know what to do. Sometimes I'll just wander around the house and smell his clothes and then I'll throw them away and then I'll get them out of the trash again. What am I doing? I feel like I'm going crazy."

"That's grief, baby," Carrie said. "It makes you do all kinds of things. Stupid things. You'll go without food for days, and then you'll eat like a horse. Or you'll shove a whole box of Oreos in your face and watch scary movies. Or you'll listen to the same song that reminds you of him for days on end and then break the album. Trust me, I've been through all of it."

"I know," Maxine said. "I've probably done all that. But I don't watch scary movies. I watch those stupid Hallmark movie rom-coms. Ugh."

"I love those," Carrie laughed. "Girl meets boy, girl loses boy, girl finds boy at the Christmas tree farm. The dog makes them kiss, they fall in love and she leaves the big city. It's the same movie over and over. I love it."

"Yeah..." Maxine trailed off. "Girl meets boy. Story of my life."

"Don't tell me," Carrie looked at her and Maxine nodded.

"Yes."

"Maxie, you're still with him?" She was incredulous. "With Joe?"

"Yes."

"Oh, Maxie," she put an arm around her friend's shoulder. "Oh honey, you gotta stop that. The sooner the better. You're in no position to be carrying on like that."

"What do you mean?" Maxine looked at Carrie, eyes wide. "He's the only thing making me happy right now. A few days ago he–"

"I'm going to stop you right there," Carrie admonished. "You can't mean, all this time, before and after? You've been carrying on? I thought it was that one time, what the hell are you doing?"

"It was only supposed to be that one time. I haven't had a chance to talk to you in a while. I haven't been able to spill the beans till now."

"Well spill it, hon."

"Okay, so well, you know we did it that one time, a few weeks before Harold. Then his wife went away, and Harold was gone in Vegas so we spent a weekend together. Then, well... you know what happened."

"Yes," Carrie said. "And it should have ended right then and there. You can't keep going like this."

"But I love him so much," Maxine explained. "He has this way of–"

Carrie broke in again, "Tell me you've never had an affair without telling me you've never had an affair. Maxine, you have to cut this off."

"Why?"

"Why?" Carrie asked. "Why? Because you're not over Harold. Besides, if this gets out, both of you will look like total jerks. It's one thing to be having an affair when both of your spouses are alive. But when one just died a month ago, and Joe is still with his wife? Maxine, can't you see the optics of this?"

Maxine thought for a few seconds, imagining the tongues wagging all over town, a local hot shot poker player's wife having an affair with some guy only weeks after her husband died. Oh, the scandal.

"I'm..." Maxine said. "I hadn't thought of it like that." Carrie got up and sat in the other seat of the booth. "I just wish he would leave her, then we could move away. You know he wants a ranch in New Mexico."

"Sweetie," Carrie sighed. "He's not going to leave her. There's no ranch in the desert, it's not going to happen. Let me ask you something."

"Go ahead," Maxine said, crestfallen.

"Why did you start this whole thing?"

"What, with Joe?" Maxine asked. Carrie nodded.

"I just wanted someone to hold me, to love me, to have sex with me. I was horny, okay? If you must know."

"Right. Do you know how many of those I've had in my lifetime? Several. They were flings. He knew it, I knew it, and we never fell in love. It was just sex. Some hot, some not."

"So you're saying that's all it should be?"

"Yes," Carrie agreed. "It was just sex, Maxine. You weren't supposed to fall in love with the guy."

"But what if I did?"

"How do you know? Has he told you?"

"He's just so generous, and good, and attentive. He touches me in a way Harold never did. I can't explain it."

"Sweetie, you can't keep this up. You have to break it off. It's not healthy. For either of you."

"It sure feels healthy to me," she thought of when she and Joe were together, the blazing fire of him overloading her senses with just a touch.

"Okay," Carrie said. "I get that you like him a lot. Do this. And I can't believe I'm saying this. Find out what he's thinking. Have a talk.

And if he's still thinking he can stay with his wife and have you on the side tell him that's not an option."

"I can't make him break up with his wife, Carrie."

"Then you're at an impasse." Carrie ate another bite of pizza. "Just try it. Just talk to the man. Make him see reason. Take a break from him. Go see other guys, be single, and live your life. God knows you can travel now. Fly to Europe. Have an affair with a guy named Andre you pick up at a bistro somewhere in Paris."

"Didn't you do that?" Maxine joked.

"Oh yeah," Carrie said. "That was me. I wonder how Andre's doing." she looked wistful for a moment and then got back to the conversation. "The point I'm trying to make here is, you're a single woman. You have your whole life ahead of you, pardon the cliche. You should go enjoy it. Have fun. God knows Harold would want you to."

"Harold would want me to go to Vegas with him," Maxine said. "I never did want to go. That's why I didn't go with him last time. I hate that place." Tears started to flow again.

Carrie stopped and stared off in the direction of the kitchen serving window. "Maybe," she said, lost in thought.

"Maybe what?"

"Okay, hear me out," Carrie focused on Maxine, a serious look on her face. "You still love him, right?"

"Oh God, yes."

"Okay," Carrie shook her head. "As much as I hate to say this, I have an idea. Follow me here. Take a week or two away. Just go out west. See if you like it. See some parks, take a look at properties. You don't have to buy anything, it's a sightseeing tour. But by yourself. Call it a trip of self-discovery."

"What does that get me, I don't understand."

"Just hear me out."

"Okay," said Maxine. She was warming up to the idea. "Go on."

"So you go out there, you take a look at properties. Say you find one. Don't make an offer. Just keep it on the down low. Keep in touch with the realtor. You don't have to do anything beyond that. And in the future, if you still like the guy, he leaves his wife, you go out there and live happily ever after. Problem solved."

"What if he doesn't leave her?"

"Then you call the realtor and say you're no longer interested. Easy peasy lemon squeezy. You had a whirlwind affair with a cute salesman, you move on, and he stays miserable. Problem solved."

"But I don't want to move on."

"Maxine, honey," Carrie got serious now. "You have to break it off. For now at least. You can keep in touch. Just don't have sex with him anymore. Keep it loose. Friends who meet in the store every now and then. Neighbors. But don't have him over to mow the lawn anymore. Distance sweetheart, distance.

"Just tell him it's a break. You have to get your affairs straight, he has to get his mind made up. That's all. You're not so much breaking up with each other, you're taking some time to figure out how you both feel with each other. That's all. It was a fling, you liked it, he liked it, and now it has to end. For now."

"That would work better than a complete break-off."

"Well, that's the ideal," Carrie said. "You shouldn't have done it in the first place, but who am I?"

"I know, you warned me," Maxine agreed. "But I didn't listen, I just went all in on the guy."

"Yes you did," Carrie said. "And now it has to stop. For now. You know I love you, right?"

"I know."

"Just do this thing. Trust me. You can't keep living this way, mourning one and loving another. It just doesn't work out. Trust me I've been down that road before and it just leads to too much heartbreak for both of you."

A BRIGHT AND HOPEFUL PLACE

"I just worry about how he's going to take it."

"Don't worry about him. You have to worry about yourself now. Especially now. If he loves you, he'll understand. And if he really does love you, he'll make a choice."

"But what if he chooses her?"

"Then that's his choice," Carrie said. "And it's a choice you'll have to live with."

"Okay," Maxine said, sadly. "I know, everything you say is true. I just don't want to hear it."

"You don't want to but you need to." Carrie gave her friend a hug. "You'll get through this, hon. Break it off with the boy. Grieve the husband. Live your life. Next year at this time you'll see I was right."

They finished lunch, Carrie paid for the meal, at Maxine's protestations, and they went out to the parking lot.

"See you later," Carrie hugged her friend. "I love you, sweetie. Take care."

Maxine said the same, went to her car, cried for a bit, and then texted Joe.

Hey. miss you. Need to see you.

> At work. Maybe after? I have a few
> Minutes. Want to run? ;)

No. meet at the park bench. Want to talk.

> Ok. got it. See you then

Ok. ILY

> <3

JEAN-PAUL PARE

Edge of a Broken Heart—Vixen

CHAPTER 35

Maxine

THEY SAT ON A PARK bench, hands briefly touching. It was a public space, situated in the community park. Kids played on jungle gyms and frolicked on the plastic slide. A couple of boys of Joey's age swung sticks like swords at each other, mocking knights slaying the evil overlord of the fantasy movies they had seen. She had asked him to meet here, under the bright sunny sky, so they could talk. The afternoon was hot, but they sat apart from each other like two spies doing the handoff of classified documents. Only their fingers touched on the plastic green park bench.

Their greeting had been chaste, and he knew why it had to be. There were people here. People who didn't know them, but people nonetheless. People who would talk. Perhaps they knew her, perhaps they knew Joe, but they could not take the chance. As far as the wanderers and passersby in the park saw two neighbors chatting, they wouldn't raise an eyebrow.

So it had to be a handshake, a simple greeting, a "Hi, I'm glad you came," from her. And a "Sure, no problem," from him.

They had sat in silence for a few minutes. He could tell she had been crying. So he asked her, "So what's up?"

"Joe, you know I love you," she started. "God, more than anything, I do. You know this right?"

"I don't think I like where this is going, Maxine," he said. She could hear the concern in his voice.

"Let me speak for a minute, please," she looked in his direction. She couldn't look him in the eyes. If she did, she would lose her nerve and this would be all over. She would jump into his arms and ask him to take her away from everything. But she knew she couldn't do that. So she kept her head lowered, her voice soft and as soothing as she could.

He smiled, and said, "Of course. Go on."

"Thank you," she paused to take a deep breath. "I can't do this anymore," she said finally. "This, you and me. We have to end it."

He looked at her and went to reach out to her, to say something. It was as if all the words were impossible to say so he said nothing. She shook her head. "Please, don't touch me," She pleaded. "please."

He brought back his hand, "I'm sorry." he said. "It's just. I—" he trailed off.

"I know you love me, God knows you don't have to say it. You show me in a million different ways," tears streamed from her eyes. She hated having to do this. The last thing I ever want to do is harm this man, she thought.

"Yes," he said. "I do."

"So you have to let me go, Joe," she looked at him again, this time in the eyes. Those pretty blue eyes, growing dark, disappointed and tinged with anger.

"Is that what you want?" he asked. "What do you really want?"

"Oh, God, no," she whispered. "It's what has to happen. For us, for you. And for me." She sighed, a shudder of tears welling up in her voice. "Don't you see?"

"See what?" he asked sharply. "Maxine, for the past month and a half I've been the happiest I've been in over ten years. And you want to take that away?"

"No, I don't," she put her hand on his. Her touch calmed him, and she squeezed his fingers, not giving a damn about the optics to wandering park goers. "Every time I look at you I want you more than the last time I looked at you. I can't keep my hands off of you, and everything you do, everything you say, the feelings I feel, I just can't stop thinking about you. I want you in my life all the way. Not half, not some. But all the way.

"But you're married, and I have to accept that. Please, don't say anything. Let me finish," she stopped his lips with a finger, shushing his coming objections. He relaxed, and let her talk.

She continued, "You're a great guy, Joe. You're the best guy I've ever been with, the best man I've ever known. I've had a crush on you from the start. But I have to go. I have to be single, to live my life, to find out what it means to be Maxine. And just Maxine, alone. Only for right now."

"I see," he said. He sighed, understanding. She could tell his eyes were wet now, and she handed him a tissue. She had brought a bunch in her purse for herself and hoped he would need some too. This brief show of emotion made her want him more.

"Do you, Joe?" she asked. "Do you really?"

"I'm going to tell you something, Max," he started. "I tried not to love you. For the first couple of weeks, I had an inkling you liked me, and not knowing if it was more than a flirtation or not. But then we did that, well, you know, the first time. And I felt in that moment I was yours to my dying day. It wasn't just the sex, even though that was amazing. It was heart, it was soul, it was a solid thing in my chest.."

She put her hand on his chest, and her palm felt his heavy heartbeat.

"But you can't have me all the way, Joe," she said finally. "And I know that. You know that. We talked about this that first time. I just didn't know…"

"Know what?" he asked softly.

"That I would fall in love with you. That everything you did, everything you said, would hit me like it has. I thought I was having a fling. I thought it would last a few weeks and we would get tired of each other, but that was before Harold, before..." her voice trailed off.

"Before he died," He finished.

"Yes," her breath came in a ragged despair. She coughed and caught her breath. "Before he died. I'm realizing now, I never really hated him, and there was some sort of affection for him. And he took care of me, of us, my daughter and me. So he wasn't a bad guy, really. Just... we grew apart. And it always felt like he didn't want us to grow back together. So the chasm widened. Every year it was deeper and wider and then I realized there was a stranger living across the rift in my house. A stranger I didn't know anymore.

"But then you came along and that chasm got filled with everything I needed, and I latched on to it, and it filled me with everything I was craving. You were that craving, you filled that need, Joe."

"So you were using me, then?" he asked, smiling at the metaphor.

"No, I wasn't using you," she said. "And you know it. Lord knows I wanted you from the start. I don't believe in love at first sight, but with you, whew. You had me from that first look."

"To be honest, so did you," he said. "I just fought back against it longer."

"You did," she said. "But when you finally gave in, I wanted you more and more." She hesitated. "But I can't have you anymore, not while there are people in your life that need you more than I do."

"I know," he said after a long pause. He was looking at her, and she felt him studying her features with his eyes. The clothes she wore, the way her skin flushed pink in the summer sun, the way her hair blew in the wind. The sorrowful way her eyes looked when they were wet with burgeoning tears. "But I don't care."

"Don't you though?" she pleaded with him. "Do you really know everything you would lose? Your kids would hate you, Arlene would take more than half of everything if she found out. Your job, I know your boss wouldn't take too kindly to you having an affair with a client, especially while you were married. Think of the scandal at the local hardware store, tongues would wag for sure. The cars, the house, you'd be on the streets with your shirt on your back. I can't ask you to go through that for me."

"What if I said I would though?" he asked. "What if I decided to go through with all of it? Tell Arlene, tell the boss, tell the kids, everything. Nike this whole thing and just do it."

"Oh, Joe, I can't ask you to do all that for me," she smiled at the thought but had to be logical. "As much as I want that, I couldn't live with myself destroying your home and family. I feel guilty dragging you in this far, actually."

"You didn't drag me in, I assure you. I didn't exactly come to your house kicking and screaming you know."

"I know, that's what makes this harder. It would be really swell if you didn't love me like you do. Then again, if you were a heartless monster, I wouldn't have done anything with you in the first place, so there's that."

"Maxine, I couldn't be a heartless monster if I tried."

"I know, and right now I wish you could be."

He shifted his body to look at her fully, "So what do we do now? Where does it go?"

"It ends. For now, anyway," she said flatly. "Maybe a break, til we figure out what this is. You understand?"

"As much as it pains me to say it," he relented. "Yes, I do."

"Thank you," she said. She reached out a hand to shake his, tears growing in her eyes. He held it, then quickly grabbed her. She felt the broad chest, the solid arms around her shoulders, the breath on her neck. She was in his arms before she could resist. He held on to her, a bit longer than he should have. She felt a tear drop on her neck and knew it wasn't hers. She smiled.

He pulled back, letting her go. She said, "God, I could get used to that."

"So could I," he said. His eyes were moist and pouty now, he dabbed at them with the tissue. "God, I'm going to miss you."

"And I'll miss you, Joe." She stood up. She went to walk away and turned. "One day you'll make a decision," she said. "And when that day comes, I'll be by the phone. Think about it. Think really hard about it, Joe."

"I will," he sat on the bench, letting her go, letting her walk away with the long auburn hair falling down her back, the tight jeans hugging her curves, watching the best thing he'd ever had in his life walk out of it, facing a decision that would alter the course of too many lives to count.

CHAPTER 36
Joe

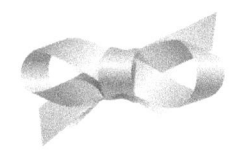

THE SMALL ACT OF MOWING the lawn brought back too many memories. It had been a few weeks since he and Max had broken up. Or took a break, as she told him. We both knew what that was, really. They would never see each other again. He knew it, and she did as well. Sure, he understood. It was for the best. But was it really? What was best? What was the best possible outcome of all this?

He knew it wouldn't have lasted. He had to have known, right? You don't get the girl when you already have one at home. Even though the one you have at home is not the one you really want. He wasn't even trying anymore. He was just going through the motions.

Taking the kids to school, soccer practice, his daughter to Meghan, going to work. Doing grocery shopping. Going to the liquor store and lying to the clerk. Getting vodka. Arlene pouring vodka. Drinking it, falling asleep too early. Household chores stacking up and neither wanting to do them.

Looking for a new life, trying to break the shackles of the one he had. Losing himself in his work. Trying to call people to sell flooring to, thinking this is the worst job in the world. Pining for wide open land, and even wider skies.

He pushed the mower down another row, turned, and started again. That's when he saw it. The gray-silver Lexus slowly drove down the street. The girl with the auburn hair in sunglasses driving past.

Looking at him. He looked at her. She almost stopped but drove by anyway.

Every time he saw her out and about in the world he remembered everything about her all over again. The way her hair smelled, jasmine and sunshine. The yellow bikini. The way she sucked the life out of him. The way her body looked on top of him, framed in the light from her bedroom window, pure and graceful riding him. Cooking for him. Moaning as he was inside her. The shower. The sycamore tree. The swimming pool, a yellow bikini shining gold like the sun.

He would have to take those memories, bury them in his mind somewhere, and never tell anyone. Never reveal that for a brief time, he had loved another woman with his whole heart. Still loved that same woman with all of his heart.

He got to the end of the row and turned the mower again. Started another row.

He should just go tell Arlene. Go tell her now. Break it off. File for divorce. Tell her the whole truth. What was stopping him?

Fear. The anger he would have to endure. But would he really? He thought. Anger is brief. But then he thought of the kids. What would they think? What would they do? How would they look at him? Joey loved his father. They were best friends. Doing all this, he would lose that respect. Cathy would hate him for the rest of her life, he knew that. Arlene would turn that girl against him and all men thereafter. He couldn't put the kids through that.

So he mowed the lawn. He thought of Max. he thought of her laugh, her body, her skin. And he would have to put those thoughts of her in a little box, bring it out at times when he wanted to and never bring her up, or her out, again. It was a nice fling. Let it stay that way.

The only problem was, he didn't want it to be just a fling anymore. He wanted her. He wanted all of her. He had a life. He had a wife. He had kids. A house. A job. All of that gone in an instant if the truth got out. So he mowed the lawn. He went to work. He went to the store. He joked with friends. He watched the Lexus turn the corner, out of the neighborhood, out of his life.

He finished the lawn, put the mower back in the garage, looked at it, and said, "You got me in trouble, you know." as if the mower was the culprit in this affair. Like the inanimate object started it. He kicked it.

"Fucker," he said to himself. The epithet was directed at the mower, but deep down he knew it was to himself. He let the tears flow then, mourning the loss of something he desperately wanted, but never having the ability to get it.

He thought of his father then, wondering what he would have done. His father, sitting in a nursing home, sitting in a wheelchair, dementia setting in, making him forget the wife that had gone so many years ago. He remembered once what his father would say about this situation.

His father used to say, Son, find a woman you'd jump in front of a bullet for. Maxine was that to him. The only problem, the bullet was a wife and two kids and a house and a car and a job.

So it wasn't just a simple matter of jumping in front of a single bullet. That killed you quick.

These other bullets killed you slow.

JEAN-PAUL PARE

She's a Lady—Tom Jones

CHAPTER 37
Maxine

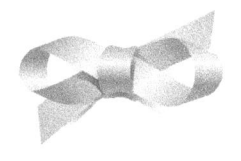

SO SHE HAD GONE OUT West. For a week. To look at properties. To smell the air. To see the desert, feel the heat of an August day. She ate in diners where Dixie waitresses called you "sweetie" and "sugar" and "hon". She bought trinkets in road side stands that were made of emerald and jade and beads. She met bought a cowboy hat at a shop where a Native American made it for her special, bending, stretching, and decorating it to her specifications.

She visited real estate agencies. She looked at properties with a salesman in a white cowboy hat looking like Boss Hogg from that Seventies show about law breaking rednecks. She drank wine, whiskey and beer in Honkytonks. She danced with a handsome cowboy and thought about kissing him. She stayed in luxury hotels in Arizona and New Mexico. And when she finally finished her trip, she got on the plane, knowing what she wanted. And she had made several inquiries with people to get just that.

They would have to wait for her choice to be made.

Just like she would have to wait on a choice from Joe.

CHAPTER 38

Joe

JOE WAS AT WORK, A week later, finishing up the Sydney job, finally. He had delivered the transitions he'd been able to find and sent Chris the handyman to go put them in personally. It had taken an afternoon. There was another job finished. He put the file in the "Finished" drawer, heaved a sigh of relief at having to never have to talk to her again and stood up to stretch.

Derrick looked out over the showroom floor and laughed, "I don't know how you do it," he said. "Getting all these hotties coming in looking for flooring."

"What do you mean?" Joe asked, looking out at the carpet racks where a tall brunette stood looking absentmindedly at the stain-resistant samples. She looked over at Joe and smirked.

Joe sighed. "Uhoh."

"Uh Oh good or uh oh bad?" Derrick asked. He straightened his tie and pulled out a business card. "Or was that Uh-oh, Derrick is going to get to her first?"

"Hold your horses, there hotshot. That's Carrie, Maxine's friend."

"Wait, that chick's been married three times you were telling me about? You didn't tell me she was hot as fuck," he whispered.

"I only met her one time and I wasn't paying attention. But now I look at her, she fills out those jeans really nice."

"Hands off, Don Juan, this one's mine."

Carrie had seen the boys talking by this point and started walking their way.

"Don't do anything stupid, Derrick," Joe said. "Who am I talking to?" He went out to meet her.

Carrie stopped a few feet away, and said, "Hey Joe. Got a minute?"

Joe said, "Yeah, are you looking for anything in particular?"

"Joe's an ace in the flooring game, ma'am," Derrick cut in. "And we have a great selection of lumber in the yard if you'd like to see some wood? What are you working on today?"

"Not wood," Carrie looked at him, and Joe could tell she was bored with Derrick already. "I came to talk to this one." She pointed at Joe.

"Let's walk around the store, shall we?" Joe said. He started walking away. Derrick pulled out a business card, put a hand through his wavy black hair, and handed it to her. "Just a thought, you're looking for lumber any time soon, you give me a call. Business and personal cell phone right there on the card," he explained.

"Are you trying to flirt with me?" She looked at the card and saw his name. "Derrick?"

"No, ma'am," he said quickly. There was no getting past this one, and that intrigued him. "Just being a salesman is all."

She smiled and told him, "If I ever need wood from a hardware store, I'll give you a call, how's that?"

"That'll be fine," he answered. "Fine as kind."

"Are you two done?" Joe asked. They looked at him together, and Carrie said, "I have to go talk to this guy, Derrick. But if I need your wood, I'll give you a buzz."

"And I'll be happy to help, any way I can." Derrick smiled his best salesman smile. She turned, put the business card in her purse, and walked to Joe.

"We need to talk," She said harshly. "You're in a lot of trouble."

"Great," He led her through the flooring section, around the outskirts of the store as they talked. They were soon in the hardware section, hammers, drills, and boxes of yellow Dewalt tools wrapped with green security tags on shelves. "Trouble with another woman. Seems like my life these days. What's your beef?"

"I want you to know one thing," she started. "Maxine is my best friend. I would die for that woman. I only want to see her happy all the time. You get me?"

"Yes," he said. "So do I?"

"Really?" she turned on him angrily. "Because it certainly doesn't seem like it, Joe."

"Hey," he tried to shush her. "Keep it down, okay?"

She breathed, trying to calm down. Then in a more subdued tone, said, "I'm sorry, I just get kind of excited when it comes to my friends and the losers who break her heart."

"My heart's broken too, you know," he whispered. "You think this has been easy for me?"

"God you two are fucking useless, you know that?"

"What do you mean?"

"She loves you, Joe," Carrie explained. "She's miserable without you. She told me yesterday, she's going to Vegas, and she's not thinking of coming back. Said, 'I can't drive by his house anymore and not think of him'. Pathetic."

"She said that?" he smiled.

"Yes, you idiot." Carrie smacked him on the arm. "And here's you, going on like it was never a thing. Just loved her and left her, living your best life all married and shit."

"Listen," he said. "It hasn't been easy for me either. You think I see her Lexus pull by real slow and leave it at that?"

"So what's your problem?" Carrie whispered angrily. "What are you doing with her?"

"Her who?"

"Maxine, dumbass!" Carrie shook her head, marveling at the stupidity of the man. "She wants you. You want her. What are you doing?"

"I'm at work. I'm trying to keep my marriage. I'm trying to keep my kids," Joe explained. "My job?"

They were in the plumbing aisle now, their conversation snapping back and forth like two pundits on a late-nineties politics show.

She stopped and said, "Okay, I understand. I get it, I really do, Joe. And it's admirable." She put a hand on his shoulder. "But you're about to lose the best woman you'll ever have in your life because you want to play it safe. I want you to know that. I came here against my better judgment. I don't like you. I don't like this situation. I don't like what has happened to Maxine. She's had a shit life with men, and now she's found what she calls a good one. I just want to see her happy. You get it?"

"Got it," he said. "But I'm kind of stuck, Carrie."

She pointed to his head. "You're only stuck up here." Then she pointed to his heart. "Follow this, the rest is easy."

"Easy, you say," he said sarcastically.

"Loving is hard, Joe," she said finally. "God knows I've had my share of heartbreaks. Call me old-fashioned, but I still think there's a guy out there for me who'll love me with everything he can. Maxine has that in you, I know it. As much as I hate to admit it, you're probably the best thing for her right now." She looked at him earnestly. "At least talk to her. Tell her how you really feel. Explain what's going on. Let her know you miss her. Maybe you two can figure something out. Who knows? Hell, if I had all the answers, I wouldn't have had three marriages and a lot of breakups.

"But I do know one thing. I love my Maxie. I want to make her happy. And if you want to do the same, you have to do the right thing."

"So she'll have me back?" he asked. There was still hope.

"Of course," she said, slapping him upside the head playfully. "God you're dense. Of course, she will. Just talk to her. But don't string her along. She wants you to choose, Joe. In your heart, you've already done that, I can see. God knows what she saw in you, but whatever. Think about it. Talk to her. Maybe then you'll see what you're about to give up by playing it safe."

"It's not that easy," he said.

"It is, Joe," she said. "Easy as pie. You just have to stop being afraid of what you'll lose and embrace what you'll gain. You'll figure it out soon, I hope."

She started walking away. "See you around, Joe. Thanks for the help."

"No," he said, lost in thought. "Thank you."

Jodi, the garden shop manager, was putting up stock in the plumbing department when she overheard Joe and Carrie talking. She wondered what the hushed whispers were about, and curiously went to another aisle to get a better understanding of the conversation. She had been a garden shop manager for years. And twelve years ago she had even tried out for the flooring department when Jamie first got the idea to sell it at the store. She was deemed too good at her job, and they brought in this guy for the job instead. Some guy off the street worked in one of those big box stores in the city.

She went to the end of the aisle, to hear them better, putting up plumbing stock, something she had just had in her hand by mistake and decided to put it up. But she had heard enough. She had heard the name Maxine. She had heard "Make your choice. She loves you, and you love her." she had gotten all she needed to get from their illicit conversation, and she decided to go out to her car for a cigarette. She didn't stay for the end of the conversation. She had enough ammo. She was going to be selling flooring pretty soon, she thought.

She speed dialed Arlene, put a cigarette in her mouth and lit it, and then the phone rang on the other end.

"Hello?" Arlene said, sleepily, as it was about ten in the morning and Arlene had probably had a couple of shots in her coffee by then.

"Arlene?" Jodi said. "Hey, girl. It's Jodi."

"Hey, hon, how are you doing?" Arlene asked. They had been friends since Arlene had worked at the store, and had kept in touch all these years. "What's up?"

Jodi spilled the tea. Explained everything. And ended Joe's decision-making process with one phone call.

A BRIGHT AND HOPEFUL PLACE

The Good, The Bad, and The Ugly—Ennio Morricone

CHAPTER 39
Arlene

SHE PUT DOWN HER PHONE. She poured another shot. She needed this one. She gulped it down, the stinging liquid burned her throat, and she wiped her mouth. "This motherfucker." she said. "This fucking motherfucker!"

Joey had come into the kitchen, stopped at seeing his mom, tears in her eyes, and said, "Hey mom, what's up?"

She didn't see him. She was lost in her own thoughts, unaware of what was happening going on around her. Anger blazed hot in her heart, and her tears stung.

She wiped her face, and said, "Nothing honey." Then turned to him. "Where's your sister?"

"In her room, upstairs," he said. He went to the refrigerator. His eyes were on his mom as he opened the door. "We got any of those cheese sticks?"

"They're in the drawer, honey," she said. "Hey, you feel like going to grandma's house tonight?"

Joey was always excited to go to the farm. To see Grandma and Uncle Tommy and said, "Heck yeah!" excitedly.

"Good," she turned, giving him a hug. "Go tell your sister to pack for a trip for a couple of days. And get your stuff too. I'm calling grandma. We'll leave in a few hours."

"Is Dad coming this time?"

"No, he's not. He'll be staying here."

Her son looked crestfallen. "Aww," he said. "He never comes with us anymore."

"It's just going to be us, honey," she explained in as soft a voice as she could. He won't be welcome, she thought. "Just go get ready for the trip, sweetie."

"Okay," he said. He got a cheese stick and opened the clear package. Bit into it. "How long are we staying?"

"Couple of days at least. I'm calling Grandma right now. I'll let you know on the way."

"Mom?" he asked. "What's wrong?"

"Nothing, kiddo," she lied. "Just go and tell your sister. I have a couple of calls to make. And I have to go run an errand. Are you guys going to be okay here by yourselves?"

"Sure," he answered. He started upstairs, his curiosity building. Mom had been calm before, but a kid senses when his mother is upset. And he got the strongest vibe of anger from her he had gotten since before he could remember. There were storm clouds ahead, he thought. Big storm clouds. He went upstairs.

Arlene poured another shot. She picked up the phone and dialed her mother's phone.

After a few rings, her mom picked up. "Hey, hon, what's up?" her mother said.

"Hey," she paused. Should she tell her mother? Later, maybe. Right now, keep it brief. Just ask. "I was wondering if me and the kids could come stay for a few days, maybe longer?"

"Sure, sweetie," her mother said. "What's up?"

"I'll explain on the way. And could you tell Tommy to come down and pick us up? I won't be able to drive. Not after doing what I have to do soon."

"Now you have me worried," Catherine said. "What's going on, hon?"

"I can't explain right now," Arlene said. "It's too big and I haven't really processed everything."

"Arlene," Catherine said.

"Mom?" Arlene said, trying to remain calm. "I can't say right now. It's something to do with Joe. I can't say anything else until I find something out. And right now I'm so angry I can't really form the words to tell you. Just trust me, okay? I'll tell you everything when I see you tonight."

"Okay, sweetie," her mother said finally. "You know you're always welcome. We can talk later, okay?"

"Thanks, mom. I love you."

"Love you too," Arlene sighed, shuddered, and tears flowed again. "Just tell Tommy to get here as soon as he can, alright?"

"I will, baby," Catherine said.

"Thanks, Mom," They said their goodbyes and she turned to the living room, went to the couch, got her purse, and headed for the door. She couldn't think of anything else to do at this moment. She was going on anger, rage, and alcohol. That would just have to see her through the day.

Twenty minutes of power walking down the street she finally came to the end of the cul-de-sac where Maxine's house sat. She stopped, looked at the neocolonial white house, and the gray Lexus SUV in the driveway, and formulated a plan of what to say. She went to the door. Rang the ring doorbell and waited.

A few minutes passed. The door opened. Maxine, in a flowered shirt and jeans, opened the door and said, "Hello, can I help you?"

Arlene paused, not really expecting what she was seeing. Here was a woman her age, a woman she would have been friends with, a woman she could have spent summer nights drinking on the back porch near the pool with. She had long auburn hair, a nice figure, and a face clear of wrinkles. She was expecting someone older, someone Joe would never be interested in in a million years.

"Can I help you?" Maxine asked again.

"Yes," Arlene found her voice. "I'm sorry," she said. "I thought I knew what I was going to say, but I got distracted. You're Maxine Colston, right?"

"Yes," Maxine was getting suspiciously curious about this woman all of a sudden.

"I'm Arlene Guillaume, Joe's wife," Arlene said. She noticed a shock of recognition or something on the woman's face. Arlene continued. "I just wanted to say, I heard about your husband, and I wanted to give my condolences."

Maxine relaxed. "Oh, honey, thank you. That means a lot." She opened the door wider and said, "Do you want to come in for some coffee or something?"

"No," Arlene said. "I have some other errands to run today. You know, before Joe gets home from work. I just was in the area, and it's been a while. Sorry I didn't come to the memorial, I'm not good with funerals."

"That's okay," Maxine said. "I'm not either. Everything was just a shock. You understand. But I appreciate you coming by."

"No problem," Arlene said. "Like I said, I just wanted to say I'm sorry for your loss."

"Thanks," Maxine said again. "Sure you don't have time for coffee?"

"No, Really. I have to go," Arlene started walking away. "It was good meeting you, though. If there's anything you ever need, you give us a call. Joe said he was helping you with the lawn, I hope that was a help."

"It was, yes. But I've since gotten the HOA people to do it. Frankly, it looks better now, don't you think?"

Arlene looked around at the grass, well-manicured lawn, and trimmed hedges, like a picture out of a real estate magazine.

"Yes, it does," she said. "They do a good job. Maybe I should have them do our yard."

"No," Maxine said. "Let Joe do it, it gives him something to do on the weekends. Men like having something like that they do for the house."

"Yes," Arlene said. "He does enjoy it." she paused, and a thought came to her. "I do have one question, though. And this might sound strange. But when Joe explained that he was doing the lawn for the old lady down the street, I didn't imagine you'd look so young."

Maxine's face went pale, and she coughed shortly. She said, "Old lady?"

"Yeah, he had me thinking you were in your sixties or something. Anyway, just had to come by and see if you needed anything."

"I'm sure there's a reason he would say something like that. For the life of me, I can't imagine why."

"Joe sees everyone older than he is as an old man or old woman maybe. I'm not sure." Arlene started backing away. "Anyway, nice to meet you, Maxine. We'll be seeing you around, I hope."

"Sure," Maxine said. She started closing the door. "Have a nice day. Thanks for stopping by!" She tried to sound as cheery as possible. Arlene wasn't having any of it.

"Bye!" She said as Maxine closed the door. "Homewrecking bitch," she said under her breath. She went back home, got an overnight bag ready, and put her toothbrush, toothpaste, and the rest of the bottle of Absolut in it as well. Then she pulled the bottle out, poured another shot and sipped it.

Then Alene texted her cheating husband.

What time do you get off tonight?

Same time as always. What's up?

She couldn't find the right response to this. Come home now, we have to talk. No, just play it cool. Let Tommy come and get the kids.

Be alone. Find out his side. Give him the benefit of the doubt. But she already knew. She could sense it. She could feel it. The past few weeks Joe had been distant, always lost in thought. When she had asked him what was wrong, he answered "Nothing, I'm just tired. Jamie's got us doing extra duty now the store's slow," or some other lame excuse.

She texted back.

Turns out i don't need you to go
to the store after all.

Everything ok?

Fine.

See you after work.

She turned off the sound on the phone. Knocked back another shot. She would have to get some more before she and Tommy left town with the kids. She looked at the clock. Three hours to go. She rage-cleaned the house, trying to keep her mind off of the fact her marriage was going to go to shit at five-thirty.

CHAPTER 40
Joe

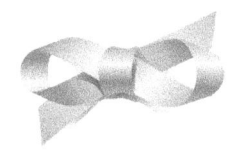

HE SAT AT HIS DESK and put the phone down after reading the texts Arlene had sent. For once, she didn't ask him to go to the store and didn't want him to stop by the liquor store. It was odd, he thought for a minute, and then the phone rang. He looked and saw "Max" as the caller. He let it ring once. Twice. He answered.

"Hey," he said, as cheerful as possible. "How are you?"

"I don't know, Joe," she said. He could sense anger there. "You tell me."

"Okay, you have me at a loss," he said. He didn't know what to say. "What's wrong? Want to talk?"

"Oh, you want to talk to the old lady now?" she spat.

"What?" he asked. "What are you talking about?"

"Arlene came by," she said. "I was wondering why? Why now?"

"Shit," was all he could say. "Honey, I'm sorry."

"Save it," she was being short.

"Max," he said, he was going to try to explain. "I don't know why she came to your house. What happened?"

"She wanted to give me condolences," she said. "About Harold. But I think there was something else there, something more sinister. And she told me you had said you were helping the 'old lady' down the street with her lawn. Is that what I am to you? An old lady?"

"Hon," he said, trying to be calm. "First of all, I'm sorry, I never meant to upset you." He explained. "She was grilling me, it was just a little white lie, I had no idea what I was saying. You have to trust me."

Maxine sighed. There was a pause. "It's okay, I guess. But we'll have to talk about it later."

"I'm sure we will," he said, relieved. "Remember, I didn't know what I was doing when we started this."

"I know," she said. "I don't hold it against you. I understand. I can't stay mad at you, you big dummy. But you may want to understand this may be it."

"What may be it?" he asked. The problem of Arlene finding out had never been a topic in their discussions. "What are you talking about?"

"I think she knows," she answered. "About us. I don't know how she found out, I don't know who may have told her, I thought we were being careful, but here we are. I think it's now or never."

His mind went blank. He started shaking, nerves making him sit down, stretching to calm his nerves. It didn't help.

He went back to the phone. "Okay," he said finally, trying to regain his composure. "So what do we do?"

"We?" she asked. "We don't do anything. You, on the other hand, may have to make a decision sooner than you think."

"I already have," he said. "I was going to call you after work. Arrange for us to meet and talk."

"Talk about what, Joe?" she said. "There's nothing to talk about."

"Goddammit, Maxine," he shot back. "About us. About what we were going to do going forward. I don't know. I've never done this. I've never had to make a decision like this."

"Well, tiger, now you do."

"Hey," he said.

"What?" she sounded exasperated.

"I love you," he answered, admitting his feelings. "I always have."

There was a pause. Finally, she said, "I love you too, you big dumbass." she paused again, letting it sink in. "Tell you what. Do this tonight. Figure it out. I'll be by the phone. If you need me, call me. Okay?"

"You promise?"

"I promise."

He relaxed a bit. One part of his life had worked itself out. "Maxine?" he asked.

"Yes?"

"Are you still sore about the 'Old Lady' remark? Because I promise I'll explain better later, I'll make it up to you."

"You're going to have to, Buster," she chuckled. "Now go, get back to work. I'll wait by the phone." He almost hung up the phone. Wanted to hear her voice some more. When they talked, it always calmed him down. And he needed it right now.

"Joe?" he heard her say.

"Yeah, babe?"

"Good luck."

She hung up the phone. He looked at it, wanting to call her back. Wanting to go to her house, wanting to do everything in the world instead of going home. He looked at the clock. It was two hours til he got off work. But he didn't care about this anymore. And he was incapable of working knowing that the executioner was only a couple of hours away.

He stood up, got some files ready for tomorrow, told Derrick he was going home for the day and left the office. He avoided anyone else, didn't want to help any customers, and didn't want to talk to any coworkers. He left and noticed Jodi giving him a strange look, but didn't think anything of it. That woman had been one of his enemies since he had started. He had found out later she was up for his job and maybe that's why she held him in such contempt. He thought about talking to her, thought against it, and went to his car.

He drove out of the parking lot and started home. Best get it on with, aye?

He took a circuitous route to get home. He had a lot of thinking to do, about what to say. About how to explain. About what he was losing. A lot. What he was gaining. A lot more.

Of all the times in his life, this was the one that made him think about drinking. He may stop by the liquor store. Get a bottle of tequila. May? He thought, no. he most definitely would. Tonight was a clear reason to get shitfaced hammered. He didn't know what he was going to do after this conversation. It was as if the floor underneath his life had been dismantled. And he was the wile e coyote falling down a chasm. But he was right before finding out that gravity was going to pull him down. Suspended in the air, running on nothing.

Oddly, he was calm. His heart beat at a normal pace. Sure, his hands were clammy from nerves, but he would get over that. He considered for a minute she would be violent, but then considered since she had never been in the past, there would be strong words. And he would take it.

He would let her call him every name in the book. Everything would be fine. He knew his kids would hate him, but they would eventually get over it. They would grow up. He would be able to explain. He would be able to tell him that their parents hadn't loved each other in years. If they ever had at all.

So he pulled up at the liquor store, walked in, grabbed a big bottle of Jose Cuervo Gold, and took it to the register. The bald fat clerk said, "She changed up, huh?"

"No," he laughed. "She still gets the vodka." He paid for the bottle. "This is for me. It's been one of those kinda days."

"Aren't they all?" the clerk mused. "Have a nice day."

"Thanks," said Joe. "You too."

He went back out to the car and drove down the street. He looked at the brown paper bag in which it had been placed, thought about taking a shot now, calmed his nerves, then said "No. it'll wait." and kept on driving.

He soon came to his neighborhood. He still remembered that stupid brochure with pretty houses drawn by architects, promising that "White Pines would be a Bright and Hopeful place for you and your family!" They had gotten the deal of a lifetime on this house when the spec houses had started being built about ten years ago. His credit was good, he got a great deal on the mortgage, and within the next ten years, they would have had it paid off. But then the neighborhood had grown. More people moved into the white and tan and gray houses and he wondered why he had bought them in the first place.

It was a far cry from what he really wanted. That was a dream he wouldn't attain now, not with Arlene taking half of it, demanding the whole thing maybe. He would give it to her. He would accede to all of her demands. He would let her go.

But hadn't he already done that? A long time ago? Hadn't he already said to himself that if it ever ended he would be okay with it? Hadn't he told himself in the beginning he would try to love her but in the end never being able to truly do that?

God, he'd tried. He just never could.

Lost in thought, he drove by the house. There was a red diesel pickup in the driveway. Tommy. He didn't want to have that conversation, didn't want to have that guy in the house at all. Tommy was one of those big dumb jock types, was the son of a farmer, and would be the farmer his dad always wanted him to be. That's the only life he had ever known, Tommy. He continued to drive around the neighborhood. The tone on his phone rang, the good bad and the ugly.

It was Arlene asking if he was coming home soon. He texted back he was right around the corner.

He sighed. Now or never, boyo. Now or never.

CHAPTER 41

Joe

• • ⚜ • •

HE PULLED INTO THE driveway next to her gray minivan. The red truck was gone. Good. he wouldn't have to deal with her overprotective brother. God knew what that hulk of muscle and testosterone was capable of.

He got out, grabbed the bottle of Jose' and walked to the door. He went in and noticed the house was immaculate. Gone were the clothes on the couch, the dishes on nightstands and coffee tables, and dust bunnies gone from corners of the linoleum flooring in the den and kitchen. He walked into the kitchen, put the bottle down on the counter and looked at her, Arlene.

She stood at the sink, looking out the kitchen window. He could tell her arms were crossed. He thought to go to her, hug her, tell her he was sorry, they could work it out, do whatever it took. Go to counseling. But she ended that thought with a word.

"I saw your whore today," she said. "You have anything to say about that?"

"Now, listen–" He started, but she cut in.

"No!" she turned. He could tell she had been crying. He wanted to explain. "You fucking listen to me!"

He put his hands up, and said, "Okay, go ahead. Get it all out." as calmly as he could.

"You want to explain to me what's going on?"

"Okay," he said. "I will." he paused. Trying to find the right words.

"Well? I'm waiting!"

"It's not easy," he said. "To explain everything."

"Start at the beginning, maybe," she said. "Do you love me?"

"No," he admitted. There it was. Then he caught himself. "I do, but not in the way you think."

"A no will suffice, Joe."

"Well, I'll ask you the same thing," he said. "Do you love me?"

"I don't know. I did at one time I think, maybe, maybe not. I don't know. But you could have done something besides going around my back with the slut down the street!"

"Don't call her that!"

"What, the old lady?" she saw his face, "Yeah, the old lady that turned out to be an attractive redhead? How long were you going to try and keep this up, Joe? How long were you and the old lady going to run around behind my back? How long were you fucking her and not me!"

She threw a glass at him then, and he dodged as it hit the patio door behind him and shattered. The tempered glass remained. "How fucking long, Joe!" she demanded.

"Now, hon," he started.

"Don't call me that! Don't you fucking call me that anymore. Ever, you hear me? Don't you fucking dare!" She went to him then. She slapped him across the face. He wasn't expecting this. But he didn't know what he was expecting. "Asshole!"

He let her rant. This was a time for her to give him both barrels. And he would let her. He was oddly calm about this. He kept his mouth shut.

"Do you know how many years I did your laundry, looked after your kids, picked up your dingleberries, vacuumed your house, washed your shitty ass underwear?!"

"Yes," he said weakly.

"Twelve years, Joe. Twelve fucking years. Did I get a thanks? Did I get any fucking gratitude from you? No! I got nothing!"

"Now wait a minute!" He started getting angry now. "I did everything for you. Everything! Went to work every day, bought groceries. Picked up when I could, and put in my own time in this house. I even lifted you up and took you to bed when you got too sloshed to move. I gave you time to grieve, to get over your dad, but then you kept on drinking. You think I wanted to come home to that? You think I want to buy your liquor every two days? Don't even start with me, Arlene. Don't even fucking start!"

"You could have said something."

"Say what? Tell you to stop? How many times did I try? Your response was always, if you were going through what I had to do you would drink too. Well, I was going through it too. You're not the only one who misses your father."

"Oh please, you don't miss shit. Don't give me that bullcrap. You didn't like him any more than the man on the moon. So give it up."

She pushed past him. "Just go away, I don't even want to be in the same room with you right now."

"You never did," he said flatly.

She turned. "What do you mean by that?"

"You don't think I noticed how you never wanted to be around me? How do we never even talk anymore? How we haven't been physical in over seven years? You don't even want me to touch you. How do you think I would feel? If you love me, then you got a piss poor way of showing it, honey."

She stopped.

"Yeah, think about it. I fucking tried Arlene. I tried to love you. But every time I tried to hold you, you would bristle. So I stopped trying. Every time I tried to kiss you, you turned your lips away from me. You think I didn't see it? You think I didn't notice the snide remarks? The passive-aggressive tone? Always with a complaint about little things. The dish towel isn't right, the toilet seat isn't clean, the toilet paper isn't put on the right way, do the dishes in the dishwasher this way, not the other. Always with a tone of "here's the stupidest guy on the planet trying to do chores!"

"Is that why you ran around on me? The toilet roll?"

"No, Arlene. That's not why. Fuck the toilet roll. That was one straw on the camel's back of your hatred toward me. Don't think I didn't notice. Don't think I didn't see it. The thinly veiled contempt you had for my very existence. Just admit it, you haven't loved me in years."

"I could say the same about you, Joe," she said.

He calmed down. He had to get that out. He didn't know where it had come from, but he had to try to make her understand the way she had made him feel all these long years.

"I know I haven't been the greatest husband. I'm sorry. I tried to be there for you and the kids. I tried to do the right thing. Yes, I admit I haven't been in love with you for a while. How could I be? I'm just selfish, I guess. I thought maybe it would happen one day. Maybe I would look at you and feel the same way I did when I looked at you the first time I kissed you but it went away. I tried to get it back after Joey was born but I couldn't."

There was a pause in their fight as the realization sank in for both of them.

"Me too," she said. "Oh God," she started crying. He went to her and she let him hold her. She cried into his chest. "Oh God, what are we doing?"

He paused. Let her hold him as another human being. He was devoid of emotion for her. He was holding a woman. Someone he had been with for twelve years. And here he was, holding no affection for her at all. He was simply holding a person who was crying. Even though he was the source of her tears.

"I'm taking the kids, Tommy will be here in a few minutes. We're going to my mother's house. I don't know if I'll be back."

"Okay," he said. He let her go. She backed up. Her face was red with anger and tears. "So what do you want to do now?"

"Fuck, Joe, I don't know." she turned around, waved her hands, and shrugged. "I don't know. What do you want to do?"

He admitted, "I think we need to get a divorce." he said. "I don't want to be married to you anymore." His words hung in the air. He had just said what he had wanted to say to her for the first time in his life, what he'd wanted to say for years, perhaps even a decade.

She turned and nodded. "Okay." She sat down. "Okay, yeah. Jesus." She looked like she was about to cry, and she brought her head up, steeling herself. Defiant to the end.

She put her face in her hands. She looked up at him, seeming to understand what he had just said. The gravity of it, and the realization that she too agreed with what had to happen. "Okay. do me a favor," she said. A tear fell down her cheek. "Go get my bottle. I noticed you had a bottle of Jose with you when you came home." He saw her eyes were red with anger, prior tears, and several glasses of vodka before he had even come into the room. "Share a drink with me?"

He said, "Yeah, sure. Why not?" He went into the kitchen and got two tumbler glasses. Filled hers up with Absolut, filled his with tequila, and took them to where she sat resolutely on the couch. They clinked glasses. "We gave it the old college try," she said.

"Yes," he said. "We did."

They drank together.

"Of course, you know I'm taking everything you've got, mister," she said.

"Yeah," he chuckled. "I kind of figured."

A few minutes of silence passed between them. They drank together, saying nothing. There was no more to be said. It was over and they both knew it. They had both accepted it. It made them both sad. But they both knew it was a necessary step.

She stood up, they shook hands, and she handed the empty glass of vodka to him. She said, "Does she make you happy?"

"Yeah," he admitted.

"Good, Joe." She gave him a hug. "Goodbye, I'll be around in a few days to get my stuff and all the rest for the kids."

They heard a honk outside, and Arlene looked out the window at the red pickup truck in the driveway. "Right on time," she said. "I'm going to go. I'll be in touch, obviously." They shared one last hug.

"Okay," he let her go to the door alone. She picked up an overnight bag he hadn't noticed when he first came in. He was so focused on talking to her and getting this over with he hadn't noticed she had already made the decision to leave him.

"Hey," she said before she left.

"Yeah?"

"You want to call her go ahead. I won't be sleeping in that bed ever again." And then she went out the door. He watched her go to the truck, get in the driver's side. She slammed the door, and then it sped out of the driveway, down the street, and was gone.

He went up to the bedroom, and looked at the sterile nature of it. The sheets were gone, and the mattress was a bare white pad. He looked at the stains left by ten years of a couple sleeping there and decided it would have to go. He wouldn't have Maxine on that bed, it held too many memories of crying nights, drunken slobber, night sweats, and sadness. He would have to make it later on. He wondered where the sheets were, realizing he would have to do all of this on his own for a while, and went to the bathroom linen closet where he remembered Arlene put the fresh sheets. He reached out to touch them, decided he would do it later.

He went back into the bedroom, unable to form any thoughts whatsoever. The astounding numbness of what had just occurred hit him and his body shook as the adrenaline wore off and he sagged. He sat on the bed, smiled as a thought came to him. Then he stood up, and started unbuttoning his shirt. He was going to go for a swim.

Alone in the house, he took off his clothes and walked downstairs naked. His heart beat normally. He couldn't think. His brain had been flooded with too many emotions in the past day, and he just needed to not feel at all.

He walked to the stairs of the pool, the blue water glittering in the summer sun. He stepped on one foot, then the other. The coldness of the water greeted him with a feeling, something he needed. Then he walked into the pool. Kept walking until he was underwater, went to the bottom and sat.

He screamed until there was no air in his lungs. He went back up, got some more air, and went back down.

He did that three more times.

Then he went inside and got drunk.

CHAPTER 42
Maxine

HER "SHE'S A LADY" ringtone went off a couple of hours after her conversation with Joe. She looked at her phone.

>Hey. its done.

Whats done?

>Arlene. Me. done. Getting a divorce.
>She left. Took the kids.

Maxine smiled. She didn't know how to feel about this. Happy? Sad? She never saw this happening. She texted back.

SO WHAT NOW?

>I'm getting drumk

Need company?

>I dont know. Maybe.
>No.

She started texting back that she understood. Give him a night to process all the emotions. Another text came.

> Yes. i want you. Can't be alone
> right now.

Ok. be there in a few

> Front doors open. Im in back.

Maxine smiled then. She went upstairs, put on the blue sundress with flowers on and nothing else. She went downstairs, got her purse, and headed out the door.

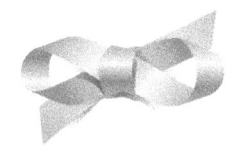

CHAPTER 43
Joe

WEEKS LATER, HE WATCHED as Arlene's Uhaul truck carrying all of her belongings left the house. In the front seat were Joey and Cathy. Both had taken to communicating with him in short sentences, giving him angry disappointed looks. He came to expect it. He tried to explain all of the stuff to them that had happened, but they either wanted to side with Arlene, or they didn't want to hear his explanations.

He knew in the intervening time between when they had decided to separate and now that she had said some pretty nasty things about him to them. She said she wouldn't, but there's always a moment when a father knows that his ex-wife is talking shit about him behind his back. He figured he had earned this level of scorn.

Arlene hadn't wanted to talk to him beyond what to do with this or that trinket. As far as he was concerned, she could take them all. Take everything in the house, he had said at one point. It was all hers anyway. She hadn't paid for it, but in the divorce decree, anything that could have been an asset went to her.

He had signed over everything, except for half the assets of the house. She had agreed. So they sold the house, he took the money and decided that he could live in an apartment for a while til he got on his feet.

This was going to prove a bit more difficult. When the news broke at work, Jamie had called him into the office, and Joe knew what this was about.

"You wanted to see me, boss?" Joe had said.

"Close the door," said Jamie. Joe did. He sat down.

"You want to explain what happened with you and Arlene?" Jamie had asked. Joe told him. He didn't leave out any details. Yep, Arlene and I are getting a divorce. Yep, I had an affair with a client. Yes, I know it was wrong, and against company policy.

"We're going to have to let you go," Jamie had said. "It's a store thing, Joe. We can't have the news that our salespeople are out there trying to seduce every customer, especially when they're married."

"Oh, but you'll let Derrick get away with it?" Joe had asked, a bit incensed.

"Derrick is my cousin's kid, Joe," Jamie explained. "And if you saw my cousin, you wouldn't fire the guy either. It's just bad for business. It's a small town. You know how people talk around here."

"I got it," Joe had said. "I understand. I'll pack up my things."

"You'll get a week's severance, and of course your retirement fund is yours. Can't do anything to take that, you've earned it."

So they stood up. Joe had shaken hands with him. They went downstairs to the floor and Joe was escorted out of the building by a security guard. As he walked out, he noticed Jodi smiling, knowing Jamie would give her a chance to sell flooring now.

He never walked into that store ever again.

He and Arlene were on speaking terms for the moment. He would get the kids every other weekend. She would get them for Christmas. He would be able to visit on Thanksgiving. Maxine told him he could stay at her house, and move in there if he couldn't find anything, but he demurred, saying "I need to be on my own for a bit before we do anything crazy like that. Even though he wanted to. It just wouldn't look right. Him shacking up with the woman who had just suffered her husband's loss only a few months before. She agreed. But they did spend a lot of time together, getting to know one another. Falling deeper in love by the day and talking about future plans.

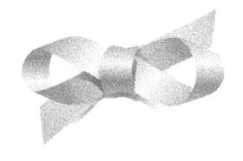

CHAPTER 44
Maxine

• • ⚘ • •

MAXINE HANDED HER DAUGHTER some paperwork. It was a simple file with a few pieces of legal papers with information about a trust they had set up for her in the event of his or her mother's death. There were two checks there. And when Maryanne looked, she stopped. She looked up at her mom.

"What's this?" she asked. "Really? This much?"

"That's only one check," Maxine said. "Take a look at the other one. Maryanne did.

"Mom," she said. "No. This is yours."

"I cut the original in half, baby. Your dad gave us a million. That's yours. Keep it."

"Mom, I can't," she said vehemently. "I... I can't. This is what Dad left for you."

"He left it for us, baby," Maxine said. "I want you to have it. For San Diego. For life, for whatever you want. You need to go out and explore the world. And I don't want you to struggle. So between that and the trust, you should be set for a while. Make the right investments, and you'll be comfortable for life."

"But I have a job now," she said.

"This gives you options. Keep the job if you want to. But if you don't like it, you don't have to worry about leaving it and going to find another. Or not having one at all."

"You mean this?" Maryanne asked. There was some disbelief still. Between the trust and the insurance, she was a twenty-four-year-old millionaire.

"Yes, sweetie. Take it. With my blessing," her mother said. "I want you to have it. I'll be okay. Trust me. Between the sale of the house and everything your dad left us, I'll be okay."

"Where are you going to live now?"

"I'm moving out west. I found a ranch in Tucson. It's only a few hours from San Diego, and I can drive to see you when I want to. And if you find a man and settle down and have kids, I can come to see the grandkids."

"A ranch?" her daughter was flabbergasted. "You've never talked about buying a ranch. What are you going to do with that?"

"I don't know," she smiled wistfully. "I have a feeling a handsome cowboy may show up there to help pretty soon."

Maryanne smiled, knowing who that cowboy might be.

A BRIGHT AND HOPEFUL PLACE

Three Little Birds—Sarah Darling

CHAPTER 45
Arlene

ARLENE HELD HER TUMBLER full of vodka, close to her chest, watching the back plot of the farm. Tommy sat on an old John Deere tractor his father had bought back in the Seventies, Joe on his lap driving it around in a circle. Cathy was on the back porch reading, something about kids fighting in a gladiator game. She had tried to explain it to Arlene, but there was too much violence and apocalyptic stuff in it so Arlene had told her to stop.

She had stayed in the room her mother had set up for her. Her old room. The one she grew up in, and she looked around at the white-painted walls. How many times during childhood had she had these walls painted white? She couldn't tell. Eighteen, nineteen?

When she had gotten to a point where she could draw, Arlene had been given permission to draw and paint on the walls of her room. Her father Thomas had encouraged it. Sometimes he would come in and watch her. If an archaeologist in painting ever came in to excavate it layer by layer, they would find many portraits of her father through the years on various points of the smooth white surface.

There was a slight knock on the door, and she looked around. Her mother, Catherine opened the door slightly. "Mind if I come in?" she said.

"Yeah, mom. Hey." Arlene said. "What's up?"

Catherine came to stand by her daughter. She put an arm around her. Tugged her close. Looked at the glass, and looked at her daughter. "Baby, it's ten thirty in the morning."

"Mom," she started.

"I'm just saying," Catherine said. "Doesn't do good for the kids to see. And that's all I'm going to say. I know you've been through some things, and I don't want to get you all in a snit."

"Thank you, mom," she said. "One day I'll get responsible. I promise."

"I'll hold you to it," Catherine said. She smiled, looking out at Tommy and Joey on the tractor. "Your dad would have loved to see this."

"Yeah, he would have. God, I miss Dad so much."

"I do too, baby," Catherine sighed. "I do too."

"Mommy?" Arlene said. She always called her mother mommy when she was sad. Catherine loved it. "What am I going to do?"

"The best you can, sweetie."

"I just.." she stopped. "What's wrong with me? Why do I pick such awful men?"

Catherine laughed, "Sweetie, if you can answer that, you'll make a billion dollars. You think you're the only one that ever made a few bad decisions around a man?"

"You and Dad seemed to do alright," Arlene looked at her. "You were perfect."

"Baby, I broke a lot of eggs before I found that particular rooster, that's for sure."

"But how did you make it work all those years?"

"When I met your dad, he just kissed me the right way to light a fire in my belly I could never put out," Catherine smiled at the memory of their first meeting. A double date in the back of Carl Weatherbee's Camaro. "Find you one like that."

She kissed her daughter on the cheek, turned and went to the door. "I found something you might like," she said, pulling in a large cardboard moving box. "Some stuff I found in the attic when I was going through your dad's things. Thought you might want to take a trip down memory lane. See if it inspires you."

Arlene approached the box, its layers of dust settled in the way only time could manage. She opened it, revealing canvases, papers, and drawing pads filled with artwork she had created in her childhood room. She looked at her mother. "Where did you find all this? I thought Dad threw it all away."

Her mother smiled. "Posh, he would never do that. He loved your art." She picked up a canvas from Arlene's Bob Ross phase—a landscape of pretty trees against a mountain stream. Arlene smiled, remembering how much she had loved that one.

Her eyes tearing up now, she said, "Oh, mom."

"Don't worry about anything, dear. You don't have to leave again. This is your home. And the grandkid's home. We'll get them into school around here, they'll find new friends. Tommy has really stepped up, and Joey can help around the house. Teach him responsibility instead of being in that idiot box all day killing zombies. Stay as long as you like."

"Okay, Mom," she looked back down at the artwork. "Hey, mom?" Her mother came back in the door.

"Yes, baby."

"I love you."

"I know."

. . ✤ . .

A FEW WEEKS LATER, Arlene sat in the front seat of the minivan, outside of a Methodist church several miles from the farm. "You can do this, Arlene. You can do this. For the kids."

She stepped out. She saw a few people going into a white door to the fellowship hall of the stately red brick church on the corner of the small town where she had grown up. There was a sign on the door, in a big block of red letters. "AA MEETING HERE," it said.

She went in the door, and down a hall. Another door opened up to a large brown paneled wall room. There were flyers on a table in front of her, telling her about AA life, traditions, and any number of ways to stay sober. Several people looked in her direction. Older men, younger women, all ages, she noticed. She was wearing a white blouse and blue jeans and suddenly felt self-conscious. She found a round table near the back. An older woman, with white close-cropped hair, petite, with spangly jeweled bracelets on her arm came over to introduce herself.

"Hi, I'm Dana," she said. "What's your name?"

"Arlene," she said. "I don't know what to do. I'm really nervous."

"We all were when we started, sweetie," Dana said. She sat down next to Arlene and grabbed her hand, squeezed it. "You'll be okay. You're in the right place."

The chairman at a larger table in the front of the fellowship hall rang a bell and introduced himself. "Hello, welcome to this Tuesday night meeting of Alcoholics Anonymous. My name is Greg, and I'm an alcoholic."

The group all said, "Hello Greg!" in cheery voices.

Greg started the meeting. Arlene looked around. These people were smiling, seemingly happy. Was this a cult? Greg said, "Before we start tonight, are there any newcomers here?"

Dana looked at Arlene, and Arlene raised her hand. The whole room looked at her. She suddenly wanted to run.

"Hi," she said. "My name is Arlene." she looked at Dianne, then looked up to Greg. "And I'm an alcoholic."

As a group, the people said, "Hello Arlene, we're glad you're here."

A BRIGHT AND HOPEFUL PLACE

When My Fingers Find Your Strings—Jeff Daniels

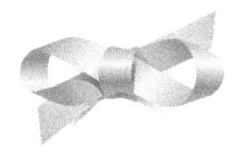

CHAPTER 46
Joe

• • ⚘ • •

HE FINISHED BRUSHING the horse, a gray mare he had named Cathy. She had long black hair and reminded him of his daughter. The kids were scheduled to come out to Tucson in the fall. It was a working name, and the horse didn't really seem to like it. But it did like the apples Joe had given it so as long as she took the apples, she was going to be called Cathy.

He went out of the barn, closed the door behind him and looked at the Arizona sky. It was the clear bright blue he had imagined in his dreams all those years of living in the city. Maxine and he had pooled their money together, found this online at the same place he had been looking at other properties so many months ago, and had bought this one for a song.

It was Maxine's idea to buy the horse. Every few days, they had a couple of guys come by and take care of her, and there were talks about getting another one to keep her company. He sighed, wondering about the journey he had taken to get him here. The lost job, the lost marriage, the kids, who would eventually come around and love him again. They were going to be teenagers soon, and there would be challenges. But with love, he thought they would figure it all out. He went up to the ranch house, which was going to need a lot of work. One of the reasons they had gotten it for the price they did was because it was a fixer-upper.

Joe guessed that's what happens when you buy a defunct ranch that had been built in the nineteen sixties on the outskirts of the city . But it was home. It was peaceful. It was theirs, together.

His and Maxine's.

He looked down at the ring around his finger, placed there in a simple ceremony a few months ago.

In Las Vegas of all places. No, they didn't have the Elvis impersonator officiating, but he had joked that he wanted one, and Maxine had given him that look. He liked that look.

He went inside the house and down the hall to the simple kitchen. He looked at the refrigerator, something from the Seventies. He would have to replace that soon, but the green thing kept on humming and worked well, so they would have to make that decision later. He saw her standing over the sink, rinsing vegetables. She wore a simple cotton red dress, zippered in the back. She looked like a housewife from the Fifties. She turned her head, saw him come in the doorway, and smiled.

"Hey good lookin', what you got cooking?" He patted her ass, kissed her on the back of the neck.

"Chicken, wanna neck?" She said, turning to kiss him deeply. He snaked a hand around her butt and squeezed.

She said, "You keep doing that, I won't finish dinner."

His fingers went up to the zipper of her dress and started pulling it down. He smelled her jasmine hair, kissed her neck and left heat where his lips had been. She looked into his blue eyes and blushed.

She didn't finish dinner.

THE END

ABOUT THE AUTHOR

Jean-Paul Pare' is called "Daddy" by some, "father" by his kids and is an absolute DILF per his best friend. As the youngest of nine children, he knew he wanted to be a storyteller at a young age. He has been an Actor, a floor salesman, a bartender, and a host of other jobs that lend themselves well to serving as professions for future protagonists.

Finally, after all these long years dreaming of it, he decided to be a writer. When asked who would play in his movie he admitted he was torn between Oscar Isaacs and Pedro Pascal and he admits his favorite album of all time is Paul Simon's Graceland.

I know, save your scorn.

When he isn't sharing his romance with the world he can be found painting miniatures for Warhammer or being a Dungeon Master for his Tabletop Role Playing Group in a small Southeastern NC.town.

You can follow him on his socials listed below.

In Fall 2024 expect the sequel where a woman with notches in her lipstick case falls for the salesman's smile when she needs some hard wood in *A Broken and Hallowed Heart*, book two of the Newton's Crossing series.

And just in time for Christmas, *A Season of Spice and Snow*, Book 3 of the Newton's Crossing series.

Share a journey from friends to lovers in this age-gap romance between a lonely widowed 55-year-old bookshop owner and a 36-year-old free-spirited lover of Emily Bronte.

It's anything but a Hallmark Christmas romance, with plenty of hot spice, just in time for your holiday reading list, with steamy scenes that will surely put you on the naughty list.

Welcome to book 1 in the Newton's Crossing series. In the heart of the suburbs of White Pines, two lives are about to intertwine in ways neither could have foreseen. Joseph Guillaume, a floor salesman at Bennet's Building Supplies, finds himself trapped in the monotony of his life and the cold silence of a loveless marriage. Maxine Colston, on the outside, appears to have it all—a beautiful home and a seemingly perfect existence. But beneath the surface, Maxine yearns for a passion long since extinguished in her marriage to Harold, a high-stakes gambler whose luck is about to run out.

When Joe and Maxine meet, a spark ignites, offering a fleeting promise of the passion they both crave. As their affair blossoms, it threatens to unravel not just their marriages but the very fabric of their lives.

Thrust into a web of deception and lust, Joe and Maxine find themselves facing the ultimate test of love and loyalty. Can they forge a new path together, or will the weight of their pasts pull them under? Set against the backdrop of an ordinary suburb, this novel is a captivating tale of desire, betrayal, and redemption where two souls must decide if the price of their happiness is one they can afford to pay.

ISBN 979-8-227-54430-8